AMAZE YOUR FRIENDS

Also by Peter Doyle

Amaze Your Friends

Peter Doyle

DARK PASSAGE

A Dark Passage book
Published by Verse Chorus Press, Portland, Oregon, USA.
info@versechorus.com

Cover photograph: Hans Bonney (1905–2005), Holden car by the side of the road, ca. 1950–1959. © State Library of Victoria.

Design and layout by Steve Connell Book Design | *steveconnell.net*

Dark Passage logo by Mike Reddy

Library of Congress Cataloging-in-Publication Data

Names: Doyle, Peter, 1951- author.
Title: Amaze your friends / Peter Doyle.
Description: First American edition. | Portland, Oregon : Verse Chorus Press,
  [2019] | Series: A dark passage book
Identifiers: LCCN 2018059431 (print) | LCCN 2018061660 (ebook) | ISBN
  9781891241789 (ebook) | ISBN 9781891241345 (paperback)
Subjects: | GSAFD: Noir fiction.
Classification: LCC PR9619.3.D69 (ebook) | LCC PR9619.3.D69 A82 2019
  (print)
  | DDC 823/.914--dc23
LC record available at https://lccn.loc.gov/2018059431

For Sue

Prologue

Even though killing Ray Waters had been a spur-of-the-moment thing, Laurie carried it off with a certain old-world grace. He poured a scotch for each of us, asked the ladies to step outside, and then shot Ray in the chest.

If Laurie had consulted me before he started blazing away I would have urged moderation, but I wasn't altogether heartbroken when Waters copped it. I helped Laurie dump the body at sea, and later I took Waters' car to Mascot airport, to make it look like he'd left the country. Which in a way he had.

We went our separate ways. Time passed. I started thinking we'd got away with it.

Chapter 1

A cold Saturday night at Woolloomooloo Bay. Three men shuffled down the gangway of the SS *King of Prussia*, along the deserted Pier 6 and out through the gateway to Cowper Wharf Road.

I flashed my headlights, wound down my window and called out, 'You're late. I was getting worried.'

The man in front shook his head, kept walking, and said out of the side of his mouth, 'The hotel, ten minutes,' without breaking stride.

I got out, walked over to Harry's Café de Wheels.

Jude, the old girl behind the counter said, 'What's on, Billy?'

I watched the three figures enter the pub across the road. 'Looks like I'll be having a drink.'

'Eat something first. You should never drink on an empty stomach.'

'Yeah, that's what my father used to tell me. Along with, Avoid bad companions,' I said.

'Mine used to say, Never trust a man who doesn't wear a hat to the races.' She handed a meat pie across the counter to me.

I told her I didn't want it. She insisted.

I moved over to the railing at the water's edge. Seagulls squawking in the darkness. I took a bite, spat it out, tossed the remains into the drink. Then I pulled a couple of dexedrines out of my top pocket and swallowed them dry.

When ten minutes were up I waved to Jude, started moving off. She asked did I feel better now? I told her too right.

The pub was a storm of noise and cigarette smoke. I bought a beer, pushed my way through the crowd to the jukebox, punched in 'Summertime Blues'.

Before the song had finished Chet Kimbrough, American seafaring gent and bad companion, tapped me on the shoulder and muttered, 'Out the back.' I followed him through to the ladies' lounge. His mates were there already, in the company of three women of the night. Chet slipped the bolt on the door, took his leather jacket off. He reached under his shirt, brought out a rolled-up paper bag, dropped it on the table, said, 'All right, fellers, give daddy-o the booty.'

Bad companion number two, a toothless Negro, grinned and took off his Canadian jacket. He put his hand into the lining, took out another bag, dropped it on the table. Then he went in under his shirt, took out some magazines, put them with the other stuff. He held up his finger like a magician, then unbuckled his belt and dropped his strides. The girls whistled. More bags taped to both legs. He carefully cut them free with a flick-knife, threw them on the table. He put his trousers back on and bowed. Then Chet and bad companion number three, a nuggety Scot with a crewcut, did the same. They all went back out to the front bar then, leaving me and Chet with the pile of reefers, *Playboy* magazines, 45rpm records and some paperbacks. I sniffed the reefers, flicked through the books: *Sintime Beatniks, Narcotics Agent, Stripper, Jailbait, Junkie, On the Road*.

I handed a roll of notes to Chet. He counted it, then nodded.

I put the stuff in my disposal store kitbag. 'Why the big production?'

'Customs guys on the wharf back there. See them? A guy on board ran out of cash, took some magazines to sell uptown. In a bag. Big mistake. Customs tracked him all the way to Ashwoods. They took him in, charged him.'

'No sympathy for the working man.'

'Nail on the head there, brother.' He held up the roll of pound notes. 'Hey, why don't you hang with us? We're going to get all messed up.'

'Nah, I'm racing the clock. I've got to sell this dope faster than I can smoke it. See you next time.'

I bought a bottle of Remy, went back to the car and drove a little way up Darlinghurst Road, into a tiny back lane, to the house of Shirley Hill, artist, stripper and dabbler in the black arts.

She opened her door wearing a paint-spattered army shirt and tights, her hair tied back with a red bandanna. She said, 'Hello there.'

'Hello, Shirl. How's things?'

'About to get better.' She stood aside and I walked past her, through a little courtyard into the kitchen. It smelled of cat shit and incense. An Yma Sumac record was playing on the gramophone.

Shirl followed me in. 'Would you like a drink? I've got some wine.'

I thought, Never mix your drinks. 'Yeah, thanks,' I said.

Shirley poured me a glass of claret from a flagon.

I took a reefer out of the bag, fired it up, took a few drags and handed it across. We passed it back and forth. When it was finished I cranked up another one. Shirley got up, changed the record.

I picked half a dozen reefers out of the bag, handed them to her. She said, 'How much?'

'Ten quid will do.'

She went to her purse and handed me a tenner.

'Would you like a palm reading before you go?'

I held out my hand. A black cat jumped onto the kitchen table and walked over to me, rubbed itself against my arm. Shirley took my mitt.

She looked closely at my palm for half a minute, then let go.

'Dark forces are gathering around you.'

'You don't say.'

'I do. Finish your wine and hand me the glass.'

I drained it and gave it to her. She peered into the glass, rolled the last drop around, then looked at me strangely. I shivered.

'There's unfinished business. A trembling hand reaches into the icy depths for an elusive quarry.'

'What's that supposed to mean?'

'I don't know. I'm just the messenger.'

'How about the daily double for Randwick next Saturday?'

'You know I never get anything as clear cut as that. You'll have to make do with Unfinished Business and Icy Depths.'

'How about Travel and a Dark Stranger?'

'Funny you should say that. They're both there too.' She reached over and took my hand again. 'And so is Bad News Arriving by Telephone. You've got the fortune teller's lay-down *misère*.'

It was dark when I stepped out into Darlinghurst Road. Shirley's connection to the other side was better than she knew. A bloke was in my car, looking in the glove box, another leaning against the mudguard.

The lookout pegged me. He said something and the other turned around to face me. They were both in their early twenties, dressed casual, but they weren't your run-of-the-mill thieves. The one who had been in the car was Italian, or maybe Greek. He had his black hair cut short and neat and he was standing up straight. The other one had blond hair, tanned skin, a surf-club type. Plain-clothes policemen.

I sauntered over with what I hoped passed as a cavalier attitude and said to the Italian, 'So Enzo, what were you doing in my car?'

'Looking for evidence of criminal activity.'

'Such as?'

He looked away and back again, then with an elaborate show of unconcern said, 'Oh, take your pick.' He started counting on his fingers. 'Sly grog and dutiable imports; SP betting slips, pak-a-pu tickets, two-up coins or other gaming paraphernalia; stolen milk money, hub-caps or V8 badges; or maybe even some of those sex drugs we've been hearing about.' He'd run out of fingers. 'From what I hear, pretty well anything small-time and crooked would be your go, including living off the immoral earnings of a woman. Would that be right, Glasheen?'

He wasn't completely wide of the mark, except for the V8 badges. There's another one for the list, I thought—Always obey the law. I shrugged.

He looked over my Customline. 'You're driving a pretty good car for a two-bob petty crim. Makes me wonder what you've really been up to lately.'

'Hard work and clean living,' I said.

He spat on the ground near my foot. 'You've never had a real job in your life.'

I looked at my watch. 'Listen, I'm in a bit of a hurry, boys. Tell me, is this official, or are you after a donation or something?'

The surf-club type stepped forward then. 'Smart bastard, eh? You feel like having a go, do you?'

I nodded, rubbing my chin. 'I get it, it's unofficial. Well, fellers, as I see it, your tough bloke act shows some promise but I'm afraid it still needs work. Stick with it, you may get there one day. Meanwhile, you, Luigi, hang on to your job in the fruit shop.' I turned to the lifesaver. 'But I really think you've got the makings of a pretty fair comical sidekick.'

I moved past them towards my car. The surfer grabbed the shoulder of my coat and threw a punch at me. It might well have done some damage, except the other bloke grabbed him at the same moment I ducked, and the punch went wide. I turned around ready to box on if I had to, sincerely hoping it wouldn't be necessary. The Italian took the blond aside, spoke a few words to him. Then they both turned to face me, grinning in a way I didn't care for one little bit.

The surfer straightened his cuffs and said, 'Yeah, you'll keep. Go ahead, give cheek all you like, gummo, because you've got some *real* surprises coming!'

I said, 'Yeah, sure, sure,' and got in the car.

I drove off, saw the coppers in my rear-view mirror still standing there, watching me. I went around the corner into Liverpool Street and stopped, opened the bottle of Remy and took a long pull. I had a strong impulse then to cancel all other engagements, go back to the Rock'n'roll and get blotto. But I fought it. For one thing, I told myself, those blokes were too junior to worry about. And regardless of how shaky my nerves were, I still had a living to earn.

I took another swig of brandy, started up the car again and drove through the city, down to Harmony House, the music store at Circular Quay, where upstairs in the recording studio my arrival was being eagerly awaited by Max Perkal and his group, the Percolators. In 1958 Max and his band of would-be hipsters between them accounted for about seventy percent of the total demand for Indian hemp in the entire city of Sydney.

They were in the main studio. I sat down with the engineer, handed him the brandy bottle and watched the proceedings through the control booth window. Max and the boys were playing back-up to the lovely Del Keene, singer, dancer, comedienne, and, as of two months ago, my ex-girlfriend.

She was singing a tune she and Max had co-written called 'Kiss Crazy'. It was intended to be their ticket to television stardom, if only they could get it arranged right. The song was a straight twelve-bar, but Max had put some stops at the end and added bongos to give it a Latin feel, he said. To me it sounded more like Charleston than cha-cha, but what would I know? I asked the engineer what he thought. He told me that in London before the war he'd worked with all the greats—Formby, Fields, Lynn—and if this was a hit record, he was in the wrong game.

They finished the song and Del came out to listen to a playback. We said hello and kissed. She made a show of waving away the alcohol fumes. I went into the studio.

Max was retuning his guitar. He said howdy partner. At the age of thirty-five he had already clocked up twenty years in the entertainment business. As a one-time Hawaiian guitarist, hillbilly yodeller, juggler, piano player, band leader, radio actor and now bearded bongo beater, Max Perkal had experienced pretty well all that show business had to offer, barring success.

Lachie the drummer came bouncing over to me, slapped me on the back and asked if l had any dope. I told him maybe, did he have any money? He said no, but he would have tomorrow, or maybe the day after, and he'd gladly pay me Tuesday for a reefer today. I thought of the 'money can spoil a good friendship' line, but kept it to myself.

I said, 'Shit, Lach, fair go. You think I'm in this game for fun?'

He said, 'Man, you're wound tight. You need to loosen up a bit. You better crank up one of them reefers fast, get mellow.' Lachie using hip talk with a broad Aussie accent.

I lit up a couple of reefers and passed them out, received assurances from the band that, too right, they'd square up with me next week, no problem.

Del came back into the studio. She frowned when the smoke was offered to her. Lachie asked did I have anything else. I left the brandy and dexes with them and went back out to the control room while they recorded yet another take, then another.

Having provided the reefers, I was more or less redundant. I hung around reading an old *Downbeat*, then took a spare guitar and went out the back to practise my strumming. Sitting there, plunking on the guitar, I sort of hit on an idea, a kind of hillbilly-shuffle thing. My guitar playing was still at page three of *The Mickey Baker Jazz Guitar Book*, but I could strum enough to get out of trouble and this shuffle feel was sounding pretty catchy to me.

Over half an hour or so I came up with some words, half sung, half spoken against a C chord.

There's no one I can talk to, they've all got troubles of their own
I try to tell how bad I feel, I'm on my Pat Malone
But I found a way to have your say, all you folks who have no one
Just sit right down and tell it all to good old number one.

Then came a sung chorus, which went up to the F chord.

Talking the blues to myself
Get another bottle down off the shelf
Tell your troubles to the wall
When there's nobody who cares at all
Tell the cat how bad you feel
Tell the pooch about your rotten deal
I'm just talking the blues to myself.

Chuffed, I scribbled the lyrics down and went back out to the studio. They were all listening to the latest take of 'Kiss Crazy'. The general feeling was that that was as good as it was going to get.

Del said she was too tired for any more tonight and went home. But the mob were flying now, full of dexes, Remy and reefer, and they were unwilling to call it a night. They went back to their instruments, jammed on 'Honky Tonk' and 'Jumpin' with Symphony Sid', and then I said here, have a go at this, and sang them 'Talking the Blues'. They thought it was sort of funny and over the next twenty minutes we worked out a quick arrangement, with the whole lot of them singing along on the chorus, sounding like a bunch of drug-addled pisspots. Max switched to steel guitar and played a solo in the middle. The engineer had a bit of tape left over, so we recorded the song right then. It was two o'clock before everyone bolted, but I hung around for a while finishing off the brandy with the engineer while he packed up.

Outside at two-thirty I had some trouble getting the key in the ignition, and when I did the headlights didn't work. I got out and looked. Both headlights had been kicked in. Then I noticed the new defect notice pasted on the windscreen and a ticket stuck under the wiper. On the back of the envelope was written in pencil 'Ray Waters, Lest We Forget'.

I drove home along the back streets to my pad at the Kia Ora flats in Moore Park Road and fell asleep in the armchair. At four-thirty the telephone rang. I fumbled with it, picked it up and said hello. The other end hung up. An hour later it rang again and the same thing happened. I left it off the hook.

I woke later with a dry mouth, still in the armchair. It was just getting light outside. I replaced the handset and five minutes later the phone rang again. Without thinking, I picked it up, said hello. There was no reply but I could hear sounds in the background.

There was a kind of laugh, then a voice said, 'We're going to get you, cunt.'

I lit a smoke. My hand shook. One more for the list: Never get mixed up in a cop-killing.

Chapter 2

I spent the next morning brooding over the events of the previous day. Whichever way I looked at it, there was no avoiding the conclusion that word had got out that Chief Superintendent Ray Waters was dead and that I was involved. A month before, quite suddenly, I'd started copping speeding tickets when I went driving, parking fines whenever I stopped. Twice I'd come out in the morning to find my tyres deflated. I'd been putting it down to coincidence, but with that anonymous phone call it was time to take action.

First off, I drove my beloved green and white Customline up to the car yard in Paddo and swapped it for a grey Holden, got two hundred quid cash back, smashed headlights notwithstanding. I took it straight out to the Motor Registry at Roseberry and told the kid behind the counter that I'd misplaced my licence and needed a duplicate. He gave me a form to fill in. I wrote down a phony name and address and handed it to him. He came back a while later, said they couldn't find my records. I huffed and puffed and they gave me a stat dec to fill out, which I did, and they issued a licence to me under the name I'd given them. Then I registered the car under the new name. It was that easy.

I went back to the Kia Ora flats, paid up a month's rent, then went straight out to find somewhere else to live. I took a lease on the first place I looked at, a flat in Farrell Avenue in East Sydney, behind William Street. It was pretty scungy and smelled of damp, but it was cheap and private and would do me well enough while I waited for the police business to die down. I moved in the same day. I left the phone connected at the old place and got it put on under the phony name at the new joint.

I spent the next day putting things in order. With my record player set up, my framed picture of Rising Fast winning the 1954 Melbourne Cup on the wall, some bottles of beer in the fridge and tea and biscuits in the kitchen cupboard, the flat didn't seem so bad. It had its own private stairs down the back of the building which led onto a laneway that could have come straight out of a gangster movie. The landlord was a Maltese bloke named Sam. He seemed inclined to mind his own business.

After lunch I opened a bottle of beer and drank a toast to the new pad, allowed myself a little pat on the back for my quick action. I finished the beer, dropped a couple of pills, and presently paddled my board onto that familiar wave of confidence and well-being.

I went into the bathroom, and while I brushed my teeth I took a long hard look at myself in the mirror. My hair was still sandy and most of it was still there, and so too were my teeth. Sure, I could have done with a couple more pounds, and maybe my face was rather drawn. For a 31-yearold, my eyes were a little more bloodshot than they might have been, but what the hell? I ran a comb through my hair and stood up to my full height, five ten. I shaped up, threw a few punches at the bloke in the mirror. I skipped around a bit, dodging behind my guard. That's the way, I thought, still every inch a champ.

Suitably geed up, I turned my attention to monetary matters. I got out my financial records-an old exercise book-to establish where I stood. It had been a big twelve months, starting with me well ahead, holding the combined take from the J. Farren Price robbery and my share of Lee Gordon's Little Richard tour. But since then I'd shouted a lot of drinks, fattened up a few bookies, and shelled out some hefty unsecured loans. Now the bank balance was looking decidedly crook. The way it was going, if I didn't get some real cash flow soon I'd be on the bones of my arse by Christmas.

But I still had a few hundred quid left and there was a chance I could call in at least some of the money I was owed. This ranged from the five quid Lachie owed me for the reefers (which I'd never get) all the way up to up to a £1200 advance that I'd made to

Jack Davey six months ago. Retrieving that one would require a careful approach. Despite his being the highest paid entertainer in the country, getting money out of Davey was harder work than brickies' labouring.

My philosophy on money had always been wait and see what turns up, but while you're waiting, do whatever's necessary. The more I thought about it, the more certain I was that the best course open to me was legitimacy, or the appearance of same. The problem was, short of getting an actual job, I had absolutely no idea how to earn a legitimate quid.

The next morning I went for a run and a swim at the Domain baths, then repaired to the Rock'n'roll for a restorative midday sherry while I considered how I might create a semblance of propriety. I sat and cogitated. Nothing came to me. I had another sherry, examined some of the things I'd previously ruled out.

Which led me to Uncle Dick, the blackest sheep of the Glasheen family.

It had been a while, but I could still remember his last words to me: 'Money won is twice as sweet as money earned—remember that, Bill.' That was just after he'd swindled me out of a hundred quid. Three or four years later he'd written to me from Adelaide to say he'd started a business and that there might be a place for me if I was interested. I hadn't replied to that letter and there'd been no communication between us since. He could be anywhere by now.

I put aside thoughts of lost uncles and looked at the jobs section in the newspaper. I was shocked and appalled to see how little money was to be made for forty hours' hard yakka. I closed the paper, ordered another sherry. I wrote a letter to Dick right there at the bar and sent it straight off to his old post box at the Adelaide GPO. It couldn't hurt, I thought.

Eight days later I received a reply.

Dear Bill
It was a very pleasant surprise to get a letter from you after so long. I'm glad to hear that you're interested in the mail

order business—after all, it's only right that family should stick together. Of course, I'd be delighted to do anything I can, even though your late father, God rest his soul, had some reservations about me. But I know I don't need to tell you about that.

I've enclosed two adverts cut from the sports pages of the Adelaide *Advertiser*. These ads are for my two best-selling products. As you can see, one is a cure for nicotine addiction, the other a cure for bad luck. The latter consists of a small booklet (which stresses the importance of mental outlook) and an accompanying good-luck charm, the patented Lucky Monkey's Paw. At the moment I have a number of different products for sale. They include Stop Now! (a cure for bed-wetting), Straight Talk (a cure for stammerers), and Love Secrets for Young Marrieds (a ringing indictment of prudery and narrow-mindedness). I also offer a nerve tonic and a series of life-study photographs for artists and students of the human form.

I have long been in favour of expanding the business into Sydney and possibly Melbourne. The only thing holding me back has been a lack of suitable business partners.

With you working the Sydney end, and me the Adelaide end, we could do very well, I'm certain. And who knows, maybe you will be able to introduce some new products to the range?

There's nothing wrong with commerce and enterprise so long as you are doing better than the other fellow. You may remember me once advising you to avoid any line of work in which you are required to join a trade union or similar association—not that I'm against the working man, heaven forbid! But the way I see it, any such occupation must by definition be strenuous, possibly dangerous, and will almost certainly be poorly recompensed. That is not for the likes of you or me (although it was for your father, God rest his soul).

Anyway, in the postal sales area, you will find that not more than a few hours' work a day, for two or three days a week, will produce a handsome return, leaving you plenty of time for the finer things in life.

I look forward to hearing from you.

Yours Sincerely
Dick Glasheen

There were two press clippings with the letter:

That night I put through a trunk call to Uncle Dick. We had a yack about the old days. About how he used to drop by to pay his respects to my recently widowed mum and see that everything was all right. Or sometimes take my brother and me to the Easter Show or the fights, and sling us ten bob each. There were other things we didn't talk about, like when he used to stay over at our place, supposedly sleep in the spare room. After lights out he'd tiptoe into

Mum's room, a bottle of scotch in hand, be gone before daybreak. Then there was the time he shot through suddenly and the house-keeping money went with him.

Anyway, we got the cherished memories stuff out of the way and then I hit him with some questions about the business. The Lucky Monkey's Paw, he said, was a plastic thing he had made up at a factory in Hong Kong. The nerve tonic was a harmless concoction put together by a bloke in Melbourne. All the items were small; you could squeeze the entire stock into a couple of suitcases.

'I'm telling you,' he said, 'the mail order business can be marvellous. Every week there's a slew of money orders in the post box.'

I said, 'But are there really that many mugs out there?'

'We call them *customers*, Bill. And yes, armies of them, have no fear. Didn't *you* have a Phantom ring when you were thirteen?'

'One for each hand.'

'I rest my case.'

'How legal is it?'

'Pay your taxes, don't send any filth through the post, it's legal enough.'

'What's in it for you? I mean, to be frank, you're being much more co-operative than I expected,' I said.

'Blood's thicker than water.'

'With the greatest respect, Dick—'

'Let me finish. Blood's thicker than water and therefore a good basis for a business relationship. This is what you do: you get some stock produced, sell it in Sydney. You pay all your own expenses and keep whatever you can make. In return you pay me a royalty for use of the idea, say ten percent of your gross sales. Twice-yearly payments would suit me. Cash, of course. And, naturally, I pay you the same for any of your ideas that I use.'

'All right then, I'll think about giving it a go, for a trial period. But listen, Dick, there's a mate of mine, he's good at thinking up schemes and shit. How would you feel about him coming in on it?'

'If you trust him, then so do I. What's his name?'

'Max Perkal.'

'He'd be of the Jewish faith?'

'Does that matter?'

'Not at all. I was just going to say, your four-by-two tends to be skilled at this sort of thing. Good money managers. He could be a real asset.'

Max Perkal was a pretty fair musician, he knew loads about the entertainment game, and he'd never once rooked me, not really. But what he wasn't one little bit of was a good money manager.

I said to Dick, 'Yeah, a real asset.'

The following week Dick sent me an ancient battered book called *The Business of Life*, by T. Whitney Ulmer. According to the cover it was a book of original mottoes, epigrams, oracles, orphic sayings and preachments for Men of Enterprise and Seekers of Wisdom.

In his accompanying letter Dick said:

Have a good look at this almanac, Bill. It has been my constant companion and adviser in business and all other areas of my life. It is the key to knowledge and financial success. It has helped immeasurably in attaining clarity of thought and prudence in action, and it may even help you make your fortune.

The way to use it is this: whenever you are facing a dilemma, are confused, unsure or otherwise at a loss, you hold the problem in your mind, close your eyes and open the book at random, and then read the preachment or motto. I cannot tell you how or why it works, but it usually comes up with an answer which is uncannily pertinent to the problem.'

I put the letter down and opened the book. It matters not whether the cat is black or white, as long as it catches mice, I read.

Max didn't take much convincing to come on board. The dance game was running dead but his cabaret show was firing, especially since he'd added the sultry exotic dancer Lovely Lani to the act. He was on a winning run, so he thought, and the time was right for expanding his enterprises.

We got together, reviewed Dick's merchandise and then decided to kick off trading with Dick's plastic monkeys' paws and the smoking cure. I ordered a dozen boxes of monkeys' paws from the factory in Hong Kong, and Max had a local printer run up two thousand copies of the smoking cure booklet.

But then Max's scheming mind really got to work, and at the end of two weeks we had a whole range of mail order items either ready to sell or in production. These included a betting system and two different courses in guitar and piano accordion. We had adverts made up, all ready to go except for a postal address. For *Trotguide* we had this:

And this one for the back page of the *Classics Comics*:

And another for *Man* magazine:

Calling All Hepcats!

Learn to play the ELECTRIC guitar in just 6 easy lessons!!!

Have you been trying to play ROCK'N'ROLL
but don't know where to begin? This is a golden
opportunity to turn your talents into money.
For a small outlay you can learn this exciting style
with the guidance of our experts.

Write to : The Bopalena School of Guitar . . .

Max had dummied up the guitar and accordion courses from his own collection of tutors, sheet music and old song books. The betting system was something he and a pal of his, Neville, had worked out years before. It had never been known to turn a quid for anyone, but nor had anyone lost too badly with it either. Neville was now a fast-rising Labor barrister, and happy to hand full ownership of the betting system over to Max. In fact, he was insistent he receive no money of any kind from the sale of the system and that his name not be linked with it, nor with any aspect of our enterprise. It's nice when your friends have faith in you, I told Max.

For our temporary office and storeroom, we had been using the downstairs flat at Perkal Towers, as Max's block of flats at Bondi Junction was known, but in our third week of business Lovely Lani arrived at his door in tears and announced that she needed somewhere to live. The previous weekend her parents, Greeks, had caught her act, the Tahitian Fire Dance, at the Maroubra Junction Hotel, and now her persona was extremely non grata in the strict orthodox household. So Max, ever the gent, invited her to move into the downstairs flat for a special mate's-rate rental. Max said we could rent a good room in the city for less than he could pull on the flat.

I checked out city real estate. I'd prefer a room with a view, I told the agent, nothing fancy, maybe Macquarie Street facing the botanical gardens. I spent an afternoon inspecting stately old buildings occupied by accountants, barristers, gynaecologists, and the like. After seeing several horribly expensive such premises, I went back to the real estate office and asked the agent, who could afford to pay rents like that? He said plenty of people. He looked at his watch, asked me did I want to think about it for a while, as he had things to attend to. I told him, listen, there must be something cheaper.

Well, he said, there *was* a room, downtown. It might better suit my budget, so long as I didn't mind sharing the premises with chows and lurk merchants. If I wanted to have a look, the place was called the Manning Building. I could get the key from the tenant next door to the empty office, one Murray Liddicoat.

It was a run-down, four-storey building in the Haymarket, backing on to the Capitol Theatre. At street level there were two Chinese restaurants, a disposal store, a shoe shop and a milk bar. There was a laneway out the back where some shifty-looking Chinese blokes were hanging about.

I took the stairs to the first floor, strolled along the corridor past a rag-trade workshop, a supplier of artificial limbs, an elocution teacher, a wig maker, an 'art studio', and two charities I'd never heard of. A middle-aged woman walked out of one doorway marked 'Association of Breeders of British Sheep'. She glanced my way. I said, 'Excuse me,' but she hurried away before I could continue.

I knocked on an unmarked door, went inside. There was an old bloke sitting at a bench, a piano accordion in pieces in front of him. I asked where I'd find Murray Liddicoat. He said he didn't know. I tried three more rooms, got nothing but suspicious looks. I walked slowly back along the hallway, taking in the atmosphere of malpractice and dubious enterprise. It wasn't Macquarie Street, but I had to admit, it was my kind of place.

I went into the sweatshop, Conni Conn Fashions. A good-looking girl with long straight brown hair was sitting at the front desk. She was reading a paperback, smoking a black cigarette. I said hello.

She slowly turned to face me. Her eyes were brown and bright, despite her serious expression. She was done up in the style that the Sunday papers were calling beatnik—black sweater, black stockings, not much makeup, eyes half-closed.

I asked her if she knew of anyone named Liddicoat on this floor.

She said she didn't and turned back to her book. 'What are you reading?' I said.

She held up the cover of her book, *Women in Love* by D. H. Lawrence.

'Good yarn?'

She said it was fabulous and returned to it.

I found Murray Liddicoat in the office two doors along. The sign on his door said 'Private Inquiry Agent'. I knocked and went in. A large, genial-looking bloke was sitting behind the desk in an almost bare room.

He sat back in his chair, his coat open over a large paunch. 'Yes?'

'I have an inquiry. The real-estate bloke said you have the key to a room for rent somewhere in the building.'

'Oh yes, I do, old son. The key's here somewhere.' He spoke out the side of his mouth, like he'd spent a lifetime at racetracks and boxing stadiums. His accent was broad but crisp. He rifled through his desk. 'Ah, here it is.' He stood up. 'Come, I will shew thee great and mighty things which thou knowest not.'

'Eh?'

'This way.'

I followed him into the corridor and along to the next office. He unlocked the door, swung it open and said, 'This is it.'

A double room with big arched windows looking out at Belmore Park. The paint was peeling, and some chunks of broken moulding were lying on the floor. There was an old scratched desk in the centre of the room, large enough to use as a work bench.

'Do you know what the rent is?'

He shook his head. 'I pay five guineas a week but this one would be a little more, in view of the appointments. Listen, old chap, I'm a little thirsty. I'm going back to my office. When you finish here just slam the door. Join me for a snort before you go, if you like.'

I looked around. This would do. I closed up and went next door to get to know my neighbour-to-be.

We had a couple of nips of Johnny Walker together. He kept the bottle in his filing cabinet. In that regard, if no other, he was straight out of your private-eye yarn. Before I left he put the bite on me for five quid. I felt like I'd known him for years.

On my way out I stuck my head into the brown-eyed beatnik girl's door. She was still reading her book.

'I found Liddicoat, he's the bloke two doors along,' I said.

'Oh, you mean Murray. You should have said his first name.'

'I found him anyway. Looks like we might be neighbours soon. My name's Bill.'

'Enchanted, I'm sure,' she said, and returned to her book.

Next day I signed a lease, paid a month in advance and then rented a box at the Haymarket post office. That afternoon Max and I lugged our just-printed stock down to the new premises in the boot of his car.

On the way I said, 'What are you reading these days?'

'All sorts of stuff. What do you mean?'

'Like, if I was reading D.H. Lawrence, say, tell me something to go on with after that.'

'For you?'

'Yeah. Or anyone. A beatnik, maybe.'

'Anything by Jack Kerouac.'

'Yeah, right, *On the Road*. What else?'

Max shrugged. 'Albert Camus, *The Outsider*.'

'What's that about?'

'A bloke shoots some Arabs, doesn't give a shit.'

'Oh yeah, like Mickey Spillane?'

'It's French. Very deep.'

'What else?'

'Marquis de Sade.'

'That's filth, isn't it?'

'Yeah, but it's French. Very deep. Why're you asking?'

'Just wondering. What else?'

'Oh, I suppose *Nausea*, by Jean-Paul Sartre.'

'Yeah?'

'There's this bloke, everything gives him the shits.'

'Don't tell me. It's French and very deep. What are *you* reading?'

'I just finished this thing called *Malone Dies*, by Samuel Beckett.'

'Hey, that's more like it. A story about an Irishman, eh? There'd be some good jokes in it, then?'

'Actually, it was written in French and—'

'So, French is the go.'

'You could say that. Especially if they're existentialists.'

'You better spell that for me.'

I gave the magazines the go-ahead to run the adverts, with the new address, and sure enough the letters and postal orders started rolling in. Over the weeks I settled into a work routine. Each day I'd empty the mailbox, then go to the office and make up the relevant packages—smoking cure, guitar tutor, lucky charm, betting system—and post them off the same day.

There was nothing too difficult about any of it, except that after a while, along with the postal orders, we began getting the occasional complaint or demand for a refund. I only answered if they wrote twice, and I never refunded so much as threepence.

The stock sold pretty evenly except for the Lucky Monkey's Paw, which proved to be a dud. There'd been a misunderstanding at the factory in Hong Kong and they'd sent me five tea chests full. At the rate they were selling, I figured we had enough to last about three centuries. So I started looking into ways of getting them moving. I got some little strips of leather, riveted them onto key-rings and carried a pocketful around with me, giving them out as a kind of gimmick. People liked them. Next I produced a deluxe version with a bottle opener as well, and took to throwing in a complimentary key-ring or bottle opener with every package I sent out. Sometimes I'd include a little thought for the day, lifted from T. W. Ulmer's book of preachments.

The daily business took me an hour or two to complete. After that, I'd do the banking then have lunch at one of the watering holes in the Haymarket area. Murray Liddicoat would sometimes join me. A man fond of a drink, he wasn't without talents: he could quote the good book, chapter and verse, on just about any topic and could reel off sports results at great length. As drinking company he wasn't too bad, although it was usually up to me to pay for the drinks.

Max kept out of the day-to-day running of the business. We had agreed on a split whereby I took wages for doing the hack work, we paid the expenses and then divided the remainder equally between us. For his part, Max was supposed to be working on expanding our product range. He talked about developing a Hawaiian guitar course and a book of jokes and magic tricks, but nothing much was coming of it. Don't worry, brother, it's all up here, he said, pointing to his head.

New Year, 1959 rolled around. The cops hadn't tumbled to my new address or phone number, and there'd been no more anonymous calls or undeserved traffic fines. Money was coming in at a rate that would see our set-up costs recouped before too long, and meanwhile I had something to keep me out of trouble. And it was all legal.

Yeah, I wasn't travelling too badly at all, I thought. I'd have that Customline back soon. Maybe I'd get a Bel Air next time.

Chapter 3

A hot Sunday in late January, I walked up to Crown Street and had a late lunch of bacon and eggs at the Italians' while I read the paper. Elvis Presley was in Germany earning $82.50 a month in the US army. Over in Cuba a 'beat-generation leader' called Fidel Castro was stirring things up. Meanwhile, the Russians had discovered a youth drug called Substance H-3. There was a picture of a bloke doing a handstand on a table, one hand. I swallowed an Aspro, paid up and left.

A bloke was waiting for me outside the cafe, leaning against a car, his arms folded. He had short, bristly hair, a round face, protruding lower jaw. I knew the face. Detective Sergeant Fred Slaney. He pointed at me.

'You, come here,' he said.

He opened the passenger door of the car. 'Get in.' I did. He walked around, got in, started the car and drove up William Street.

'Where are we going?' I said.

He didn't answer. He drove into the city, off Pitt Street into a laneway called Central Street.

'Are you taking me to the CIB?'

'When I want you to talk I'll let you know, maggot.'

He drove through an archway into a courtyard. He parked the car, got out, said, 'Come on,' and we went into the old building next to Central police station.

We went upstairs to a small room, bare but for a table and two chairs. Slaney went off and came back in less than a minute, carrying a folder.

He sat down, indicated for me to sit in the other chair, opened the folder and flipped through some papers. Then he leant back and looked at me.

'September 1957. Someone knocks over the J. Farren Price vault. Forty thousand quid's worth of jewellery. Six weeks later Chief Superintendent Ray Waters disappears. His car is found at Mascot airport. Items from the Price robbery subsequently turn up in Los Angeles. Why do you think that was, Glasheen?'

I said nothing.

'Well? What do you think happened? Don't be shy.'

'I believe there were rumours to the effect that Waters had bundied with the gear, that he was somehow mixed up in the robbery.'

He said, 'I worked with Waters on a number of cases.'

I nodded.

'And I *know* he didn't organise the Price robbery.'

I nodded again.

Slaney closed the folder, sat back. 'But I also know he had an interest in it. He was in line for a half-share of the fenced value.' He paused. 'Ten thousand pounds, so he reckoned.'

'A lot of money.'

'And I was expecting half of *his* share. That's how we used to work, sharing the take.'

'That's very touching.'

He leaned forward. His fist shot out, caught the side of my jaw, knocked me right off the chair.

'I'll let you know when I want your smart-arsery. Get up.'

I did. He continued like nothing had happened.

'So, I was expecting a half-share of Waters' ten grand.'

'You must have been upset when he disappeared.'

'I was more than surprised, you might say. So I personally looked into the matter of Ray's disappearance, on my own time.' He smiled at me. 'Among Ray's notes I found an address in Pittwater. And naturally I—'

There was a tap at the door. A voice called out, 'Mr Slaney?'

He got up and left. Ten minutes later he returned with another bloke, a grubby little feller. Slaney left us together in the room, said

32

he'd be back shortly.

The little bloke hardly looked at me. He walked around the room, blew his nose into a dirty hanky.

'It's not fuckin' fair. I fuckin' told him what happened, I told him the truth. I didn't give him up. He doesn't give a man a chance, that bastard.'

'Who, Slaney?'

'Yeah, fuckin' Mr Slaney. You got a ciggy?'

I gave him one. He lit it and looked at me for the first time. 'Thanks, mate. What are you here for?'

'I don't know.'

He nodded like he didn't believe me, then went back to pacing the room, muttering to himself.

After twenty minutes, Slaney came back with another copper.

'All right, come on, you two. You get to know each other, did you?' I looked at Slaney and he laughed. 'I mean, you'd've been wasting your time if you did.' He walked over to the grubby bloke and punched him hard in the stomach. He fell to the floor. Slaney kicked him.

'Get up, you scum.'

The little bloke slowly got to his feet. 'It's not fair, Mr Slaney, I never—'

Slaney head-butted him and then gave him another kicking.

It went on like that for five minutes or so, then Slaney said, 'All right. We'd better get going now.'

The little bloke was lying on the floor, bleeding. Slaney said to me, 'Give the little cunt a hand up.'

I helped him to his feet. The four of us went out to the court-yard. Slaney said, 'You come in the car with me, Glasheen.'

We got in his car and he drove off. The sun had gone down and there was a gritty wind blowing. The bible bashers were in Park Street singing songs to a crowd of idlers. We drove into Clarence Street and over the Harbour Bridge. Sunday evening, it was quiet on the roads.

We took the first exit off the Bridge, left into Lavender Street and along to Blues Point Road. Slaney said nothing the whole time. But he was breathing noisily through his nose and his eyes were wide. Alcohol on his breath.

The police radio was on: there had been an accident at Broadway, a disturbance in a boarding-house at Redfern, a break-in at a gift shop in Mosman.

Slaney drove down to the end of Blues Point Road and pulled up outside a big building site, right down on the harbourfront.

'Get out,' he said.

The building site was surrounded by a white-painted ply fence. Slaney walked over to the entrance, a gate with a big chain across it. He pulled out a bundle of keys and tried them each until one opened the padlock. He pushed the gate open a couple of feet.

The other cop pulled up in his car then, with the shivery little bloke on board. They followed us in. There was a gatehouse, but no one there. The site was a huge hole in the ground, blasted out of the Sydney sandstone to a depth of maybe a hundred feet. There were a few lights about the place, but it was pretty dark.

Slaney and the other cop had a quick whispered conversation, then Slaney pulled the gate closed behind us.

'All right, come on, you two.'

We walked down a steep, rough roadway which spiralled around the edge of the excavation, all the way to the bottom of the pit. There was earthmoving equipment down there and the ground had been roughly smoothed out, ready for construction to proceed. Steel reinforcing was in place over half the ground.

At the bottom of the roadway I stopped and said, 'Are we going to talk business, Slaney?'

He punched me in the face. 'Mister Slaney, maggot. So you think you might be able to say something of interest to me, do you?'

'The way this seems to be developing indicates to me, you know, that maybe you're considering acting on what you think the situation is, when maybe you're not in possession of all the facts, and I was—'

'Shut your mouth.'

Slaney turned to the little bloke, who was whimpering now, and pushed him in the chest a couple of times, away from the roadway.

Slaney turned his head away, spat on the ground, then pinched his nostrils closed. 'Phew, this little prick has shat himself.' He put his hand into his coat, brought out a gun and shot the bloke in the head. He seemed to crumple in on himself. He twitched once and then was still, bent over in a position that no living body could ever have achieved. Slaney fired twice more into the body, which gave a little shake as each bullet went in. Blood trickled out from under the body, black and oily in the dim light.

'Okay, Terry, you better put a couple in him too.'

The other copper was looking none too spry now, but he took out his gun and fired twice. Slaney pulled a half-bottle of scotch out of his back pocket and took a swig, handed it to the other copper. 'All right, Terry, let's see what you're like with a bulldozer. The keys are supposed to be in it.'

When the cop had gone, Slaney looked around, rubbed his chin and said, 'I did this in the wrong place. All right, Glasheen, it's time to see how fit you are. Pick up that piece of shit there—' he walked over to a pit, grave-size, which had been cut into the sandstone—'and drop him into this hole. I'd be careful though, that feller's leaking from everywhere.' He laughed, a short, ugly sound.

I took the body by the feet, dragged it over to the edge of the pit, stopped.

'Go on, drop him in.'

The body fell to the bottom, about four feet down.

'Life is short and full of woe,' said Slaney. He laughed again, turned around. 'What's holding Terry up?'

Right then the front-end loader started. The cop drove it towards us. Ten yards away he put the blade down and pushed a load of rubble into the pit, reversed up and did it again until the top was level. Then he drove over the spot a couple of times with the blade down to smooth it out and square it all off. He stopped the vehicle, got out and had a spew. But Slaney was in good spirits now.

'The concrete pour is on first thing tomorrow. Fifty tons of concrete should shut the little fucker up. All right, Terry, you did well. You can shoot through.' He turned to me, put his hand heavily on my shoulder. 'Now, young Bill, you said something about doing business.'

Slaney drove us back to East Sydney. On the way he finished his account of his investigation into Ray Waters' disappearance.

'So I found this address among Waters' things. It was a place up at Pittwater. I went there, took the ferry across the bay. No one home. The ferry driver recognised a photo of Ray Waters, remembered taking him across. But he couldn't remember taking him back to Church Point.

'I found out that you're the owner of the place, and before that old Laurie O'Brien was. I knew who he was, but I'd never heard of you.' He smiled at me. 'But I know a bit more about you now.

'So I had a bit of a walk around up there at your place, thought about it all. I saw the boat down there in the shed, looked at the water, the open sea just a few miles away. And then I pretty well knew what had happened: you and O'Brien killed him and dumped him in the briny. Now, I admit, it seemed unlikely, a bodgie petty crim and a broken-down old bookie taking on Ray Waters. But I was certain that was what happened.'

'What if I didn't kill him? What if I just happened to have been there? Hypothetically.'

'Doesn't matter a flying fuck. You were there and you failed to prevent it. That fact alone makes you as guilty as the perpetrator. And then, you benefited from it—maybe a judge would give you twenty years instead of life. You want to put it to the test?'

'No, not really.'

He pulled up in William Street, turned off the engine.

'Don't get me wrong. As far as I'm concerned, your relationship with Ray Waters is your business. He was nothing special to me, and knowing Ray, he probably asked for it. Spoilsport old cunt that he was.' Then he turned to me and leaned right over until he was inches from my face.

'But you see, Glasheen, I never got my money. *That's* what gives me the shits. I was counting on it.'

'So what do you want from me?'

'Ten thousand pounds. Obviously.'

I stared at him. 'You can't mean it. I've got less than a thousand.'

'I do mean it.'

'It would take me years to make that much. And what's stopping you from killing me anyway, even if I do pay you?'

'Absolutely nothing.' He brought his gun out, put it to the side of my head. 'It's up to you. If you think I'm asking too much, we'll drive back to the building site, take care of it all right now. That way, you won't have to bother yourself with raising the money, or with anything else. The alternative, have a go at getting the money. If I was you, I'd have a go.' He put the gun away. 'That way you have a chance at least. What have you got to lose?'

I thought hard. 'I need time.'

'I understand that. Since this is a kind of settling of accounts, an appropriate deadline would be the end of the financial year. I'll give you until the first of July. See it as a kind of race against the clock. Now, I'll let you choose how you do this. You can either give me fortnightly instalments, or a lump sum at the end.'

'I'll go for the lump sum. How do I get in touch with you?'

'You don't, I'll keep in touch with you. You live in a flat up the back there, work down at the Haymarket, drive a grey Holden. Yeah, I know your movements pretty well, Glasheen. I'll keep in touch, don't worry about that. Off you go now.'

I stayed indoors with the blinds drawn for the next three days. I'd never crossed Slaney's path before but I'd heard the stories. About how he was a loner in the force but had a hand in nearly everything bent that was going: abortionists, pros, bludgers, thieves, standover men, bookies—a whole army of crook operators made regular payments to him just to stay in business. Then there was his other job, the New South Wales Police Force's unofficial assassin.

I slept badly or not at all. My appetite vanished. I tried to read, couldn't concentrate; turned on the television, couldn't sit still. I had a nearly constant headache and a cold feeling in my guts.

Towards the end of the week, my nerves started to settle down. It was pay up or die, and the longer I spent shivering in my burrow, the nearer the deadline would get. I opened Uncle Dick's book of wisdom. The preachment said, *Put fear aside and go forward.*

I turned my mind to the matter of the ten thousand pounds. A huge amount of money. You could buy a row of terrace houses for that much, or three new American cars.

First off, I'd have to call in all my debts. If I did the rounds I could probably collect half of what I was owed, or maybe more. And there was the Jack Davey loan. That might add up to one and a half or two grand. But I knew my only chance for the really big money lay in high-risk, high-return endeavour—lawbreaking.

The fact was, however, I was sadly underqualified for day-to-day criminal work. The rorts I'd done in the past had been other people's jobs that I'd tagged along on, or else spur-of-the-moment things I'd stumbled into. I had no real idea about the routine business of crime. For the life of me I wouldn't have known how to open a safe, pick a lock, or shimmy up a drain pipe.

I got on the phone to Teddy Rallis, slippery man about town, dealer in stolen property, and prime mover of the J. Farren Price deal. I told him I was on the loose and interested to hear of any business on the go, and that I wasn't averse to trying my hand at the semi-skilled, meat and potatoes aspects of the trade. He said he'd keep in touch.

Then I got out and pressed the flesh, visiting those places known to be frequented by the lawless element. I started at the Bognor, moved on to Monty's at Pyrmont. I mingled, got into shouts, dropped hints here and there. I wasn't exactly overwhelmed with offers, so I moved on to the Ancient Briton at Glebe. I asked the bloke behind the bar if he'd heard of any, you know, 'jobs' going anywhere. He kept a straight face, said he understood they were looking for an offsider on the brewery truck.

I went to the Victoria at Annandale where I spotted Ronnie Cosgrove. Just after the war, when Ron had been a Newtown publican, I'd run sly grog for him. Nowadays he was the acknowledged expert at hoisting cigarette trucks. So lucrative was the ciggy truck business, three or four such jobs could get me square with Slaney. I renewed my acquaintance with Ronnie and let him know I was available. He nodded, said he'd be happy to have me on board but he had nothing on right now. I read in the paper next day that a Rothmans truck had gone off that very evening.

But I didn't panic yet, I had five months. Christ, anything could happen in that time.

Chapter 4

Back on the mail order front, things had been let slide. Not that a few days mattered so much—the mail was so slow, I could let the post office take the blame for my tardiness. But mail order was my bread and butter, and it would be a mug act to leave it any longer. So on the Friday of the second week after my encounter with Slaney, I went back to the Manning Building.

It was the wrong day and the wrong time. When I got out of the lift a rough-looking hoon was knocking hard on my office door. He was forty or so, wearing a yellow sports shirt with big green blotches on it. I couldn't place him as anyone I knew. He grew more impatient, banged harder.

I walked down the hall. He looked at me as I drew level. His shirt was a map of Hawaii, the green blotches were the islands. I nodded good day and walked past him.

He called out to me, said, 'Do you work here, pal?'

'Ah, yeah. Why?'

'I'm looking for the bloke who works in this office.' He pointed to my door. 'Do you know him?'

'Oh, I see him now and then. Do you want me to give him a message?'

'Yeah. Tell him to ring this number.' He handed me a slip of paper with a phone number on it.

'Can I ask what it's in connection with?'

'About a betting system I bought from him.'

'I'll pass it on,' I said.

After he'd gone I went inside, watched from the window as he got into a light blue Zephyr convertible and drove away. If that goose thinks he's getting a refund from me, I thought, he's having himself on.

But coming on top of my other troubles, the episode unnerved me. So instead of going to work straight away I nipped over to the Chamberlain for a calming draught. An hour later, suitably calmed, I cautiously made my way back to the office.

Five minutes after I arrived back, the brown-haired beat girl from Conni Conn tapped on my door. She said there'd been a bloke looking for me earlier.

'Oh yeah, a bloke in a yellow shirt? I saw him. It's all okay.'

She shrugged like it didn't matter much to her either way. Then she stopped, walked over to the desk, picked up the copy of *On the Road* lying there.

'Jack Kerouac. Is this yours?' she said.

'Sure.'

She nodded. I asked her name. She said Trish. I offered her a ciggy. She accepted, I lit it. She took a puff and said, 'So, you've read Kerouac?'

'Yeah, of course. Not bad really. But right now I'm rather more taken with the French existentialists.' I pulled out the copy of *The Outsider* that Max had loaned me.

Trish looked at it, nodding. She said, 'Albert Camus. I hear it's good.'

'Have it,' I said.

'No. Wait till you've finished it.'

I said sure, and then hit her with a couple of questions. Turned out she was a student at Sydney University, studying arts. A North Shore girl, working at the sweatshop for the holidays.

She finished her cig and said, 'A couple of the girls back in the workshop were talking about you the other day.'

'Really?'

'Yeah. They were trying to guess what it is you actually do. Sometimes you're here, then you're not. So what *do* you do?' she said.

'Oh, you know. Kind of a businessman. I sell things.'

She nodded, then glanced at her watch. 'Gee, I'd better get going. Hey, a gang of us are meeting for a drink after work, up at the Vanity Fair. Pop in if you feel like it. Saloon bar, five o'clock.'

I told her I might just be there.

I called Dick in Adelaide and asked him did he ever encounter dissatisfied customers. I mean, *very* dissatisfied. He said, sure, just never let them find out where you work or where you live. Everything by mail. They can't thump you through the post, he said. He asked me if everything was all right. I told him sure, everything was sweet.

That night I met up with Trish and her friends, three girls and a bloke, university people. At six-thirty we went up to Pitt Street for a Greek feed, and afterwards I walked with Trish to Elizabeth Street, put her on a bus to Randwick, where she said she flatted with two girlfriends.

I had a drink at the Elizabeth Hotel and then caught a cab to Wentworth Park Dogs.

I had no real idea of greyhound form, but I bet a few quid while I moved around, refreshing old contacts and making new ones. I had a yarn with George Freeman, shared a drink with Lenny MacPherson, passed on a tip to Chicka Reeves. No one told me to piss off, but nor did they welcome me into their confidence. For all my past lurkery, I suppose in their eyes I still hadn't done the apprenticeship: a life of break-and-enters, bashings, shootings, ring-in rorts and standovers. Nor had I attended the right schools: Mt Penang, Gosford or Tamworth boys' homes, Parramatta, Grafton or Long Bay jails. Involvement in a cop-killing might have impressed them, but I didn't feel like skiting about that one.

At ten-thirty I was taking a leak. A couple of louts came in behind me, one of them singing 'Heartbreak Hotel'. The other sidled up next to me at the trough and said in a stage whisper, 'Pssst. Want to buy a transistor radio, sport?'

I buttoned up, turned around. A twenty-year-old bodgie in a red shirt was grinning at me. I looked across to his mate standing at the mirror, carefully combing his black hair.

'Hasn't anyone told you the bodgie look is *passé* now?'

'Billy Glasheen! Jesus, how are you?'

'G'day, Les. No complaints. How about you?'

'Killing 'em.' He called out to his companion, 'Hey Kev, Billy Glasheen's here.' He turned back to me. 'You remember Kev, do you?'

'Yeah. G'day, Kev.'

Les said, 'Hey, what does *passé* mean?'

'It means gone, but not like real gone. More like finished. It's French.'

'Yeah? What would those gigs know? I'll tell you what, it's really lucky us running into you like this.'

'Lucky for me or for you?'

'For all of us. What I said before about the radios—'

A couple of old blokes came in right then, gave the three of us a suspicious look.

'Let's meet over at the pie stand after the next race, okay?'

I looked at the two of them, at their loud clothes and couldn't-give-a-fuck manner, then I glanced over at the older blokes giving them the dirty looks. Before that year was out, most of Australia would be viewing Les Newcombe and Kevin Simmonds the same way. But I wasn't to know that then. What I did know was that young lairs so keen to draw attention to themselves did not make ideal partners in crime. On the other hand, I needed every zack I could make. Les was waiting for my answer.

I told him all right.

I'd first met Les Newcombe back in 1955 at the Aloha Milk Bar when Max and I were trying to promote rock'n'roll music. Back then Les had been among the inner circle of early rock'n'roll devotees. He turned up again at the Stadium shows with Kevin Simmonds when I was road managing for Lee Gordon. They used to steal cars parked outside. A couple of times I'd slung them comps, on condition they left my car and Gordon's alone.

I joined up with Les and Kevin after the fourth race. We talked about chances in the next and they asked me what was coming up in the way of rock'n'roll shows. I told them I didn't really know, I'd lost touch with Lee Gordon.

Then Les got to the point. He asked if I knew anyone who could get rid of some gear. What sort? I said. Twenty German cameras, a whole lot of watches and a dozen transistor radios.

'Surely you blokes know people,' I said.

'We're in a hurry,' said Les. He explained that he and Kevin had been working hot for a while and the coppers were on Kevin's hammer. I said is that why he's hanging out so inconspicuously here tonight?

So, Les said, could I do anything for them? There were no telephones on course and I wasn't about to give anyone's telephone number to Les without permission, so I said meet me later outside, at the public phone in St Johns Road. I got out before them and rang Teddy Rallis, told him the story. He asked me if Les and Kevin were all right, I said as far as I knew they were. We arranged to meet the next day at the Welcome Inn, more commonly known as the Bunch of Cunts.

We did. They all got on okay and everything went off swimmingly. Teddy arranged to collect the gear that same day and I collected a cut for acting as go-between. But the whole business didn't involve more than two hundred quid, and although Les and Kevin indicated they had more work on, their league was too junior even for me. Or so I thought.

The following week I went to work for two days, got my stuff done as quickly as I could. I kept an eye out for thuggish customers seeking refunds.

Murray Liddicoat's office was unattended the first day, but he was there when I knocked on the second. He was pale and pasty, sitting there at his desk staring out the window.

I said, 'Murray, I need some professional advice.'

'Come in, Bill, sit down. What can I do for you?'

'Do you ever do debt collecting work?'

'Within certain limits, I do whatever my clients want me to do. That sometimes includes mercantile management work. Why do you ask?'

'Jack Davey owes me twelve hundred quid. I may need help in levering it out of him.'

'A tough nut to crack, from what I hear. I hope you're not asking me to go around and shake him up.'

'No, no, nothing like that, I was thinking of using psychology. If Davey thinks I need it urgently, which as it happens I do, I'm worried that he'll give me the bum's rush.'

Murray nodded. 'It's a sad fact that most people are decidedly reluctant to give their money to the truly needy. A beggar in a business suit will out-earn the poor wretch in rags every time. What do you want of me?'

I told him. Later, after I'd made a trip to the Chamberlain for a half-bottle of scotch, Murray added some touches of his own and made some suggestions about how I should follow up. By the third snort of Johnny Walker the colour had returned to Murray's face and he was ready to go. He rang Davey's number. I sat there, listened to his side of the conversation.

'Hello, Mr Davey. Keith Barnstable here. How are you today, sir? Glad to hear it. I won't keep you long. I'm a chartered accountant and I've been appointed by Mr Bill Glasheen to look after his accounts . . . What's that you say, *bankruptcy*?' Murray chuckled indulgently, winked at me. 'Hardly, Mr Davey. Rather the reverse, in fact. Mr Glasheen's business affairs are nowadays of an order that demands a professional to do the books. Which is why I'm ringing. I see here an outstanding item of twelve hundred pounds. No pressure, of course, but I was wondering if you could give some indication as to when we might be able to finalise this . . . I see, I see, yes, of course. I quite understand. Now, Jack, I don't wish to be indelicate, but if you're having difficulties, let us know and I'm sure Mr Glasheen would be amenable to a rescheduling of the debt. He may even be able to advance you a little more, if necessary, to see you through.'

This last bit was Murray's idea, the theory being that by patronising Davey, we might just goad him into an extravagant gesture, like paying me the twelve hundred.

Murray gave him my new phone number, cheerily told him not

to hesitate to call and then hung up. To me he said, 'There you go. Time the follow-up correctly and you might just have him.'

I met up with Trish at the West End in the evening. She wasn't with her friends this time. We had a drink, then went to dinner at a steak house in Taylor Square.

It was never meant to be a date as such, but things were cooking. Our knees bumped under the table. She didn't smile once, but kept looking out from behind the long hair that hid half her face. After the meal we walked down Forbes Street to the El Rocco and sat around drinking shitty coffee, listening to the group play Blue Note–style jazz. During a break we smoked a reefer outside and then came in and danced to the bop. She closed her eyes while she danced, and still didn't crack it for a grin.

Afterwards we walked back to my pad. We stopped for a kiss on the way. If Trish hadn't spoken much all night, she sure made up for it with that kiss, which was fantastic. Her lips were soft and yielding, but there were little tremors and return pressures which said all kinds of things.

The furnishings in my flat were still pretty basic—an armchair and a small bookshelf, my TV and record player. Trish looked around. She picked up one of my paperbacks and read aloud from the cover blurb, 'They made wild beatnik love to a crazy bongo beat!' She shook her head, put it down, and then flipped through my records. She ignored the country and rock'n'roll, pulled out John Coltrane, then a Ray Charles, and some Brazilian thing I'd forgotten I owned.

I poured drinks for us. Trish sat on the floor resting against my knees as we smoked more dope and played the records. I leaned over, smelled her hair, pushed it aside and kissed her neck. I reached around and undid the buttons of her blouse. She moved forward as I slipped it off over her shoulders. I undid her bra, cradled her breast in my hand, brushed my thumb over her nipple. She shivered, breathing fast and shallow. She whispered, 'I really should go or I'll miss the last bus.'

She turned around to face me, kneeling on the floor, her face serious, her eyes heavy.

'Don't go. I still haven't seen you smile,' I said.

And then she did. She stayed. We made wild beatnik love to a crazy bongo beat.

Trish was gone when I woke up. I lay in bed for a while, feeling pretty good. But as I awoke more fully, the evil chill that had settled in my bones the past few weeks returned.

I got up, made a coffee with a shot of scotch in it. That helped a little, so I had another. I was still tossing up whether or not to pop into work when I got a call from Jack Davey. He asked how I was, if I was busy. I told him I always had time for him, what was on his mind? He said would I like to drop by his pad later that morning, he had a bit of an idea he wanted to talk over with me. I told him I'd be there.

I knew that if this little bit of confidence-trickery was to work, I had to come across like a fair dinkum winner. So I tubbed, shaved close, bunged on some aftershave, and ironed the cleanest shirt I could find. Then I ate a couple of dexes, strolled up to Angelo De Marco's and got myself a square cut.

Angelo gave me a good trim. He showed me the back of my head in the mirror, took the sheet off me, brushed me down, smiled and said, 'Now is champion, eh?'

I said, 'Yeah, too right, that's great, Angelo.' But try as I might, all I could see in the mirror was a hunched-over, narrow-eyed feller, a man running scared.

I drove the Holden down to Wolseley Road, Point Piper, parked it well away from Davey's waterfront flat. He answered the door himself. At fifty years old, he was still dapper but the demanding schedule, the grog, and the drugs he took for his 'back pain' were catching up with him. He shook hands and brought me inside.

'Good to see you again, Billy. Listen, I'm running a little late on a press conference. Come on through and have a drink. But first, I've got something for you.' He handed me a small paperback book. It was called *The Wonder Book of Australiana*.

I looked at him and said, 'What's this for?'

'That book, my friend, is the key to knowledge and unheard of financial success.'

'Another one.'

'I'll explain later. Come on in. Best keep the book out of sight.' I followed him into the large lounge room. There was a bunch of blokes hanging around the bar, where a white-coated feller was pouring drinks.

A little bloke in a Sinatra hat and a bad jacket came over to Davey and said, 'Ready when you are, Jack.'

Davey moved over to a bare wall and called out, 'Could I have your attention, gents. On behalf of the Australian Wool Board, may I present the lovely Sabrina. Hang on to your hats, fellers.'

A blonde woman in a tight-fitting woollen dress walked out of the bedroom doorway. She took little mincing steps and wobbled her large breasts, Jayne Mansfield–style. A couple of blokes whistled. Sabrina posed this way and that while flashes popped, always careful to push out the tits.

'Say hello to the boys, Sabby.'

'Hi, boys, how are you all?' Her accent was Brit, broad northern. Someone called out to her to turn side on. She did, silhouetting the cantilevered superstructure. More flashes. Then Davey stood next to her, mugging and making a big show of eyeing her off.

After a couple of minutes of that he said, 'Okay, now make sure you get this, boys: on behalf of Channel Seven and our sponsors, the Australian Wool Board, I'm proud to announce a new television program, *The Australian Wool Show*, the biggest, richest, most star-studded event this country has ever seen. The program will feature a quiz show and top-line variety entertainment. Next week I'm off to America to promote Australian wool products and line up talent for the show. Off the record, we are currently negotiating with Marilyn Monroe, Jack Benny, Bob Hope, Sammy Davis Jr, Elvis Presley, and many other stellar attractions. Sabby herself will be the guest star on the first show, on which she will perform one of the most daring song-and-dance acts ever witnessed in this country. Hey, Sabby, why don't you turn around, show the fellers the rear view?'

She did. Then the little bloke in the Sinatra hat stepped forward and said, 'All right, gentlemen, now there'll be an opportunity for you to conduct private interviews in the other room.'

He led Sabrina away again, came back out and one by one took press blokes into the room.

Davey came over and said, 'Come outside a moment, Bill.' On the balcony he said, 'What do you think?'

'Crazy.'

'No, I mean my new show, *The Australian Wool Show.*'

'Yeah, it'll be a killer for sure, no risk.'

'This is something new. Simulcast, they call it—on radio and TV at the same time. International stars, and a quiz with *big* prize money.'

'Oh, yeah. Tremendous.'

'The sponsors are ready to go for broke. Two thousand quid prize money, every week. Jackpotting.' He paused, gave me a meaningful look.

'Why are you telling me this?'

'Well, Bill, there's the business of the money I owe you . . .'

'Oh, yes, I do seem to remember something.'

'Don't try to con a conman. I'll get right to it.

The thousand I owe you —'

'Twelve hundred.'

'Whatever. I can't pay it. I'm broke. Sorry, but that's how it is. I've got a desk full of letters in there, every one of them begins with the word "unless". But I want to do the right thing by you.'

'And?'

'And I have a little plan which could earn us a lot more than that piddling thousand.'

'Twelve hundred.'

'Do you want to hear it?'

'Go ahead.'

'You appear on the Wool Show, as a contestant.'

'Doing what? Animal, mineral or vegetable? Twenty questions? Come on.'

'Australian sport and general knowledge. There's a big waiting list but the final choice of contestants rests with me. We'll wait till the jackpot gets right up high and then I'll slot you in.'

'I left school after the Intermediate. There's no way I could do it.'

'I can't give you the actual questions because they don't exist yet. But I can do the next best thing. That book I gave you . . .'

'The key to knowledge and unheard of financial success.'

He nodded. 'You get the picture. The answer to every question we'll ask is in that book. Learn it and you're home and hosed.'

'It's a bit risky, isn't it?'

'Well, this is the way it's usually done, if you understand me.'

'It's fixed?'

'Put it this way: modern quiz programs more resemble the wrestling than they do real life. In real life, as we know, by and large winners keep winning and losers keep losing, with only occasional exceptions. In wrestling and in quiz shows, the battler has a chance, and vice versa; last week's winner could, and should, be this week's loser. If it's run right. You could say we iron out some of the shortcomings of real life, improve on it.'

'Blimey. Rigged!'

'Keep your voice down. Look, I'm telling you this off the record. Not *rigged*. Stage managed. Just enough to make it a good show. And that's where you come in. It's like in the fights, a good guy goes up against a bad guy, an abo against a fair-headed bloke, dago against Englishman, and so on—you know the drill. Well, it's the same in the quiz show racket, we work hard to maintain the balance. Anyway, you'd make a good winner—a decent Aussie bloke making a go of a small business, not too thick, but not real bright either.'

'Thanks.'

I'm talking about image here, Bill. By the way, what business are you in?'

'Mail order.'

Davey laughed. 'We'll say sporting goods.'

'How much would have to I kick back to you?'

'You don't "kick back" anything. However, if you were to let that grand drop—'

'It was twelve hundred.'

'Of course. Anyway, you let it drop and maybe later on you can loan me a few thou, if you get my drift.'

'But what if the jackpot doesn't get up high enough?'

'Oh, it will. You don't have to decide now. Take the book with you. You've got a few months to think about it. We'll launch the program later in the year after I get back from America. Meanwhile, you study that book. Hey, do you want to interview Sabrina before you go?'

'Why would I? I'm not a journo.'

'There's a special deal her manager gives the press blokes, just to prove there's no trickery topside. A couple of minutes alone with her. They cop a quick look, a feel if they're lucky, satisfy themselves the tits are real. Christ, it's getting her some great publicity. You want a go?'

'Some other time, I've got to shoot through. But tell me one thing, with this quiz show business, am I the good guy or the bad guy?'

'The good guy, of course.'

I went home and browsed through *The Wonder Book of Australiana*. I found out that the lowest temperature ever recorded in Australia was −8°F at Mt Kosciusko on 14th June 1945; that Australians drink 238,000,000 gallons of beer per year; and that the biggest black marlin landed in Australia weighed 680 pounds, caught at Bermagui in 1940 by one C. Starling.

At five o'clock I was tossing up whether or not to go hit the greyhounds again that night when Max rang, all excited, telling me to be sure to tune my television in to *Six O'Clock Rock*. He and Del had landed a spot, he said. They were going to perform 'Kiss Crazy', give it a bit of a flying start for its release next week. Max said if I felt like tagging along afterwards, they would be kicking on with the television crowd at the 729 Club. I said I might, and wished him luck.

Six O'Clock Rock had only been running a couple of months

but already it was the most watched program on Australian television. Johnny O'Keefe was fronting the show. His career had passed its peak, but he was hanging in. He'd still sing like Little Richard, and Jerry Lee Lewis had had a minor hit covering Johnny's own song, 'The Wild One' the year before. But he was mixing in more and cabaret.

He was admired as a powerhouse businessman, but was popping more pills and smoking more reefer than even Max and me. The show was all live music, no lip-syncing. Motley acts came and went, and often as not O'Keefe had forgotten their names by the time he was announcing them. 'Put your hands together for . . . a cat who needs no introduction!' he'd say.

I tuned in to Channel Two at six o'clock. O'Keefe booted off with 'Wild One'. Ten minutes into the show he introduced Del and the Percolators, just like that—left Max's name right out of it. The camera cut across to Del and the band, who were on a low rostrum. Kids were dancing on the studio floor. Del looked good, and did a better than passable job of 'Kiss Crazy'. Max at the piano behind her played standing up, Little Richard style. The other Percolators were wearing sharp suits but Max looked a sight in a Hawaiian shirt, sunglasses, beret and Bermuda shorts.

Del and O'Keefe finished the show with a duet on 'Love Is Strange'. O'Keefe's band, the Deejays—and not the Percolators—supplied the back-up.

I met them later at the 729 Club. Del was on top of the world. O'Keefe had made it clear that they wanted her to make a repeat appearance on the program, and hinted that there could be a regular spot for her, minus Max. Max was peeved about not playing back-up guitar on 'Love Is Strange', which had long been part of his and Del's stage act. He was steadily getting drunker.

Later on, when the party split up, Del and I were left together. We got talking, and without me engineering it, Del ended up coming back to my place for a reprise of our stalled love affair. She had a quick glance around the new digs, was not greatly impressed.

The next morning, when I brought in a cup of tea, she was sitting up in bed holding a long strand of Trish's dark brown hair between her fingers, peering at it. She turned around to face me, waiting.

I put the tea down, went and had a shower. When I came back Del was walking out the door. She stopped, turned around, pointed at me and said, 'You're going nowhere, Bill. See you, I'm off. Don't call.'

Thursday of the following week I slipped in to work at eleven, raced through the orders. At lunchtime Murray tapped on the door looking red-eyed and liverish. He came over to the desk, sat down, avoiding my eye. I asked how he was, he said fighting fit. Then he asked me how *I* was. I said all right, why was he asking? He said no special reason.

Then, on my suggestion, we adjourned to the Goulburn, sup-posedly for a counter lunch of curried snags. Once there though, we kept to liquid sustenance. Murray's outlook brightened with each nip. Mine got worse.

After a little while Murray leaned over and said quietly, 'Listen, old sport, there was a chap here asking about you the other day.'

'Oh yeah? Maybe it was a customer.'

'He didn't look the hillbilly guitar type.'

'What type *did* he look?'

'The policeman type.'

'Fred Slaney?'

'Heaven forfend. No, this was a New Australian cove.'

'What did you tell him?'

'That I'd never heard of you.'

'Thanks.'

Murray finished his drink, bit me for a tenner and left. I killed another hour at the pub, then went back to the office. I finished wrapping the last package, took the whole pile down to the post office and sent it off.

I went back to straighten things up, drew the blinds, locked up and left by the goods lift at the back of the building. It let me out in a loading dock on the ground floor. The dock opened onto a crooked laneway which ran between the Manning Building and the Capitol Theatre. The only people who used the lane were garbos, truckies, and some shadowy blokes who came and went at odd hours. I tapped on a green doorway where an old sign said 'Chinese Christian Seamen's Welfare Association'. An aged character opened the door, then stood back to let me in. He closed the door behind me, put the bolts back in place and said, 'Pipe?' I nodded.

Mr Ling ushered me into the small room at the back. There were four blokes there, pretty beaten-looking Chinese guys of indeterminate age. They ignored me. Mr Ling directed me to a couch. I gave him ten bob and he brought out the makings. They had recently installed a record player in the room and 'Quiet Village' was playing. Which was an improvement on the Mantovani they'd had playing last time.

Mr Ling held a flame under the gooey stuff in the bowl. I drew on the pipe and felt a warming deep inside me. I sat back and drifted off while Fred Slaney, the yellow-shirted bloke, and every single member of the New South Wales Police Force quietly joined Ray Waters at the bottom of the sea.

Chapter 5

To avoid unexpected meetings with coppers, customers, or whom-
ever, I thought it best to enter and leave the Manning Building by
the back entrance. The Chinese downstairs were pretty wary, having already had one run-in with Cec Abbott's drug squad, and these
days they kept a watch out permanently. Not that you'd know. The
few times I bumped into Mr Ling in the back lane, he gave a tiny
nod which I took to mean something like 'I note that you now
regularly use the back entrance; you no doubt have your reasons
and they are probably associated with crook goings on. We respect
your privacy.'

Murray got sent off the field around that time. He told me he'd
be in St Luke's Hospital for a short stay, would I clear his mailbox
while he was gone? I told him no risk.

A week later the estate agents sent a bloke around to change the
lock on Murray's door. Was there a problem? I asked. Apparently
the tenant was going bad, the locksmith said, hadn't paid any rent
for months. Next day the agent came around to clear out the office. I asked him had he tried to contact Murray. He had—Murray
rented a flat in Bondi from him as well and he had skipped out of
that weeks ago, also owing back rent.

I said, 'I've heard he's been unwell, that he's getting medical
attention.'

'He'll bloody need it if I catch up with him,' the agent said. Then
he asked if I'd hold on to the new key, to let in any prospective
tenants that he might send over. I told him I wasn't always here,

but he said that didn't matter, it might save him a trip sometime. I said okay.

That afternoon I went down to St Luke's. Mr Liddicoat has checked out, the sister said. She said she couldn't say where to, but then she followed me out and asked if I was a friend of his. I told her I was and she said that as far as she knew, Mr Liddicoat had gone into the new 'hospital' at Moore Park, down the road in South Dowling Street. I asked her why Murray couldn't be treated here. She hummed and ha-ed, then told me the Moore Park place was better for Mr Liddicoat. They specialise in the treatment of alcoholics down there, she said.

Down at the Moore Park clinic they treated me with open suspicion. Who was I and what did I want with Murray? I told them I was a friend. Wrong answer. To them that meant drinking mate and bad influence. I had to sweet talk for five minutes, quote a couple of Mr Ulmer's epigrams to show what a solid citizen I was. I told them how I was managing Murray's business affairs while he took this much needed time out. Finally the old duck consented to see if Murray was available. She came back a minute later and said he'd checked out that morning. Against the doctor's recommendation, she added. They didn't know where he had gone.

So I couldn't tell Murray about the winding up of his business in the Manning Building. I'd done my Christian duty by him, to hell with it, I thought.

But I took to doing my work in Murray's former premises, figuring it wouldn't hurt to keep out of my own office for a while. It was because of that I became a kind of half-arsed private eye.

I had been in there writing letters and parcelling up orders, and had just decided to have a cup of tea before I went to the post office. After that maybe I'd call it a day, drop by Mr Ling's.

A tap at the door, and a tall, thin, nervy-looking feller stuck his head around. He was looking for Murray Liddicoat he said. I told him he wasn't available at the moment. He asked when he'd be back, I said I really didn't know. He asked if I was a business partner of Murray's and I said not exactly, but I was sort of keeping an eye on things. He advanced into the room and I gestured for him to sit down.

He said that his solicitor had given him Murray's name, told him Murray might be able to help him with a certain matter, and was I sure I didn't know when Murray would be back. No idea, I said. The electric jug came to the boil. I filled the pot, asked him if he'd like a cup of tea. He said all right.

I poured two cups and gave him one. His hand shook as he took it. He was a little older than me, maybe late thirties. But his hair was completely grey and he was stooped. He was large boned and may have been athletic once, but he couldn't have weighed more than ten stone now. He wasn't wearing an RSL badge but I knew the look well enough.

He sipped his tea and said, 'Rodney Irving's my name.' He held his hand out across the desk. I gave him my name and shook.

He smiled and said, 'Well, since Mr Liddicoat's unavailable, would you be able to suggest anyone else in that line?'

'What line exactly, Mr Irving?'

'Please call me Rodney. Well, you know, the "personal and missing friends" sort of thing.' He smiled apologetically.

'You want to find someone?'

He nodded. 'Yes.'

'Do you mind me asking who, exactly?'

'A, ah, lady friend has . . . well, she's gone.'

'I see.'

'The solicitor warned me that it may cost quite a bit to hire a good man, but he said Mr Liddicoat had a good reputation for this sort of thing.' He shook his head, took a last sip of tea, smiled and said, 'Thanks for the tea. Sorry to have bothered you.' He put the cup and saucer on the desk, stood up.

I said, 'Listen, Rodney, if you're prepared to let me know some of the details, I may be in a better position to make an assessment of your case.' I opened one of the ledger books there on the desk, made like I was scanning the pages and said, 'I may be able to refer you on, or it's just possible that I may even have sufficient time over the next week or two to look into it myself.'

'Could you?'

'I'm not a licensed agent in the same sense that Murray is, right, but we've worked together on a number of important projects'—like elbow-bending at the Chamberlain Hotel, I thought—'and I may be able to assist you in the event of Murray not being able to.'

'Well, you seem a decent enough chap,' said Irving, 'and I'm not afraid of acting on my instincts. But, with all due respect, are you, ah, personally experienced in this sort of work?'

'I've stood in for Murray in some *very* important inquiries.' Like three weeks ago, I thought, when Murray sent me into the Covent Gardens to find out whether or not he was still barred.

Irving said, 'Well, I suppose that'll be all right then. What happens next?'

'You tell me all about it.'

And so it all came out. He and his 'lady friend' had had 'an understanding' for the last eight years, but now she'd gone.

Irving opened his wallet and drew out a snapshot. Him and a good-looking, dark-haired woman, dressed in evening clothes. They were sitting at a table, people on either side. The woman was smiling, composed. Rodney was slightly behind her, his face half in shadow. I handed back the photo.

He said, 'Her name's Fay. Fay Small. She cleared out a month ago.'

Just like that, I said, with no warning?

No, there had been warning, Irving said, but he didn't offer any more for a moment.

Then he said, 'I have these . . . attacks sometimes. Sort of nerves. When they happen it's hard on me.' He smiled weakly. 'But I'm afraid it's even harder on those around me.'

I looked at his sunken cheeks and deep-set eyes. 'Rodney, you're a returned man, aren't you?'

He nodded.

'And a former prisoner of war?'

He nodded again, looking surprised.

'At Changi?'

'Hong Kong.'

'Are these "attacks" connected with your experiences as a POW?'

'I suppose so, yes, they are. Cripes, you're as good as my quack.'

'You're getting treatment then?'

'I am now.'

'You weren't before?'

'Well, Fay always told me I should see someone, a head shrinker. But I kept, you know, putting it off. I thought with time, everything would come good.'

'But it didn't.'

'No. But now I'm seeing a chap, a top man in the field. And it really is helping. I want to tell Fay that things are different now.'

'You're seeing, what, a specialist?'

'A head bloke named Harry Bailey. He gives me special medication. His method is to cure you with sleep. It's very much the latest thing, I believe.'

I knew Bailey well enough. He was one of the quacks around town who gave me prescriptions for dexes.

'Well, if Harry's half as good at making you go to sleep as he is at keeping me awake, you're in business.'

'You know him then?'

'Yeah, I know him. If you don't mind me asking, why don't you just go and find Fay yourself? Why hire someone else to do it?'

'For starters, I wouldn't know where to look, or how to look. And I have my own day-to-day business to attend to. I need expert help.'

'What makes you think she'll come back, assuming we do manage to track her down?'

'You probably think I'm deluding myself. But I know she really does love me, as I love her. Fay's a stayer by nature. I just want one more chance. Once she sees that things really are different, maybe . . .'

'This could cost you a bit.'

He looked at me square. 'I'll pay five hundred pounds to the man who finds her.'

'That's a hell of a lot to pay for a matrimonial matter, if you don't mind me saying so.'

He smiled a little, nodded slowly. 'I'd pay five times that if I thought it would get me to her.'

I picked up a pen and a pad. 'Better give me some details. If I can make the time, I'll have a crack at this myself.'

There wasn't much. Fay had come over from New Zealand as a young war widow. She'd lived in Brisbane first, then Sydney. She started work at a place called Victory Press, a magazine publishing house, which was where she met Rodney. Their 'understanding' had commenced a bit later. She'd kept her flat in Elizabeth Bay but spent most of her time at his place at Fairlight.

We shook on it and Rodney took off. I figured if I could track down this woman in a week, then five hundred quid was a pretty good pay rate, and it would make a healthy addition to the Fred Slaney Benevolent Fund.

An hour later I finished up and slipped out. In the hallway I walked straight into Trish. I hadn't seen her since she'd spent the night at my place three weeks before.

'Hi. What's happened to Murray?'

'He's split. I don't know where.'

'Second question. What's happened to Billy?'

'Ah, well . . .'

'Three weeks and I haven't seen you once.'

'I've been flat out.'

'With your girlfriend?'

'What girlfriend?'

'The singer, Del, is that her?'

'Yeah. Well, sort of, but . . .'

'Anyway, that doesn't worry me. I think monogamy's really out.'

'Stereo's here to stay, for sure. But me and her are through anyway.'

'Not on my account, I hope. I think everyone should just do what they want to do, follow their heart's desire. Don't you think so?'

'Yeah, that's the principle I've always tried to live by.'

'I better get back to work. Coming for a drink on Friday?'

'Yeah, probably, maybe. See you.'

I headed down to Mr Ling's.

I started making like an investigator. I took a ferry across to Manly to see an old pal of Fay's, a single working woman named Judy. She couldn't tell me much about Fay's disappearance, other than she hoped I found her. That afternoon I drove to Kensington, saw another friend of Fay's, a married woman named Cath. Keen to help but she had no clue.

Driving back to East Sydney I was pulled over in Anzac Parade, booked for speeding and failing to give a hand signal. I'd been driving at twenty-five miles an hour, in a straight line. So much for the grey Holden disguise and the bodgie registration. Or maybe it was a coincidence. Just to be sure, I gave the cop my real licence. He grinned the whole time he was writing out the ticket.

There was one name left on the list, Michael Keogh, a 'fairy', according to Rodney. He worked at Dymock's Bookstore. I found him easily enough, working behind the counter in the non-fiction section. I told him what I wanted, he said he couldn't talk here but he was going to lunch in half an hour, he'd be at the Harris Coffee Shop.

Where the other two had nothing much to report, Michael Keogh had too much—hints, insinuations, veiled references. I asked him was Rodney on the up and up. He said there was a *lot* more to him than you first saw, you know. How about Judy and Cath, were they what they seemed? Was anyone what they seemed? he said. Was it possible Fay had another bloke stashed away somewhere? With Fay *anything* was possible, truly.

Well, where did he think she might have racked off to? He couldn't say, but one thing was for sure, if Fay didn't want to be found, no way was I going to find her. I thanked him and gave him my phone number, asked him to ring if he heard anything.

That afternoon I went to the address Irving had given me in Elizabeth Bay, Fay Small's flat. It was in a large block which faced the water, but her flat was on the other side of the building. It had already been relet. The new tenant, a sales rep, didn't know anything about the earlier occupant. Did any mail ever arrive for her? Nothing, he said. I went to Kings Cross post office to try the obvious: had she left a mail redirection order? She hadn't.

I rang Irving that night. The phone was answered by a girl, or young woman. I asked was Rodney Irving there. Sure, she said, hold the line please. He came to the phone. I wanted to ask him who the chick was but he saved me the trouble by saying straight up that she was his daughter, Pauline. I didn't know he had a daughter, I said. Yeah, from his first marriage.

I told Irving what I'd done so far and asked him how he felt about me making inquiries at Victory Press. He told me to do whatever I thought necessary but it would be better from his point of view if I didn't let on to the mob at Victory that I was working for him. But how should I act towards him when I visited, pretend not to know him? Oh, that won't be a problem, he said, he'd left Victory two months ago and gone into business for himself.

I got a few more details from him then finished up saying, 'I feel I should be up front with you—right at this moment, the cherchez la femme business doesn't look all that terribly promising. I mean, if you want to call it off, I'd understand.'

He was silent a moment, then spoke quietly. 'Please stay with it. Other than you, I am without allies in this.'

Next morning I made the scene at Victory Press. It was in a back street in Chippendale, behind Cleveland Street. Big place, with the printing works on the ground floor. I went upstairs to the office. There were half a dozen blokes at desks scattered around the room. They were smoking, talking into telephones. No one so much as glanced my way. I told the girl at the front desk I'd like to speak with the manager. She asked me to wait.

I sat down, picked up a magazine, an engineering trade paper. After a couple of minutes the boss came out, apologised for making me wait, introduced himself as Cec Lewin and asked what he could do for me. I told him I was trying to contact Fay Small. Well, he said, she wasn't there any more.

I asked him if he had any idea where Fay was now. Why did I want to know? I said her friends wished to contact her but couldn't find her. He looked at me pretty closely for a few seconds, then said, truly, he didn't know. She just disappeared. Which was a pity, he said, because apart from being a good stick, she was the best checker they'd ever had. Checker? Yeah, he said, you know, to ring back and confirm advertisements with clients, make sure the wording is right and all that. In this game, he said, it's vital to keep in close touch with your advertisers.

'Is that what you do here, then, *sales* work? I thought you were a publisher.'

'We are. The clients supply the editorial material and we do the rest, the advertising and printing.'

'What are all these blokes doing?' I said, gesturing to the room.

'They're our blowers. They sell advertising space. If we don't get that space sold, there's no magazine.'

'And that's what Rod Irving used to do here?'

'Yes, well, Rod's not with us any more, but that's right, he was a blower.' Cec Lewin looked at his watch. If there was nothing else, he said, he had things to do. I said no there wasn't, thanks for the help.

Before I left Lewin said, 'If you find Fay, tell her to get in touch, will you? We're still holding pay for her.'

Max phoned me at the Manning Building that day, told me he was backing up for a repeat appearance on *Six O'Clock Rock* the next night and that I should get along to the studio, see how TV programs were made.

I got to the studio an hour before show time. Max was on the bandstand tuning up. Even from across the studio I could see he was off his dial. He was dressed in a black sweater, corduroy trousers, sunglasses and a beret. He was in need of a haircut. He had shaved his goatee, then let it grow again, but on the monitor screen he looked unshaven.

Johnny O'Keefe came on the set, grinding his teeth, half mad on yippee beans. He saw him and said, 'For Jesus' sake, Max, you're not going on looking like that, are you?'

'Like what?' he said.

'Like a wash-up egghead, beatnik, jazz-dag.'

Max said, 'What would you know about clothes, music or any

other fucking thing, John?'

The producer separated them, led O'Keefe away for a quiet chat.

Max went and took his place with the Percolators. A minute or two later O'Keefe came back, found his mark in front of the camera. The producer addressed the studio crowd. 'All right, kids, you're here to have fun, so enjoy yourselves, okay? But the folks at home won't know you're having a good time unless you show it. And remember, no smoking, no fighting, no girl-girl or boy-boy dancing. Okay, remember, keep dancing, keep smiling.' He signalled to a tech bloke, then called out, 'Thirty seconds, everybody. Quiet please.' He turned to O'Keefe. 'You okay, John?'

O'Keefe said yeah, dad, he was fine. He took a swig from a paper cup, washed down a pill. He handed over the cup, patted his hair as the pre-recorded music played. The producer counted down the last five seconds. The theme music died down as the cameras glided around the floor filming the crowd. O'Keefe gave a big smile to the camera, said, 'Hello, viewers, it's time to rock!' and went into 'Roll Over Beethoven'. He shook his head around, let his hair get messed up like Jerry Lee Lewis.

He finished the song sweating and puffing. 'Now cats, we have the fantastic, wild and frantic Del Keene with her band,' at which Max hit a loud chord on his electric guitar, 'and Del's going to sing "Fujiyama Mama". Let's hope her band can keep up with her. All right cats, let's rock!'

After the show Max said to me, 'I'm going to hit the little cunt,' and took off. He didn't get to lay a hand on him in the end, but the two of them managed to stage a screaming match in the corridor. I got out there to hear Max calling O'Keefe a jumped up, talentless pip-squeak.

O'Keefe said, 'Max, you're a mug and a fool. You're half mad. You need help.'

Max said, 'Take a look in the mirror, gate. Everyone else can see it, you're ratbag number one. You're silly as a two-bob watch. And you sing flat.'

Which meant no more *Six O'Clock Rock* for Max Perkal.

Chapter 6

In between dodging in and out of the Manning Building, I killed time boning up on Australiana. I learned that the Australian continent has nearly a thousand separate species of ant, and that a certain Joe Garcia of Melbourne held the world record for oyster eating, four hundred and eighty at a single sitting.

One Friday afternoon, after a couple of pipes at Mr Ling's, I went to the Royal George in Sussex Street. The bar was half full. The blokes had beards, the girls wore no makeup. I found the feller I was looking for, a uni bloke named Gavin, and gave him some reefers, got ten quid from him. I had a beer. The mob in the corner started singing a version of 'On Top Of Old Smoky' with blue lyrics. Fuck these imbeciles, I thought, and went down the road to the Bunch. I had a couple more beers, thought about my money situation. It was crook. Nearly halfway to Slaney's July deadline, and I didn't have much more than what I'd started with.

I rang Trish from the phone outside the pub, arranged to meet her later. I went back into the pub, had a couple more drinks. At seven o'clock Les Newcombe tapped me on the shoulder.

We had a beer together, him glancing over his shoulder every minute or so. I asked him what he was up to. He was still working hot with Kevin Simmonds, he said.

'If you happen to need another hand on one of your jobs with Kevin, let me know.'

'I didn't think robbery was your go!'

'It is now. I need some fast money, a lot of it.'

'If I didn't know you better I'd say you were worried.'

'Who, me? Fair go.'

'You going to be here for a while?'

I told him I was and he went out to make a phone call. He returned after five minutes.

'You got a car, right?'

'Yeah.'

'Well, I just rang Kevin. Funny you asking when you did. You see,' he leaned close, 'we're doing a safe tonight. Kevin's too hot to drive a car. We need a driver. Do you want to do it?'

'Where's the job?'

'Over the north side. Belrose.'

'I'm a bit hot myself. Some of the cops around Paddo and Dario know me and they book me every chance they get.'

'It'd be your car they know, wouldn't it? Can you borrow another one?'

'Yeah, maybe I can. How much is the job worth?'

'Kevin reckons there's at least four thousand quid in the safe. Split three ways.'

'All right. I'm in.'

I was to meet Kevin and Les at Paddo after ten o'clock. I rang Trish straight after Les left, cancelled for that night and made a date for the next evening. Then I got onto Max, arranged to borrow his car for the night. He said okay, but on condition that I help out at a dance he was putting on the following night.

'I thought you were through with rock'n'roll dances,' I said.

'I was, but after that bullshit with O'Keefe and those shitheads at Channel Two, I thought to myself, Why not go west, to Bankstown, the Shire, Penrith? Are these places not chocka with bodgies and widgies looking for something to do?'

'You round up some talent?'

'All local attractions. Fortnightly dances right through winter. We'll split the take, naturally, fifty-fifty. You want in?'

'Yeah, I suppose so. On a no-obligation basis.'

'Copacetic!'

I swapped cars with Max, then spent the next two hours back at

Mr Ling's establishment. When I left there, I was pretty calm—too calm in fact, so I ate a couple of dexes. I drove to the meeting place, a terrace house near Paddo post office.

Les said, 'Are you all right?' I told him I was sweet. Les said to drive around the back lane to load up. Load up what? I said. The gear.

Three heavy boxes. Tools of the trade: gelignite, hammers, chisels, drills, bolt-cutters, bicycle inner tubes, gloves. I said is the gelignite really necessary?

Yeah, said Kevin, we're having an early cracker night. Les said don't worry, we're pretty handy with this stuff now.

We drove to the North Shore. The boys were quiet. I turned the radio on. Ronnie Self came on singing 'Ain't I'm a Dog'. I wound down the window, sang along with the chorus. Kevin said you're really into the spirit of it, aren't you? I told him I like to make the most of everything I do.

I said would you blokes like a pill to help you get into the swing of things? Kev said he wouldn't, thanks. He didn't drink, smoke or take drugs. Not that he was a wowser. No, I said, wowsers don't rob bowling clubs.

I dropped the boys near Chatswood station, where they were to steal a car for us to take on the job. That way, if anyone did happen to notice the car parked outside, there could be no link to us later on. I went to Roseville Bridge to wait for them. They arrived fifteen minutes later with a new Chevrolet. We transferred the gear into the Chev and drove up to Belrose. I was at the wheel.

We parked around the back of the deserted Belrose bowling club. There was no one around and a strong southerly had blown up. There were lightning flashes in the distance. Couldn't be better weather, said Les.

We climbed onto the roof, cut a hole in the tin and dropped into the club, right in the middle of the rows of poker machines. We found the safe, an ancient Sampson, in the manager's office. Les and Kevin set to work rigging up the charge, told me to keep a look out.

I went out to the club proper, strolled among the pokies. I felt in my pocket, pulled out a zack, put it into a machine and pulled the handle. Nothing. Les called out what the hell was I doing? Passing the time, I said. I put another zack in, saw two, three, four aces line up.

I called out, 'Hey, you blokes, how do you like this? I just pulled the jackpot!'

Les said, 'Well, if you care to wait a moment, I understand the acting manager will be opening the safe very shortly.'

When the boys were ready, they closed the office door and ran the wires out to near the bar. While they got ready for the big bang, I poured a middy of black label Johnny Walker for me and one for Les, and a soda water for Kevin, and toasted them. Les touched the wires and blew the safe. Even though I was braced for it, the bang shocked me.

'They'll hear that in fucking Cronulla!' said Les.

We went in. The room was filled with dust and smoke The door was hanging open. There was about four hundred quid in paper money and another, smaller strong box inside the safe. We tried to pry it open, with no success. Stuff it, said Kevin, we'll take it with us and blow it open out in the scrub. There were also boxes and boxes of silver coins in the safe, wrapped up in paper tubes. We transferred the shrapnel to bags. Kevin went to work disabling the burglar alarm so that we could leave by the door. Les found a locked cupboard, smashed it open. Cartons of ciggies. We loaded it all up.

The thunderstorm was a mile or two away now. No one was about. We drove north into Kuringai Chase. Les directed me down a dirt road. We parked and lugged the strong box into the bush. Les and Kevin discussed how they might blow it open. Finally they jammed a screw driver under the lip, wired some jelly to it and rigged up a detonator. Les set it off. The strong box flew over our heads into the bush, raining down shredded, burning pound notes. We never found the box.

We dumped the Chev at Roseville and headed home in Max's car. On the Harbour Bridge I handed the toll collector a quid note. Got anything smaller? he said. Kevin reached out the back window, handed him a big handful of silver, said keep the change, pal.

I was shaky and cold when we got back to Paddington. We carried the tools and the money inside. I poured drinks while Les counted the cash.

It came to seven hundred and thirty pounds all up, or just over two hundred and forty quid, a couple of bottles of scotch and ten cartons of cigs each.

'You're kidding!' I said. 'I was expecting a thousand, for Christ's sake.'

'Yeah, the big money must have been in that strong box. That was a bit of bad luck.'

'Don't worry about it.'

Kevin said, 'Les reckons you got some trouble or something. Not prying or anything, but if it's any help, me and Les will just take fifty each from this job, you take the rest. We'll even up on the next one.'

'Nah, that's all right, thanks anyway, but I need a whole lot more. Just whack it up three ways, even.'

'Hey, you did all right tonight. Cool under pressure, I'll give you that. We've got another job lined up. Do you want in?'

'I suppose so. Where and when?'

'A butcher shop at Lakemba. There's a safe out the back. By Saturday close it's fairly stuffed with money. We'll hit it late next Saturday night, a week from tomorrow.'

Peakhurst School of Arts was a shabby, turn-of-the-century building next to a vacant lot, pretty much in the middle of nowhere. Thirty or forty bored-looking kids were hanging around outside the hall, revving their cars and motorbikes. In the hall musos were tuning up, testing the PA.

I parked a little way down the road, smoked a reefer with Trish. She stared out the window, shook her head and said, 'Yobbo land.'

'This is your big chance to see the glamorous world of rock'n'roll from the inside.'

'I'm not sure I want to.'

'Just an hour or so. I promised. Hey, it'll be an education for you.'

Max met us at the door in a beret and shades, looking frayed around the edges. He gave me a strange look.

I said, 'Max, this is Trish.'

They shook hands, then Max went inside. Trish and I stayed at the door taking money.

After about fifteen minutes a kid came out and introduced himself to us as Paul, said Max was letting him help out for a while. He said we should go on in, see the show. He'd mind the door.

There were about fifty teenagers inside. Max came to the mike and announced the sensational Sandy Garufi and the Prairielanders, a guitar and piano-accordion combo, who started their set with Eddie Cochran's 'Nervous Breakdown'.

I said to Trish, 'Let's dance.'

We moved around the same part of the dance floor for a while, but it wasn't really working between us. Every time I tried to lead her into a jive, she'd move away, groove around all on her own, dancing some Latin kind of thing.

Max played guitar with the band for twenty minutes then disappeared. Shortly after, I saw the kid from the front door standing in the crowd, watching us dance. Watching *Trish* dance. She saw him, dragged him onto the floor. I left them dancing together to 'Cherry Pink And Apple Blossom White' and joined Max outside.

'Going okay in there?' he said.

'I want to boogie, she wants to cha-cha-cha.'

'Sounds like a Chuck Berry song. Listen, there's something we've got to discuss.'

'What?'

But right then a flurry of people arrived and for the next ten minutes we were flat out taking money and trying to prevent smarties from slipping past. Every few minutes Max would carefully add the fresh takings to the fat roll of notes in his pocket. The door went quiet. Then the kid came out, agitated, and said, 'Mr Perkal, people are getting in through the fire escape.'

'Cripes. I better go and bolt it.'

The kid said, 'I've already padlocked it.'

'Have you? Good work, Paul. You're doing a great job.'

He beamed. 'Am I? Thanks, Mr Perkal.'

'I told you, it's Max.'

Max peeled off half a dozen ten-bob notes and handed them to the kid. 'You know what's good about these? Each one of them has a meaning all its own.'

'Yeah, I, ah, I see. Thanks a lot, Mr . . . Max.'

He waved away the thanks. 'But next time lose the school suit, will you?'

'I didn't want to look scruffy.'

'A crease in your daks, sharp haircut, thin tie, shiny shoes, you can't go wrong.'

The kid nodded like he'd just been given the mail by the Pope himself. 'Crease, haircut, thin tie, shiny shoes. Got it.' He turned around to go back inside.

I said to him, 'Hey, pal, is my girlfriend okay in there?'

He grinned. 'She's been teaching me how to do the cha-cha-cha.'

'Good-o.'

As soon as he'd gone Max said to me, 'So, what exactly have you been doing to put the coppers onto us?'

'What do you mean?'

He ran his hand through his hair. 'The rozzers were here before you arrived. They were going to shut us down. I had to give them twenty quid.'

'I detest corruption.'

'Yeah, well that's funny because they mentioned your name. They asked me wasn't I in business with you. I said what if I was?'

'At least you didn't deny me thrice.'

'They said you were very bad luck.'

I took a big breath, exhaled slowly. 'There's a bit of a story behind this and I suppose it's time you heard it.'

He waited.

'Go back a few years. Just say there are three hardheads who happen to come by a large quantity of stolen jewellery—'

'OK.' He nodded slowly. 'Like you, me and Teddy?'

'Could be. Hypothetically. Just say that other interests are trying to get their grubby hands on the jewellery as well, and only by dint of great tenacity and ingenuity do our hardheads get to keep the jewellery long enough to sell it.'

'Yeah, yeah, get to it.'

'And say these hardheads meet at Laurie O'Brien's holiday cabin to divide up the proceeds.'

Max watching me intently, nodding.

'Laurie plays genial host, for no reason other than to be a good sport, while our intrepid hardheads whack up the money. Everything goes off swimmingly. Two of the three sharpies—not unlike you and Teddy—go back to civilisation a few thousand quid richer, another criminal enterprise successfully completed, so they think, while the one who looks like me hangs around the cabin for a few weeks' rest.'

'Go on.'

'Then the day after the whack-up, someone not entirely unlike Chief Superintendent Ray Waters arrives on the scene.'

'Jesus, Mary and Joseph!'

'He knows all about the rort, even how much the sharpies made, near enough. He settles in, has a drink. Makes some pretty taste-less remarks to and about Laurie's beloved, Molly. Laurie keeps his own counsel, but he's spewing.'

'Why didn't you tell me about this before?'

I ignored him. 'Then it comes out: Waters wants half the whack.'

Max was staring.

'This Waters type of fellow is getting more threatening all the time, and more personal about Molly. Then out of the blue, Laurie produces a gun, shoots him dead as a mackerel.'

'Holy shit!' Max walked away quickly, came back, lit a gasper, drew deeply. 'You shot a copper?'

'*I* didn't.'

'What happened to the body?'

'We dumped it at sea. There didn't seem to be any point telling you and Teddy about it.'

'Then why has it all come up now?'

'There seems to be a rumour about among the coppers that Waters is dead and that I'm responsible.'

'Then they know about the jewellery robbery?'

'Well, let's say it's not quite the secret it once was.'

Max turned away, rubbing his forehead. Then he made for the door without looking back at me.

'Hang on, Max, there's more.'

He shook his head. 'Not tonight there's not, padre.' He went inside, passed Trish coming out.

She was flushed. 'Wow. Those boys! Hey, Bill, do you mind if we call it a night? I've seen enough.'

So we split in my car. On the way back to town I was stopped at Newtown and given a defect notice by a cycle cop.

Chapter 7

I hadn't laid eyes on Laurie O'Brien since the Waters business. He and Molly were now running the Ocean View Hotel at South Coogee, which was where I went the following Sunday afternoon. The pub was a between-the-wars building in Malabar Road, across from the cemetery.

Laurie himself opened the side door, nodded hello, not seeming at all surprised to see me. He showed me upstairs to the residence, where Molly greeted me. Her hair was very blond now, and her skin tanned, going leathery from sun and wind. Laurie was the same as ever. His thin silver hair was brushed neatly back, his skin shaved so close you could see the blood vessels underneath. But he was thinner and more watchful than before. He poured me a drink, had water himself. Molly poured herself a big gin.

They asked after Del. I told them we'd parted company. We chatted on. On the coffee table in front of me was an open paperback by Lobsang Rampa. Laurie saw me looking at it, reached forward and picked it up, took it over to the bookshelf.

'So, Laurie,' I said, 'we have a bit of a problem. Fred Slaney.'

Molly took a gulp of her gin, watching me closely.

'He's worked out what became of Ray Waters.'

Laurie nodded.

'He spoke to you?'

'Yeah, he, ah, demonstrated his powers of persuasion to me. Waters was a pussycat compared to this bloke.'

'The fact that you're not in jail and not dead means he must want something. How much?'

'Ten grand.'

He stood up, walked around, ran his hand through his hair, shook his head.

'It's the law of karma,' he said.

Molly looked quickly at me, then at him.

'I can't help you out, not that much. I haven't got it.'

I looked around, put my hands out. 'How can you say that, Laurie? You're a publican and an ex-bookie! Nearly every quid in circulation winds up with either or both of those. Add prostitution and you two have the mugs' money hat trick. No offence intended, Molly.'

'None taken.'

Laurie said, 'I'll contribute what I can. But there is no way I can cover you for ten grand. I'm in debt. A lot. When does this bastard want the money?'

'He's given me until the first of July.'

'I'll see what I can raise. But don't count on me.'

'Well, I sort of thought in view of the fact that *you* killed Ray Waters, you might feel some responsibility for this balls-up. Presumptuous of me.'

Laurie plucked a book from his shelf. 'Leave it with me,' he said gravely. 'I'll examine the matter,' and walked out.

Molly poured us both another drink and said, 'We saw Del on the telly.'

'She's moving up in the world. How about you, Molly? Liking married life?'

'Well enough.' She straightened up. 'Well enough to see it through, whatever it may bring.'

'Fair enough,' I said. I had a look around the room. The furniture was on the old side. I walked over to the bookshelf, read some of the titles: *The Wisdom of the Ancients, The Mystic Secrets of the Rosicrucians, Destiny Explained, Black Elk Speaks.*

I said to Molly, 'Has Laurie joined the grippers?'

'No. He reads a lot now. It's sort of a hobby.'

'What did he mean "examine the matter"?' I said.

'He kind of, you know, *meditates* about things. Looks up his books and charts.'

'Christ. Going soft in the head?'

She tightened a little. 'It's not as crazy as it seems. You know his old bookie's philosophy: every piece of information is important. Even the lies.'

I finished my drink. 'Well, tell him to meditate on this: If Slaney knocks me off, it won't end there. Laurie'll be next. You don't need Black Elk to know that. See you later. I'm glad you're well.'

Next day when I went to the post box the kid behind the counter called out to me that the posties were having trouble sticking mail in the box, would I mind clearing it? I said sure, and racked off.

I went to the Chamberlain to sort through the mail. Just fifteen quid's worth of orders. Final notices from *Man* magazine and *Trotguide* for unpaid bills, as well as the usual bunch of complaints, some well-founded, most of them asinine. Fuck them all, I thought. I went to Mr Ling's.

After I'd got my head straight I popped upstairs to see that all was okay in the office. There was no sign that Murray Liddicoat had been back, but there were two notes under my door. One was from Rodney Irving asking that I give him a ring. The other was a pencil-written note on the back of a betting ticket.

It read, 'Why are you never hear? I nead to speak to you urgently in conection with a betting system I brought from you. Ring FJ 5349.'

The old dear from the Association of Breeders of British Sheep told me there'd been a bit of a row a couple of days ago. A chap had knocked on my door, and when he found no one was there he got angry and came out with some terrible language. I said what did he look like? Large, cranky chap, she said, in a bright yellow shirt sort of thing. I told her thanks. She said are you all right, Mr Glasheen? I told her I was fine thanks, and then I shot through.

Les Newcombe rang me on Tuesday to ask if I was still sweet for the job on Saturday night. I said I was. Lachie the drummer rang the next morning to say he had some comps for the Grand Ole Opry Show playing at the Sydney Stadium this Saturday. He didn't much care for hillbilly but thought I might want them. I told him I had something on, but to hang on to a couple for me just in case, I'd be in touch. I rang Les back but there was no answer. I tried again later, did no good.

That evening his girlfriend Margie answered the phone, said Les had been pinched the day before and was in remand now. They got him selling cigs from a robbery. Where's Kevin? I asked her. He's in Brisbane, she said. I rang Lachie, said I'd probably be going to the Stadium show after all.

On the Thursday Rod Irving rang me at home. 'I was wondering how things were going with that particular matter.'

'Nothing since I last spoke to you. Still working on it, though.'

'I may be . . . away for a little while. But I'd like you to keep with it while I'm gone.'

'Yeah, sure.'

'I know in a situation like this, if nothing happens for a while, even with all the will in the world, your enthusiasm is likely to wane a little.'

I launched into a 'nothing of the sort' spiel but he cut me off. 'So if you're agreeable, I'll put you on a retainer. How would fifty pounds be for starters? I could write a cheque now.'

'Yeah, all right. Where are you off to, if you don't mind me asking?'

'That quack I told you about, Bailey? He's putting me into hospital. For a sleep cure.'

'Yeah?'

'It's not like a rathouse, Bill.'

I didn't say anything.

'Well, I suppose it *is* a rathouse actually. But . . .'

'That's OK, Rod. Harry will see you right. Sweet dreams.'

I popped by Mr Ling's after the last race that Saturday, then went uptown to collect Trish at the Royal George, to go to the Stadium show. She gave me a funny look when I arrived, asked if I was okay. I said yeah, tiptop. On the way to Rushcutters Bay she asked me again why was I so quiet? I said no reason.

The crowd at the Stadium was down on expectations and the mood in the barn was low. Roy Acuff told cornpone gags, sang 'Great Speckled Bird' with tears in his eyes. The audience was unmoved. Tex Morton came on to huge applause but then croaked his way half-heartedly through a set of the old favourites. The star of the night was Jimmy Little. He sang 'I'll Take You Home Again Kathleen', and the crowd ate it up.

Trish didn't get any of it. Twenty minutes in she was looking at her watch. When Jimmy Little sang she just shook her head.

Outside the Stadium I said to Trish where'll we go? She said she was pretty tired, she thought she'd go straight home tonight.

I said, 'Do you want to get together next week?'

'I don't think so. Bye.' She smooched me quickly on the cheek, hopped in a cab and split.

It was the kiss-off. But I had to admit, even that was better than most.

Things got more shitful the following Monday. I opened my door to Fred Slaney. He walked right in, threw his hat down on the couch.

'Got anything to drink?' he said.

'There's some whisky in the cupboard there.'

He took out the last bottle of Johnny Walker. 'Black label, no less. You must be doing all right.'

'What do you want?'

He picked a glass off the sink, wiped it out carefully with a tea towel and poured a double nip.

'I came by to see how much you've raised.'

'You gave me till July.'

'Never mind that. How much so far?'

'I'm working on it. I'd have to check.'

'In my book that means you've got nothing.'

I didn't reply. He reached in under his jacket and brought out a gun, put it to my temple and jabbed me with it. He was breathing hard.

'I could kill you right now, cunt.' He jabbed again. The barrel poked me painfully in the eye. His hand was shaking.

'Well, what do you say?'

'Like I said, I'm working on it.'

He held the gun there, his face red, his hand shaking. After half a minute he put his hand down.

'What *have* you got?'

'Altogether?'

'Yeah, everything.'

'Less than a thousand.'

He shook his head. 'Not much chop, are you? What about the property at Pittwater?'

'What about it?'

'What's it worth?'

'I don't know, a grand or two.'

'You could sell it. How much cash have you got on you?'

I opened my wallet, took out a hundred and twenty quid. He took a hundred.

'What about in the bank, under the bed?'

I got my bank book. Seven hundred and thirty quid there. I showed it to Slaney.

'I'll have that. How about the business?'

'The books are at the office. A few hundred quid there. I need that to keep operating.'

'All right. Go up to the bank and withdraw that seven hundred. I'll make myself comfortable while you're gone.'

He looked around the flat, nodded in the direction of my LP records.

'You got any Frankie Laine among that lot?'

I shook my head.

'Never mind.'

When I returned he was reading Jack Davey's book of facts and figures. He took the cash from me and put it away. 'That's eight hundred down; nine thousand, two hundred to go,' he said. 'With a little bit of application, I'm sure you can make that deadline.'

'And if I don't?'

'Don't even think about that.'

'I need more time. There's no way I can get nine grand together by July.'

'You ever hear of working hot?'

I didn't reply.

He went to the door.

I said, 'Before you go, I'm getting harassed by the police. Can you stop it?'

'What sort of harassment?'

'Traffic fines, phone calls late at night. Annoying bullshit.'

'What do you expect me to do? You're the cop killer. Waters was admired in the force. But I doubt that anything much will happen. If anyone seriously wanted to off you, they'd come to me first.'

'That's reassuring,' I said. 'How about this then: I've got a stack of defect notices on my car. They book me every time I go out. Can you pull them? I'll be stuffed without a car.'

'I'll see.'

I got out my rego papers. 'Here you are. It's registered in this name.'

Slaney shook his head. 'Jesus. Couldn't lie straight in bed, could you?'

I hadn't slept a night in the house at Pittwater since the Waters killing, but for a while Del and I used to spend weekends at the converted boatshed down on the water. The possums and rodents had been in the house. I spent a couple of hours cleaning up, then went down to the boatshed. I looked at the spare clothes, fishing gear and basic kitchenware and thought, Stuff it, leave it for the next owner.

I took the last ferry back and drove to the real estate agent at Newport, signed a contract for him to put it on the market. He knew the house and thought it might bring a couple of thousand, but with the cooler weather coming on sales were dropping off, he said. He hoped I wasn't in a hurry.

I drove to Mr Ling's and had a pipe, shrank my problems down to manageable size. Hawaiian guitar music was playing today. I drifted away with it. I calmly thought about Slaney, the money, what I should do.

I came to a decision. I needed Teddy Rallis and Max Perkal on my side, staunch and committed, and ready to make a contribution. Equal parts. I'd have to tell Rallis the whole saga, and Max, whether he liked it or not, was going to hear the last bit of the story.

What were friends for, after all?

Max didn't answer his phone. I kept trying. Next day I drove over to Perkal Towers, had a look around. I knocked on the door of the downstairs flat. Lani opened up. She hadn't seen Max for over a fortnight, she said.

Teddy Rallis was out of town. His wife told me over the phone he'd be away for another week. He and his brother had taken the train that morning. She said she didn't have a number for him. I didn't hold that against her. Ted was a career criminal, and caution and suspicion were second nature to them both.

Before I rang off I said to her, 'When you do speak to Ted, tell him that we need to discuss some outstanding matters from September '57—he'll know what that means. Something has come up. Tell him it's big.'

Chapter 8

I pissed the week away. I heard nothing from Teddy Rallis or Max. But I got a phone call from Max's young apprentice.

'Mr Glasheen, it's Paul here.'

'Eh?'

'Paul. We met at the Peakhurst School of Arts. Mr Perkal gave me a message to pass on to you.'

'Where is he?'

'I don't know. He rang my mum yesterday, said he'd be busy for a while and wouldn't be able to do the next dance.'

'That's the message?'

'Yes, that's all.'

'He's not in jail, is he?'

'I don't know. You can't make phone calls from jail, can you?'

'I suppose not. If he rings again tell him to contact me immediately, it's really important.'

'Yeah, sure thing, Mr Glasheen.'

'Call me Bill. Thanks for the message, son. So, I guess that means the dances are off?'

'I thought I might go it alone. I know some of the artists from the Nicholson School of Music out here, and I've booked the Croydon Roller Rink for next Saturday. You never know. Actually, I was wondering if you still wanted to be involved.'

'Thanks for the thought, Pete—'

'Paul.'

'Sorry, Paul, yeah, but you better leave me out. Best of luck though.'

I made one more big effort at pulling the business together. I sent off cheques to *Man* magazine and *Trotguide*, sent out the back orders, and replied to twenty or so complaints.

But there were other problems. I needed new stock. The betting system had run dead; the guitar tutors still did business but were declining. For us to kick on again Max would need to get his book of magic tricks together, and maybe we could move into the patented medicine caper. With all the talk about youth drugs in the papers, I figured now would be a good time for such a line. But I needed Max for that one too, to get the legalities straight. The nerve tonic that Uncle Dick ran in Adelaide might do, except that 'nerve tonic' didn't have the same ring as 'youth drug'.

A solid day and a half's work got it all pretty well up to date. I ate dexes and took little sips from a Johnny Walker bottle on the desk. I resisted the urge to visit Mr Ling's, but the idea of having a pipe or two was at the back of my mind the whole time. I'd caught a cold and my joints ached.

After I'd squared the most urgent debts, six hundred and fifty quid remained in the account, of which five hundred was earmarked for Dick. I withdrew it all in ten-quid notes and took it back to the office. I poured another drink and spread the cash out on the desk. I sat there looking at it for I don't know how long.

There was a light tap on the door. Outside it was nearly dark. I called out to come in. The old dear from down the hall nervously put her head around the door.

'I thought I heard someone moaning. Is everything all right, Mr Glasheen? Will I turn the light on?'

'Oh, yeah, thanks. Yeah, everything's fine. I was just, you know, humming while I worked. Sorry if I disturbed you.'

She came into the room, put a paper bag down on my desk. 'There are some sandwiches and a piece of rainbow cake in there. You should eat something.'

'Yeah, thanks, I will. Ta. Well, better get on with it.' She backed out again.

I put the stuff away, picked up the money and locked up. The light was on in the hallway. As I turned away from the office door the big bloke in the yellow shirt arrived, puffing at the top of the stairs.

He saw me, pointed and called out, '*You!* Wait there a minute, I need to talk to you!'

I said, 'Here, catch!' and threw the paper bag of cake and sandwiches to him. He fumbled it, grabbed it, dropped it.

I scooted to the back stairs, down the fire escape and straight into Mr Ling's. He closed the door behind me, quietly slipped the bolt.

Outside I heard the bloke lumber into the alley. Then there was a loud knock on the door. I looked at Mr Ling. He remained placid. The door was cop-proof.

I heard the bloke swear and then stride off. Mr Ling said, 'A pipe?'

I told him not today thanks. He shrugged and walked off, leaving me there in the hallway. A minute later he came back, indicated for me to follow, led me into the kitchen and pointed to a bowl of noodles sitting on the table. He gestured for me to eat it. I said thanks, sat down and ate what I could.

A young bloke came in. I'd seen him around the place before, assumed he was Mr Ling's son, maybe grandson. He said to me, 'Why you come here?'

I put my hand on my heart. 'Because I believe that one day the white man and the yellow man might walk together as brothers.'

He pointed to the door. 'You bring your enemy.'

'Him? Nah. A customer.'

The kid shook his head, said, 'Bad.' He left the room and came back with a bowl of biscuit things. He offered them to me.

'What's this?' I asked.

'Fortune cookie. Tell your luck. From America cousin.'

I took one, crunched into it, and removed the little rolled-up slip of paper inside. Typed on it was *You will information the horse mouth*.

The kid smiled, nodded. 'New business. Will sell plenty.'

I said to him, 'What's your name?'

'Edward.'

'Did you write this?'

'Yeah, I write. Okay?'

I shook my head. 'Stay with it, Edward. You'll get there.'

I got up and found Mr Ling looking at a form guide.

'Maybe just one pipe,' I said.

I went to Max's place the next day, and spoke to Lani again. She still maintained she hadn't heard from Max, but wouldn't meet my eye.

'Listen, Lani, I'm Max's oldest friend. If you know something, you better tell me.'

'I wasn't supposed to tell anyone. But since it's you.'

'Go on.'

'He's in hospital.'

'What's wrong with him?'

'More a sort of rest home.'

'Another one gone troppo. What happened?'

'He had a kind of breakdown thing.'

'What hospital?'

She hesitated a moment, then said, 'I don't know. It's in Roseville, I don't know exactly where.'

'Who do you pay the rent to, then?'

'An agent at the Junction. He's not as understanding about the rent as Max was.'

I checked the phone book, made some calls. There was only one fair dinkum rathouse in Roseville, Buena Vista House. I drove straight there.

They let me in to see Max, no sweat. He was in a dressing-gown, shades. He was drawn-looking, and hadn't shaved for a couple of days. But full of smiles all the same, and eager to talk about the future—an expanded dance circuit, a television variety program, a leather jacket and Levis importing business, and a hot-dog stand outside state parliament.

I had to interrupt to get a word in. 'So how are you, like, you know, in your head? You really nuts?'

Max laughed. 'Never been better. A bit of time out, recharge the old batteries. I'll be back to work in a week or two.'

'Well, I'm glad to hear that. Now listen, what I was telling you about at Peakhurst. There's more. Upshot is, I, *we*, need a lot of money. Fast. It goes back to the Farren Price robbery. You see—'

Max smiled, half closed his eyes, looked at me in a strange way, put his hand up. 'Don't worry about money. Very soon, all our money problems will be over for good.'

'You got something on?'

He looked around, leaned forward and whispered, 'I wasn't supposed to tell you.' He was grinning from ear to ear. He slapped his knee. 'Oh well, the cat's out of the bag now. Just wait a few days. Next Saturday, the big day.'

'Big day for what?'

'Just get up like it's a normal day, take the bus to town, to Hyde Park. There'll be a big party on. My band will be playing. Jack Davey will be there, master of ceremonies. What's going to happen, all the arseholes in the world are going to disappear overnight. Just like that. Gone. All the good people, you, me, Del, Lani, Trish, Jack and all our friends, we'll all meet up there at Hyde Park. The Salvos will be making sandwiches and cups of tea for everyone. Jesus is going to put some money in your bank account and in mine and we won't have to worry about bread ever again. There'll be a jet plane taking people to space for a picnic on Sunday, but that's up to you if you go or not. There'll be beautiful strippers walking around handing out drinks and reefers. Jesus likes reefer, by the way.'

He smiled and patted me on the shoulder. 'Don't look so glum. All our troubles are about to blow over.'

All I could think to say was, 'Why Jesus? You're not even a Christian.'

Max shrugged. 'It's out of my hands.'

We sat in silence for another couple of minutes until a male nurse came and led him away.

I phoned Lani as soon when I got home. 'Max is completely round the twist,' I said. 'What happened?'

'He went berserk on TV. I'm surprised you didn't hear about it.'

'I've been busy.'

'He did a spot on that show, with Ray Taylor. You didn't see it? Well, Ray interviewed him, asked him about the state of play in the music business. Max went into a tirade about certain ingrate rock'n'roll stars. Taylor tried to make a joke of it, but Max kept on and on. They cut to an ad. When they came back, Max and the trio were on stage. Taylor announced that they were going to sing "Embraceable You", but Max said something to the band and they went into an after-hours blues kind of thing. I think it was called "Fool's Paradise".'

'He'd know about that, all right.'

'Max's singing voice isn't the greatest, as you know, but funnily enough this time he wasn't too bad. He really got into it, like he was telling his life story. You know, about doing everything wrong, smoking reefers, gambling, staying out all night, making a goose of himself. Then suddenly he stopped and just stared into space. The musicians were looking at him, waiting. He slowly stood up and—get this—he smashed his guitar.'

'Eh?'

'He swung it around by the neck and smashed it onto the studio floor, again and again until it was just kindling and broken strings. Then he stomped on the broken bits. Wouldn't stop. He had to be dragged off the set by members of the crew. They scheduled him that same night.'

'But what's actually wrong with him?'

'Supposed to be a nervous breakdown. But he's been acting strange for a long time.'

'Like, since 1943 at least.'

I woke the next day fighting the urge to panic. I got up, made coffee, put a nip of brandy in it. That helped, so I had another.

Over breakfast my mind kept straying back to Number One Son's nonsensical prediction, *You will information the horse mouth*. I thought about Laurie's philosophy of all the mail being important, even the bullshit. I thought about it more over another coffee.

After breakfast I scrubbed up and headed out to Alison Road at Randwick and took up a place in the public bar of the Racecourse Hotel. Not quite the horse mouth, but close. I stayed there all afternoon, talking to every jockey and stable hand I knew, buddying up to others, and in between I studied the form for Saturday's meeting. I gave some pills to an apprentice and bought drinks for anyone who might conceivably be in the know.

At six I rang Laurie O'Brien to see what sort of dough he'd managed to come up with. He could do two thousand, he said. I said okay, I'll come around tonight.

Out at the Ocean View, Molly was working in the bar. She said Laurie was upstairs, go straight up.

He was tight-lipped, didn't offer me a drink. Without ceremony he handed me a large envelope. I peeked inside. Bundles of notes in rubber bands.

I said, 'Well, I guess I'll be off then.'

At the door Laurie said, 'I hope this is the end of it.'

'So do I. But this isn't enough to get us out of trouble.'

'It's all I can get hold of.'

'Yeah, well I'm still about seven grand shy.'

'What about Teddy and Max?'

'I can't find Teddy. Max has flipped.'

'Always was half yarra, if you ask me.'

That night I got a call from Kevin Simmonds. You heard about Les then? he said. Yeah, that was bad luck. He said yeah, it was. I asked if he was still working.

He said, 'Well, actually, that's why I rang you.'

'I'm not so sure about robbing those butcher-shop and bowling-club safes. It's a bloody slow quid.'

'Yeah, bugger that,' he said. 'Frigging around with gelignite and so on. I've got a much better way of opening safes. And better safes at that.'

'Yeah?'

'You walk into the bank, make a big withdrawal.' He giggled.

'Eh?'

'I mean you wave a roscoe in a bank manager's face. Get the safe opened quick fucking smart.'

'Oh.'

'I'm doing the Commonwealth Bank at Rose Bay next week. You want in?'

'A bit out of my league.'

'How do you know if you never tried it?'

'What's the earn?'

'Sixteen to twenty grand. Conservative estimate. Half each.'

'Let me think about it. I'll ring you Sunday.'

I hung up and opened the Ulmer book. The preachment said, *Blessed is the man who has found his true work.*

I made the scene at the Racecourse again, shouted more drinks, did some more research, then drove over to the Doncaster Hotel in Anzac Parade and did the same. By the end of the day I had a fair sense of the field for the meeting next day. But I hadn't got any absolutely red hot mail. Mainly opinions. Not even good ones at that. If I had a bet, it would be on the same basis as the rest of the mugs out there having a go.

At five o'clock I was about to call it quits when Joe 'the Boot' Buetscher came in. He was a jockey, notorious for his use of the persuader, the battery, cocaine, elephant juice, sleeping pills, and anything else that might cause a horse to move faster or slower than it otherwise would. As crooked as jockeys come. He said hello to the mugs around the bar, then came over to me and shook hands.

'How are you, Joe?' I said.

'Fit as a Mallee.' He stood back. 'But if you get any thinner you'll be able to do trackwork yourself.'

'Yeah, I'm in training.'

'As a greyhound?'

I ordered a couple and we drank for an hour or so.

The Boot stopped at the third scotch. 'That's it for me. I'll be no good tomorrow if I drink any more piss.'

'Of course.'

He dropped his voice. 'But tell me, do you still get those funny ciggies?'

'From time to time, yeah.'

He leaned closer. 'Because if you had any with you now . . .'

'I just get them for a few regulars. American entertainers. It's not something, ah, I mean, I'm not out looking for new customers. You know, it's more a show business thing.'

'If horse racing isn't show business, I don't know what is.'

'You want me to get you reefers?' I shook my head and turned back to the bar.

'Hey, I'm not a kid. I've had that stuff plenty of times.'

'Like when?'

'Like the other day with Johnny O'Keefe, for instance.'

'I haven't got anything with me. Can you wait till next week?'

He whispered, 'Do the right thing today and I'll give you a bit of braille for tomorrow. Could be *very* much to your advantage.'

'I'd have to go to the city.'

'I'll come with you.'

Chet wasn't due in port for a couple of weeks, but there were some Taiwanese blokes that I sort of knew from Mr Ling's. They smuggled in transistors, cameras, and sometimes a bit of dope as well. I'd seen them just that week at the opium house.

So I went to Mr Ling's, and in a roundabout way indicated to him what I wanted. He made a phone call, then gave me an address out at Matraville.

We drove out there. The place was an old tin shed behind a five-acre garden plot. I left the Boot minding the car, walked along a muddy track beside the paddock, up to the shed, which seemed to be in darkness. I knocked, and the door opened. A bloke nodded, let me in, took me out the back. One of the seamen I knew was there. He said hello and led me to another room, a store room. He went over to a stack of wooden boxes and brought out a biscuit tin. He handed it to me. I prised off the lid. The tin was packed with dark green weed.

He nodded, held up his clenched fist, gave it a shake and said, 'Very good. Sex drug.'

How much?'

'Twenty quid.'

I haggled him down to eighteen just to make him happy and left.

The Boot and I went back to his place at South Coogee and I made up half a dozen reefers.

'I better give my girlfriend a ring,' he said. 'Once this sex drug starts working, look out!'

'Don't believe everything you read in *Truth*. It's just as likely you'll want a chocolate Paddle Pop.'

'Yeah, sure, sure.'

'Before I hand these over and you smoke your way to seventh heaven, what was this thing you were going to line up for me?'

'OK, put a quid or two on Strictly Taboo in the sixth race tomorrow.'

'It's not much of a conveyance. Unplaced last five starts. Never won a race.'

The Boot looked at me. 'You've been studying form.'

'Enough to know that horse has Buckley's.'

'Good odds, though. And I'll be on it.'

'So?'

'So place your bet *on* course, and don't leave it too late, 'cause there'll be some smart money coming in later.'

I shook my head. 'Every other starter in the race would have to die for that camel to win. I don't care how fit it is, that horse just doesn't have a win in it.'

'No, *that* horse doesn't.' He gave me a look. 'But mind what I say. Put your hard-earneds on the horse called Strictly Taboo tomorrow.'

'Oh, right. You're running a ring-in!'

'Just make sure you're on it. And pray there's no rain to make that white paint run. Now give me that silly-weed. And how about some go-faster pills?'

'For the horse?'

'For me, for Christ's sake.'

On race day I left my car at home and walked up to Taylor Square, along Burton and Forbes Street, past the tech. Darlinghurst Police Station was on a wedge-shaped block at the end of Forbes Street, where it ran into Taylor Square. Had I been more on the ball, I'd have taken another way.

But I wasn't and I hadn't, and I walked straight into the two young coppers who'd bridged up to me outside Shirley Hill's place. Of all the bad spots in Sydney to end up, the cells at Darlinghurst were among the worst. Bashings, verbals, shakedowns, and even killings all went on there, and no one much gave a shit.

The dago copper was standing, arms folded, twenty paces in front of me. I detoured around him, pretending I hadn't noticed him. As I drew level he said to me, 'We've still got unfinished business, Glasheen.'

I stopped and looked at him and said, 'Listen, Luigi, if I want a pound of peas or a cauliflower, I'll go to your fruit shop. Otherwise, we have no business with each other.'

He slowly shook his head. 'Go on, be a smart-arse all you like. It's going to catch up with you.' He walked up close. 'And my name's not Luigi.'

'Then what would it be?'

'My name would be Constable Sidoti, and this,' he gestured to his left, 'is Constable Rheinberger.'

'All right, Constables Sidoti and Rheinberger, I've got things to attend to, so I'll be running along. But I've got a tip for you before I go: if you're planning some sort of standover, forget it. I've already come to an arrangement with a certain bloke.' I paused, gave them a look. 'Someone way over your heads, who wouldn't take kindly to your interference.'

Sidoti laughed. 'You're hopeless, you know that? You think Fred Slaney will protect you? For a bloke who's supposed to be in the know, you're way behind the game. Off you go now. We'll be in touch.'

I didn't catch the tram out to Randwick straight away. Instead I hopped a cab down to Mr Ling's, fixed my nerves with a couple of pipes.

I got to the track at three o'clock and went directly to the betting ring. Strictly Taboo was starting in the sixth and I was surprised to see that the odds were down to fifteen to one. Given its rotten form, it should have been in the hundreds. I walked over to where I could see the Tote odds. It was showing twelve to one there.

Laurie's two grand, the money I took from the business account, and the retainer from Rod Irving came to a little under three grand, and I had the whole lot in my kick. All I had to do was get four to one on it and I was out of bother. Anything above that would put me ahead.

I did a quick circuit of the ring. Homer Smith was still offering fifteen to one, but across the ring Swannee Schwartz had it now at eights, and another had it at twelves. It was time to act.

I pushed forward to Smith and said, 'Three grand for a win on Strictly Taboo.'

He looked at the money in my hand and coughed. 'What was that, son?'

'Three thousand on Strictly Taboo!'

'Strictly Taboo, you say?'

'Yeah, you want me to spell it? Strictly Taboo!'

He wrote out the ticket and took my money.

I checked the betting slip. He'd written £18,000 as the win payout.

'Eh? That's only five to one. You've only given me five to one!'

'They're the board odds, son.'

I looked again. Strictly Taboo was showing five to one. His penciller had changed the display odds while he'd been stalling me.

'Stuff that, dad. Give me fifteens or give me the money back!'

He shrugged. 'Now, now, don't get narky. Ladies present. Do you want your money back?'

Off to my left I saw Perc Galea placing a bet with Les Tidmarsh. Tidmarsh immediately put the price of Strictly Taboo back to two to one. The bookies either side of them were shortening their odds, and runners were frantically signalling back and forth across the ring. There was a panic in progress and there was no bookie even offering five to two any more.

I said to Smith, 'You and your mate should be working at the Tiv with that sleight-of-hand act. No, I don't want my money back, I'll stick with this, you old mongrel. I'll see you after the race.'

I joined the crowd down the front. The Boot came out on the horse which for today was called Strictly Taboo. A good-looking nag, ready for a big run. As the horses cantered past the Leger, round to the starting gate, the Boot looked my way, gave me a nod.

I went back to the stand to watch the jump. Strictly Taboo got away pretty well but something happened in the first furlong. It was hard to see at that distance, but it seemed that the Boot was turning around in the saddle to look behind. But they sorted themselves out and Strictly Taboo took the lead by the second furlong. It stormed into the straight three lengths in front, and despite myself I started waving my fist in the air and belting the bloke in front of me with my race book. When he told me to steady on, I calmed down, headed for the betting ring, didn't even watch the finish. When the race caller announced Strictly Taboo the winner by six magnificent lengths, I was already first in line behind the bookie's stand, waiting for the payout.

I held my ticket out, whistling 'She'll Be Coming Round The Mountain', while I waited for the correct weight to be posted. Then over the public address came the announcement that a protest had been entered on the previous race and dividends would be withheld.

The rider of Strictly Taboo had been accused of interference by the apprentice on the favourite, Misty. A minute later the news came through that the appeal had been upheld, Strictly Taboo was disqualified, and Misty was declared the winner.

Homer Smith heard the news, said, 'Sorry, son. Perhaps I can set you for an investment on the next race?' smiling from ear to ear.

I told him to stick it up his arse. I ended up losing my last thirty quid on the final event and had to cadge my tram fare home.

The Boot rang that night.

'I hope you didn't get too badly hammered.'

'What happened?'

'That little cunt got the shits because we didn't let him in on it.'

'Who?'

'The apprentice on Misty. All the others had something on Strictly Taboo. But I forgot to give the young bloke the mail. As soon as he saw the horse he knew it was a ring-in. He didn't dare dob me in but, so he rode into the back of me at the start, made it look like interference on my part. One of the stewards wasn't in on it and he stuffed it up for everyone, insisted on upholding the little bastard's appeal. That's a lesson for next time.'

'You mean the stewards knew the nag was a ring-in?'

'Not all of them. That was the problem, you see.'

'I see.' I hung up.

When Kev Simmonds rang later to ask me how I felt about the Commonwealth Bank job, I said I'm in. It's the only bank job I'm ever likely to get. Well, he said, this one has better hours than the regular kind. And a better pay rate, like twenty grand for five minutes' work. He'd see me on Monday and give me the gun, he said. Then we could go and check out the bank.

Kevin Simmonds was at my place first thing Monday morning.

'You know guns?'

'Shot rabbits with a .22. I've waved a pistol about once or twice. Never fired a shot in anger.'

'We should get you some practice,' he said.

'I thought it was for effect, get the teller's attention.'

'It is. But those tellers have a pistol under the counter. And if we get some mug who's been watching *Gunsmoke*, then, you know . . .'

'You ever shoot anyone, Kev?'

'No.' Shook his head firmly.

'Would you, if it came to that?'

He looked at me. 'Nah. Let's have a squiz at that bank.'

We walked separately into the bank in Old South Head Road. I entered first, went up to the counter and asked for a form to open an account, filled it in while I looked the place over. Kevin came in and deposited ten quid in the account he already had. The teller laughed at something Kevin said, and behind them I saw two bank girls whispering to each other, apparently about Kevin.

Kevin jerried and took a comb out of his back pocket, ran it slowly through his hair like Edd Byrnes on *77 Sunset Strip*. The girls loved it.

Kevin had told me to memorise where the manager's office was and all that. I took in all I could, handed the form back. Five minutes later I met Kevin down the road.

In the car I said, 'Tell me, do you happen to be at all musical?'

'I can sing a bit, and I play piano accordion and mouth organ. And I've been learning guitar out of this book I sent away for.'

'From the Bopalena School of Music, by any chance?'

He turned around to me. 'How'd you know that?'

'Lucky guess. How good's your singing?'

'Not too bad, if I say so myself. You know Johnny Horton? Dig this: Weeeeeellllll, we ran through the scrub and we ran through the jungle, we ran through places where a lizard couldn't go.' He sang with rockabilly-style hiccups, a sneer on his face. 'We ran so fast that law couldn't catch us, down the Murrumbidgee to . . .'

He stopped singing. 'To wherever the hell it was that they ran. What do you reckon?'

'You should pay more attention to the words. But yeah, that's not bad. Can you flick your hair around like Elvis?'

'I used to practise in front of a mirror.'

'Did you ever meet my mate Max Perkal?'

'Who?'

'Boogie-woogie piano bloke, put some records out a few years ago? "Bondi Bop". Remember that one?'

He shook his head.

'You and Les nearly stole his Dodge once, from outside the Stadium.'

'Did we? What about him?'

'He's a bit crook right at the moment, but if and when he gets well, and if we get through this with our carcasses intact, I'll introduce you. See about getting you a start in the music biz. I tell you, Johnny O'Keefe and Col Joye make more money in a couple of weeks singing, drinking piss and rooting sheilas than you ever made robbing people.'

He nodded. 'That'd be a pearler, eh? Singing on *Bandstand* and that.'

That afternoon, after I'd paid a visit to Mr Ling's, Kevin and I drove over the bridge to French's Forest for some shooting practice. We headed a couple of miles down a bush track, parked and set up the obligatory beer bottles on a stump.

Kevin was a country boy and a pretty good shot. My shooting was indifferent.

After we'd each had a go Kevin said, 'You need more practice.'

'Not something I want to get good at.'

He walked over to a smooth-barked gum tree, picked up a rock and roughly gouged out the shape of a man in the bark.

'Imagine that's some cunt who's after you. It's you or him. What do you do?'

'Run like the billy-o?'

'It's a copper with a gun.' I did nothing.

'Well, go on, have a shot at him!' I did and missed.

'Try again. You or him. Shoot to kill. Go on!'

I shot three times. Two of the bullets fell inside the outline.

'That's better,' said Kevin.

'I think it's you who's been watching too many westerns.'

'Well, I'm not Australia's Elvis Presley yet, and meanwhile we both have a living to make.'

Chapter 9

With a big earn coming up, I didn't see much point in going to work that week, so I put in some extra hours at Mr Ling's establishment.

On the Thursday he said, 'You everyday man!'

'I missed last Monday.'

He shook his head. 'Every day!'

'Yeah, well, I'm on holidays this week,' I told him.

On the Saturday afternoon when I drove down to Mr Ling's place, the pubs were filled with drunken returned men in suits, all their medals on. It was Anzac Day and I hadn't even known.

I went home after a couple of pipes, found the two crook pennies I'd had since the war. I'd last used them in a lurk on Victory in the Pacific Day. They were standard two-up pennies, polished heads, blackened tails, except they'd been 'dished'—that is, tapped ever so slightly concave on the head side. Over time they would strongly favour a tails result, if you knew how to toss them. It was the simplest of all the two-up lurks, and it was only good for mug games, such as were held in every pub in the country on Anzac Day.

If I could find an offsider, then one of us could get a game going while the other backed tails. Problem was, I couldn't find anyone. Kevin Simmonds didn't dare go pub crawling and Max Perkal was still off the scene. So in the end I had a bet, just like everyone else, with no advantage. I managed to work my five quid up to twenty-seven, moving from game to game, along Elizabeth Street, up Liverpool and Oxford Streets.

There was a sing-song in progress at the Burdekin and old diggers were talking, fighting, crying, spewing in the gutter. I fell in with a bunch of ex-Air Force blokes, pissed rotten. We were shouting rounds, and returned men were dropping like flies. Worse than in the war, one of them said. Every time another drunk collapsed, the remaining lot would buy a round and call out, 'To fallen comrades!'

One of the men in that mob, pissed as the rest, asked me every few minutes, 'Which arm of the services did you say you were with?'

Women's Land Army I told him once, another time I said a fifth columnist, I was third time he asked I said I was a Jap.

Finally the penny dropped and he said, 'You weren't in the services then? That's all right, I won't say anything to these chaps about it.'

As if I gave a shit. But he annoyed me, that bloke, and he kept tapping the side of his nose and saying, 'They also serve, eh?' in a stage whisper.

Finally I said, 'Listen, nitwit. I did more to keep the Japs out of George Street than you and your silvertail mates ever dreamed of.' He stared at me dumbfounded. It was true, but I'd never told anyone about the Billy Glasheen contribution to the war effort. I'd been warned back then never to skite about it and I still took that warning seriously. At least while old Doug MacArthur was still alive.

The prick he was.

'What was that about MacArthur?'

'Eh?'

'You just called him a prick.'

'No I didn't.'

'Yes you did, I heard you, you shirking bodgie bastard!'

'All right, he *was* a prick. And fuck you, imbecile!' I hit him. Another fallen comrade. I walked out of the pub, left his stupefied pals toasting him.

It was nearly dark in Oxford Street. Drunks everywhere, slumped on the footpath, or propping each other up, trying to hail cabs, hanging out of the trams rattling up the hill. I cut through Hyde Park, past the old naval cannon.

I fell over near the War Memorial and tore my trousers at the knee. I sat for a minute on the steps. Possums were running up and down the Moreton Bay fig trees, fruit bats squabbling up top. In front of the War Memorial building was a large rectangular pool. They called it the Pool of Reflections. I sat there and reflected for a while. An old digger hawked and coughed into the pool.

He called out, 'Oh, bloody hell!'

A moment later he came over to me. 'Excuse me, son. Could you help me? I haven't got my glasses with me. Could you just have a look over here for me, for me dentures?'

'Eh?'

'My plate. It fell in the water when I coughed.'

I walked over and looked in.

'Over there somewhere.'

Amongst the slime on the bottom of the pool there were hundreds of silver and copper coins. And a partial plate, grinning evilly back at me.

'There it is,' I said.

'Where?'

I pointed. 'There! Can't you see it?'

'I haven't got my glasses. That plate cost me twenty-seven guineas, too. Repat should've paid for it but they never.'

I said, 'All right, don't cry, uncle.'

I took my shoes and socks off, rolled up my trouser legs and stepped into the water. It came to my knees. The bottom was slippery and I had to walk carefully, sliding my feet along the bottom. The dentures were fifteen feet or so from the edge.

'Jeez, digger, it must have been an almighty heave to get them this far out,' I said, but he didn't reply.

My movement stirred up the mud and slime and when I got to the vicinity of the plate, the water was too murky to see the bottom. I rolled up my sleeves, bent over and felt around. I found the dentures an inch from my left foot. 'Got 'em!' I said.

When I turned around the old bloke was gone. Sidoti and Rheinberger were standing there in his place.

'Actually, shithead, we've got *you*.' Sidoti said to Rheinberger, 'Go and get the local blokes. I'll keep an eye on him.'

Rheinberger said, 'Will you be right?'

Sidoti laughed. 'He's not going anywhere.'

Rheinberger went off into the darkness.

I skated slowly over to the side of the pool, to the left of where Sidoti was standing. He moved over to intercept me. I went the other way, he did the same. He stood in front, two feet above me.

'I want to get out of here.'

'Have a go.'

'You're in my way.'

'Am I?'

'Will you move aside?'

'Make me.'

I turned around, scratched my head and said, 'Well, Sidoti, you see,' and made a grab for his coat, hoping to pull him over into the water. But he was ready for it and he kicked me. I fell over backwards into the pool. I got up and tried again, and went over again. This time I picked up a good handful of slimy algae and threw it at his face as I turned. I almost got around him onto dry land, but a wild kick from him got me in the mouth and I went over again, back into the water. I got up, spat out a broken tooth.

Rheinberger came back with two uniformed cops. He looked at the slime hanging off Sidoti and said, 'The Creature from the Black Lagoon. He had a go, did he?'

Sidoti picked at the wet green stuff on his jacket and muttered, 'He's piss weak.'

I was still standing there in the water, dripping wet, bleeding from the mouth.

The uniformed copper said, 'Come over here, you. You're under arrest.'

I asked, 'What for?' but no one answered.

The uniformed copper said, 'Come on, now. There are two ways of doing this: the hard way or the very hard way.'

I stepped out of the pool and they put handcuffs on me. Sidoti and Rheinberger conferred with one of the uniformed blokes out of earshot, while the other stood with me. 'You smell like a brewery,' he said.

Sidoti came back and stood off to my left. They had cuffed my hands in front. 'Not so clever now, eh?' He pushed my shoulder roughly.

'Don't do that,' I said.

'What? This?' He pushed me again.

I clasped my cuffed hands and swung them upwards. There wasn't much force in it but it caught him under the chin, made his jaw click loudly as his teeth came together. He fell backwards, holding his jaw.

Then they were all on me and I went out.

The smell of piss and sweat and vomit woke me up. I was in a cell with a bunch of drunks and stiffs. I had no shoes, my clothes were torn and wet. There was blood down the front of my jacket and I was cold to the bone. I passed out again.

A yell woke me next time. 'You going to eat this?' A copper holding out a tin dish of steaming slop. I shook my head and spewed.

At some point that night I was fingerprinted, made to sign something.

Next time I woke, the mob in the cell were all either asleep or groaning. I called out. Someone said, 'Go bag your head,' and I called out again.

A cop came to the door. 'What's the row?'

'Let me out. I shouldn't be here.'

'You've been charged, sport.'

'Well, let me bail myself out.'

'You already tried that. You haven't got a farthing.'

'What's the bail?'

He called outside. 'Ern, what was the bail on . . .' To me he said, 'What's your name again, son?'

'Glasheen.'

'The bail on Glasheen.'

Another cop strolled in, looked at me and said, 'Twenty pounds. A bit better mannered today, is he?'

'Twenty quid bail? I should be on a self-surety.'

'Not for your charges, mate. It's cash if you want to get out.'

'What are the charges?'

'Theft by finding, assault, resist arrest, goods in custody, offensive behaviour.'

'Where am I?'

'Central cells.'

'I need to make a phone call.'

'We'll do it for you.' He went out and returned with a piece of paper and a ballpoint. 'Write down the number. The sergeant will ring when he gets a chance.'

I wrote some names and numbers, handed it back to him. 'There's a few there, in case any of them aren't at home.'

He took the list, put on a pair of glasses and read aloud. 'Who've we got here? Lee Gordon, Chad Morgan, Johnny O'Keefe, Neville Wran, Max Perkal.' He looked up at me. 'Well, son, the only people missing from this list would be Bob Menzies, Eddie Ward and Queen Elizabeth II of England.' He chuckled as he spoke. 'And what about Jack Davey? Wouldn't he be a mate of yours? You want us to give Jack a ring?'

'Don't bother. He's overseas.'

Someone behind me said, 'Try Don Bradman.'

I said to the cop, 'Just contact anyone on that list. They'll come down. I don't belong here.'

Over the next couple of hours the other blokes were all let out.

I said to the cop, 'What about me?'

'You're staying till you get bail.'

'What about my phone calls? Did that other bloke ring up for me?'

'Buggered if I know.' He left.

I shouted until the sergeant came in.

'Got the horrors, have you son?'

'What about my phone calls?'

'I'll go and check.'

I didn't see him again. At lunchtime a different cop brought around another plate of slop. I was shivering and sweaty at the same time.

'You crook, are you?'

'Got a cold from being left here soaking bloody wet,' I said.

'Watch your fucking mouth, you. Do you want this food?'

I shook my head.

'I want to make a phone call.'

'I'll ask the sergeant.'

'Hang on. Do you know who Fred Slaney is?'

'Of course I do. What's he got to do with it?'

'Get word to him, tell him I'm here. He'll fix this all up.'

The cop looked at me doubtfully and left.

I slept fitfully for I don't know how long. Another bunch of rowdies were put in the cell. The next morning we were all cleared out, led down a passageway through iron doors to yet another cell.

After an hour a cop came to the cell and said, 'Glasheen? Who's Glasheen?'

'I am.'

He opened the cell door. 'Come with me.'

He led me to a small room. 'Wait here.'

Fifteen minutes later I was joined by a smiling, red-faced bloke in a suit. He shook hands and said,' My name's Leo Royston. I'm the duty solicitor today. Do you want representation?'

'Where am I?'

'Don't you know? This is Central Court of Petty Sessions. You'll be going before the magistrate soon.'

'Bullshit! I need to ring my friends, get some help. I've been denied my rights. I've got a fever, I need a doctor.'

'Well, regardless of what you think should or shouldn't happen, you will be going before the magistrate to answer serious charges. As for your rights, the desk sergeant said they tried to ring the numbers you gave them but got no result.'

He waited for me to respond. I was shaking. I needed a drink. Shit, I needed a few. And a pipe. And some money and a real lawyer. I tried to get a grip.

'All right, one thing at a time then. What am I charged with?'

He opened his brief and looked down the page. 'Theft by finding, first off.'

'Theft of what?'

'It is alleged that you unlawfully took monies from the Pool of Reflections—'

'What?'

'To wit, twelve pounds, thirteen shillings and threepence. That's what it says.'

'It's bullshit. What else?'

He read, 'Assault. Resist arrest. Goods in custody—that'd be the money you took—'

'I didn't take any money.'

'Of course. There are also three offensive behaviour charges.' He looked up. 'So how do you wish to plead on these?'

'Not guilty, of course. Listen, that's all beside the point, anyway. I need you to contact someone for me, Detective Sergeant Fred Slaney. You know him?'

'I know *of* him. But you must realise he can't help you in this matter.'

'Just give him a call.'

Royston shook his head, looked skeptical, said, 'Well, I'll give it a try. But meanwhile, if I were you, I'd think about how I was going to plead. You'll be before the magistrate within the half-hour.'

He came back ten minutes later looking almost pleased. 'Apparently Fred Slaney is somewhere outside Narrabri at the moment, working on an investigation. I left a message with the Narrabri police but they don't know when they'll be seeing him. So, to matters at hand. How do you wish to plead?'

'These charges are a complete fabrication! Two cops are behind this, Sidoti and what's-his-name.'

He studied my face and nodded slowly.

'I see.'

'So tell the beak that. This is a conspiracy against me.'

He took his glasses off. 'It's my duty to tell you that if you plead not guilty and get convicted it will be much worse for you. On the other hand, if you plead guilty, you'll probably just get a fine and then you can go home.'

'What about the cops who are setting me up?'

'It's my professional opinion that to mention this business about

Sidoti and Rheinberger in court would not be in your best interests. It could do you great damage.'

I leaned across the table, grabbed him by the collar, dragged him forward and punched him in the face. 'You're with them. I didn't mention Rheinberger's name. Rack off, I'll defend myself. If I ever run into you outside, look out.'

Royston cried out and a cop came in, asked what's the trouble? Royston straightened his tie and said no trouble, this mug doesn't want legal help, so fuck him.

They led me into court barefoot and unshaven, with blood and dried mud and slime on my shirt and jacket. The magistrate wrinkled his nose and examined me over the top of his glasses. The charges were read and I was asked how I would plead. I said not guilty.

One of the arresting cops was brought in. He said how they'd found me drunk in the pool, picking up coins. When they interrupted me, according to his telling, I'd said certain words. What were those words? the prosecutor asked. The cop handed a piece of paper to the clerk who showed it to the prosecutor, the magistrate and then to me. It said 'Get fucked you mug fucken copper.'

The prosecutor asked about the coins. People throw them into the pool, the cop said, and the council collects them every so often, passes the money on to Legacy to aid their charitable work among war orphans. Had he ever heard of anyone thieving the money before this? The cop said never in his experience. Even common thieves respected the Pool of Reflections, he said.

I put myself in the dock, stated that I'd done none of the things claimed, that I was the victim of a police conspiracy. The magistrate sighed audibly. The prosecutor asked me if I'd been celebrating that Anzac Day. I said yeah. He said who with? I told him Air Force. He said then you'd be ex-Air Force, Mr Glasheen, is that correct? I told him well, no. Which branch of the forces had I served with then? I told him I had no war record.

The magistrate then asked me what my occupation was. I said businessman. He said what business? I said mail order.

The police prosecutor took over again and told the magistrate that police had been observing the accused for some years and he was known to them as a supplier of illicit sex drugs and the like, and was a frequenter of dives of the lowest sort.

Even I knew that wasn't cricket, so I objected. The magistrate agreed and said he'd disregard those last remarks. Then he asked me was I a beatnik, and was this beatnik attire I was wearing? I said no. He said well, it certainly isn't businessman's attire either. He smiled indulgently as the prosecutor and courtroom staff all had a little giggle. I told him I had been held in the cells all weekend, hadn't been given a chance to clean up, had been denied bail, that's why I was like this.

'What's this conspiracy business?'

'Two cops called Sidoti and Rheinberger,' I said, 'they have it in for me. They rigged up the charges.'

'*Did* they? I see no mention of these gentlemen in the papers before me.'

'They were there. They stage-managed this.'

'And why are you unrepresented here today? Didn't the duty solicitor see you, offer to represent you?'

'He's part of it too,' I said.

'Saints preserve us,' he said. So then I objected to that. The magistrate asked me what exactly was I objecting to. I said to you, the prosecutor, that goose writing it all down and the whole effing lot of you. I said this court's a joke, you mob aren't fit to run a chook raffle. I said I wanted the hearing adjourned so that I could hire a proper solicitor. The beak said it was too late for that, I should have spoken up at the beginning. He asked did I have any more to say. I said fucking plenty. He said that sort of language wouldn't help me at all in this court. He found me guilty. He said it was a despicable and unmanly act, all the more so happening as it did on Anzac Day.

He gave me six months' hard labour.

They led me handcuffed to the holding cells out the back. At the cell door the copper undid the handcuffs. I asked him what happened now. He said when it was a full house here, the breadvan would take us out to Long Bay Jail.

There were half a dozen blokes in the cell, all new faces. A lair called out what was I there for? I sat down, lit a cig. When he realised I wasn't going to answer, he asked someone else the same question. Talk went on around me and after thirty minutes I had an idea who everyone was and what they were about: there were three bodgies who'd been done for brawling, offensive behaviour and resist arrest, and another for car theft. There was a shoplifter; a couple of pervs; three old chats pinched for begging of alms; a nondescript, middle-aged bloke for goods in custody; and two Chinamen.

They gave us a rissole and a piece of bread around lunchtime, and afterwards it sat like a river stone in my stomach.

As the afternoon wore on the talk in the cells died down. Some time after three the loudest lair called out to the cop on duty could he have that newspaper when the constable had finished with it. The cop said sure, passing it over to him.

The lout looked at the back page first, then turned it over and read the headline, opened it up. After a minute he called across to me, 'Hey matey, is your name Bill?'

'Yeah, why?'

'I thought so, you're the only one here who's barefoot. You made the arvo papers.' He walked over smiling, handed me the paper.

I was on page three.

ANZAC DAY OUTRAGE

'I WAS HELPING OLD DIGGER,' SAYS THIEF

A man caught stealing coins from the Pool of Reflections in Hyde Park told Central Court of Petty Sessions today that he had entered the water to retrieve a set of dentures on behalf of 'an old digger'.

Bill Glasheen, 'businessman' of East Sydney, claimed that the mysterious 'old digger' had said he lost his dentures in a coughing fit.

Glasheen's testimony was directly contradicted by Constable G. Pringle, who had earlier told the court that he and Constable Venables had surprised Glasheen in the pool 'furtively filling his pockets' with threepences and sixpences from the pool.

Pringle told the court that on being disturbed, Glasheen let fly with a torrent of obscene abuse, and had made a feeble attempt to assault him and Constable Venables.

In sentencing him to six months hard labour, Mr MacDonald declared that he was sick and tired of 'barefoot beatniks and bodgies' coming before his court. He said that Glasheen at his age should have known better, and that to steal from a charity on Anzac Day and claim that he was aiding a returned man put a particularly sordid twist on the offence.

I folded up the paper and put it down. The lout was looking at me. 'You'd have to be a low mongrel to steal from Legacy kiddies,' he said.

'Yeah, ain't I'm a dog?'

An hour later three cops came down to the cells. One of them called out, 'All aboard for the Malabar Mansion express. Come on, you lot, look lively, on your feet.'

They shepherded us out to a loading dock. We walked out single file and into a large, dark blue van.

They bolted the door. The only light in the back of the van came from two small vents near the roof. Nothing happened for fifteen minutes or so. Then another door slammed and the van started up. The trip to jail took half an hour. It was nearly dark outside when they opened the door again. I could smell the sea.

Long Bay Jail was set on a hill above the cliffs out past Malabar, near the tram tracks. It was a bleak, scrubby, snaky bit of ground, and in winter the winds off the Tasman Sea blew in so hard it felt like south of New Zealand. I'd passed the old brick outer wall of the jail maybe two hundred times, but this was my first time inside. Shit, I sure hadn't missed much.

They called us out of the van and had us line up. The driver passed a clipboard over to one of the warders. No one spoke to us, and when one of the lairs called out, 'Hey, mate, have we missed our tea?' a warder said to him, 'Shut up, you.' And that was the most personal interest any of the warders showed in us. They could have been looking at a row of housebricks.

We were led through a caged walkway, which led into a kind of assembly hall. They had us line up in front of a table where a screw was sitting filling in forms. When it was my turn the bloke scarcely glanced at me.

'Name?'

'Glasheen.'

'Christian name.'

'Bill.'

'William. Religion?'

'None.'

'You can't have none.'

I shrugged.

'This is required for the burial arrangements in the event of your death while here. I personally couldn't give a shit, but I've got to complete this form. What were you brought up?'

'Nothing.'

'When was the last time you were in a church, not counting weddings or funerals?'

'Can't remember. Must've been when I was in kindergarten, when the nuns took us to Mass.'

He nodded. 'That'll do. RC.' He wrote it down. 'Normal occupation?'

'Self-employed.'

He looked up at me. 'You haven't got a trade then?'

'Businessman.'

I saw him write 'unemployed' on the form. 'Next of kin?'

I gave him my brother's name and the last address I knew, which was over ten years old.

Then the screw told me to empty my pockets onto the table. I pulled out a packet of smokes, a dirty hanky, my wallet, and from my jacket pocket *The Wonder Book of Australiana*. The screw picked up the wallet, looked through it and put it in a manila envelope.

He picked up the book. 'What's this?'

'Think and grow rich.'

He thumbed through it. A piece of folded paper that I'd been using as a bookmark fell out. He carefully unfolded the paper, which was a page that had come loose from Ulmer's book of preachments. He examined the fancy Gothic printing.

'You rip this out of a library book, did you?' He looked at the page and read aloud. '*Seek a suitable place for retreat and contemplation.* Looks like you've found a suitable place.' He put the paper back in the book and handed it to me. 'You can keep that.'

'I urgently need to contact someone,' I said.

'Listen, son, your busy social round will have to be put on hold for a little while.'

'A cop. Fred Slaney. I've got to get in touch with him.'

The screw looked at me funny. 'You've never been here before, have you?'

'What's that got to do with it?'

'You can write a letter to anyone you wish.'

We went to another queue and were each given a grey boilersuit, a pair of brown shoes, socks and underwear, a hat and a thin blanket. Then they sent us to a shower block to tub and change into the jail threads.

The prison warden came out and gave us a little speech about what would be expected of us here: how we must observe certain standards of behaviour and we'd be accorded certain privileges, which were *not* to be mistaken for rights; that if we acted the billygoat we'd get a lot more than we bargained for. He finished up by saying that here, as everywhere else, we'd be judged by the company we kept, which might have almost been funny.

We were led out into the jail proper. It smelled of sweat, soap, disinfectant, damp concrete and stale cooking. There was a continuous murmuring and even little noises echoed loudly, so that it was hard to tell where any single sound was coming from.

A screw took me up a set of stairs into a long corridor. There were solid iron cell doors off to the side. He stopped near the end of the passageway, unlocked a door and gestured for me to go in.

I entered and the door closed behind me. A short dark bloke was sitting on the bottom bunk. He glanced at me and said, 'You have that one,' pointing to the top bunk.

I put my stuff down on the bed.

'Bill Glasheen's my name.'

He nodded but didn't look at me, nor did he say anything more. After a ten-second silence he stood up, walked around me and moved over to the door, which opened a couple of seconds later. He walked out. 'Teatime,' he said back over his shoulder.

The screw who opened the door said, 'Come on, get a move on, you.'

I followed my cellmate back along the corridor. The screw proceeded along the row, unlocking cells. At the other end of the passage there was a bain-marie on wheels where two blokes were serving out food onto tin plates. Half a dozen prisoners were queuing up. I picked up a plate and waited behind my cellmate. When it was my turn the first server put some grey stewlike muck on my plate. The other one scooped out some potatoes and veg.

He looked at me and whispered,' Bill?'

'Les!'

'Jesus, Billy, I thought you were too smart to wind up in this shithouse.'

'So did I.'

He looked around and lowered his voice. 'What'd they get you for?'

'Some minor bullshit. It's a long story.'

'You're not the money-in-the-fountain bloke, are you?'

I didn't say anything and he said, 'That's wild, dad. Billy Glasheen pinching zacks from orphans!'

'Come on, Les, you really think I would?'

The line had grown and the screw called out, 'What's the hold-up? No talking there!'

Les put some cabbage on my plate and said quietly, 'Keep your chin up. But look out. Some of the blokes here are crooked on people who hurt kids or steal from them and that.'

'High principles.'

'Don't worry, you've got mates here too. You're in with Jim Swanson, eh?' He turned to my cellmate and whispered, 'Hey, Jim, Bill's a mate of mine. You'll do the right thing by him, won't you?'

Jim nodded joylessly.

Les put a knife and fork on my plate and handed me a half-loaf of bread. As we moved away Les said, 'I'll catch up with you later.' He nodded in Jim's direction. 'He won't say much but he's all right.'

I went back to the cell carrying my plate, and ate in silence. The veg was edible but the only solid bits in the stew were bones and lumps of fat and gristle. I ate a mouthful and put it down. Jim kept working away methodically at his meal.

When he'd finished he looked up at me and said, 'Not too good, is it?'

'The bread's all right.'

He said, 'Put your plate under the door there, with the cutlery on it. They'll be along to collect it in a minute. Would you like some golden syrup for your bread?'

'Okay.' I still had the best part of a packet of cigs with me, which they'd let me keep. I offered Jim one. He took it, nodding, and put it behind his ear. 'I'll have it later.'

I said, 'Take another one for now.' He did and I lit it for him.

He smoked about half and carefully put it out. Then he bent over and pulled a wooden fruit box out from under his bunk. He brought out a tin of golden syrup, a billycan, mugs, bits of wire bodgied up with insulation tape. He filled the billy at the little basin by the wall and placed the shit bucket in the middle of the cell. He carefully stood on it, reached up to the light, then looked down. 'Now hold that element in the billy, but for Christ's sake don't let it touch the sides.' He pointed to the end of the apparatus, a twisted electric-jug element. There were a couple of wooden clothes pegs near the end. 'Hold it by those pegs. Dangle it over the water, but don't let the wires touch or else you'll blow the fuses and bring the screws down on us. That insulation's pretty ratshit.'

He removed the globe and plugged the end of the rig into the light socket. He waited there for two or three minutes until the water in the tin boiled. Then he replaced the globe, got down and threw a half handful of tea in the billy. He put everything away again and sat down.

'I've got some milk here.'

'Black will be all right.'

He poured it out. I drank it.

'You never been here before?'

'No.'

'It's a cunt of a place. But there are ways of getting by. You'll learn.'

116

Chapter 10

My health wasn't great. I was feverish for the first week and had all sorts of strange aches and pains. I was desperate for a drink, or for a smoke of chow treacle. I didn't sleep well and when I did I dreamed the same dream every night. I was knocking on the Chinaman's door but there was no answer.

I sent a letter off to Slaney at the CIB. I asked to talk to the prison warden but I was told my request for an interview had been refused. I was forced to adjust my standards of personal hygiene and what I considered to be reasonable medical and dental care—the dentist only did extractions, the quack didn't do anything, and they only let us shower and shave once a week.

The few luxuries you could get—extra tobacco, tailor-made cigs, toothpaste, shaving cream, lollies, butter, jam or golden syrup—were prized items of trade. I had come in with nothing but a pack of tailor-mades, the clothes I was wearing and my book of facts. Les loaned me ten quid, which helped me through those first few weeks.

Time passed with a slowness I couldn't have conceived of before. Like the song said, the minutes seemed like hours, the hours seemed like days. When it became clear Slaney wasn't coming to the rescue, I settled into a permanent state of combined boredom and terror, if you can imagine such a thing.

Blokes inside coped with the boredom in different, sometimes strange ways. One feller endlessly built houses of cards. Another told me he was trying to sleep his way through his lagging. My cellmate Jim kept strictly to his daily routine, like a monk. Every night at exactly the same time he'd brew up his tea, eat his bread and golden syrup. In the daytime he'd read and reread his little stack of photography magazines. I was sure he knew them off by heart, but each day he read through them like it was the first time.

I laughed at him inwardly at first but then I took a leaf out of his book, so to speak, and started putting in some time on my own little self-improvement project, *The Wonder Book of Australiana*. I read it cover to cover once, twice, many times. I memorised it the way rockchopper schoolkids learn their catechism. As time passed it became a bit of a thing for people to throw questions at me, like, 'Hey, Bill, what's the current sheep population of Australia?'

'Approximately 158,000,000.'

'What trotter won the first Inter-dominion?'

'Evicus, from Perth, 1936.'

'What is an Australian triantelope?'

'The so-called Australian triantelope is a large, flat-bodied, long-legged, hairy spider, commonly known as a huntsman.' And so on. If it was in the book, chances were I knew it. Otherwise, I was the same dill I'd always been.

Jim kept to himself, but every day he'd ask me one thing about myself, beginning with the standard what was I in for.

'My enemies have plotted against me,' I told him.

He nodded, said nothing more that day, but the next night, after we'd brewed up, he said, 'You didn't pinch the kiddies' money, then?'

I told him no, I hadn't, and he said, 'So what, you're a cleanskin then?'

'No. But I didn't pinch the money.'

Next night: 'So what do you normally do?'

'I'm a man of enterprise.'

Jim nodded, said, 'A man of enterprise, eh? I like that. Does that mean lurk merchant?'

'I suppose so.'

At a rate of one or two questions a day, Jim got to know a fair bit about me. What I found out about him was that he was a 'short-story writer', a forger. He'd been trained for the printing trade but his true calling was crime. He'd been in for three years, was due for release in the next few months. He got a weekly visit from his wife and oldest son. The only time he ever really opened up was when he talked about his hobby, photography. He had his own darkroom at home. He showed me photos he'd taken, of his family, of sunsets, race horses, football games. He was always looking at shadows and lighting angles, at rough-textured walls and interesting shapes, saying that would make a beaut photo. He even gave me his photography mags to read so I could better understand what he was talking about. I flipped through the pile, came to an issue of the *Women's Weekly*.

I said to Jim, 'How long did you say you've been inside, Jim?'

'Very funny. Turn to page twenty-seven.'

I did. A full-page colour photo of a bird, a green parrot of some kind, between two tussocks of grass.

'That's a ground parrot. They used to think they were extinct. They're not, though, they're just bloody shy. You've got to keep very still to get a photo like that.'

'You took this?'

'With a special lens. I got twenty guineas for that picture.'

One night over a mug of tea Jim said, 'You say you're a local lad and you've never lived anywhere else, but you haven't had a single visit yet. As far as we know you're not a child molester, mass murderer or Liberal voter, so what's the story? You say your enemies have plotted against you, but what about your friends? Where are they?'

'Good question.'

They assigned me to the vegetable patch. It was on a slope southwest of the main jail, inside the perimeter wall. It was supposed to be hard labour but it was pretty easygoing, even by my standards. Each day the work party would collect garden tools from the sheds, walk out to the vegie patch and piss around for three or four hours, hoeing out weeds.

I didn't see much of Les Newcombe. He was in the boys' jail, where the under-25s were kept. But he was often given jobs around the jail proper and he was a great one for carrying news and gossip. It was on one of his little official errands, my third week inside, that he whispered to me, 'Look out for Mulcahy, he's going to have a go at you,' and walked on. I gaped after him, not sure what he meant.

I asked Jim later on.

'Tommy Mulcahy, that must be. You better get tooled up if he's got it in for you.'

'I don't even know this bloke. What could he have against me?'

Jim shrugged. 'Who knows? If Les gave you the word, though, you better take notice.'

I had to get someone to point Mulcahy out to me. He was a big, ginger-haired feller, always hanging around with a gang of three or four blokes. I'd noticed him giving me a hard stare on a couple of occasions. Not the inmate I'd have chosen for an enemy.

Once I'd become aware of him, our paths seemed to cross twenty times a day. One time Mulcahy sprung me looking at him. He came over and muttered, 'What are you looking at?'

'Nothing.'

'Nothing, bullshit. You keep out of my way, cunt.'

Next day in the lunch queue they gave me three sausages, but Mulcahy, who was further behind me in the line, missed out on his full ration.

He said loudly, 'What, I get one snag and that kiddie-robber gets three!' He sidled up to me and said, 'I'm going to get you, Glasheen. I'm going to kill you and fuck you while you're still warm.'

I stayed clear of him. But a week later, at the end of an afternoon working in the garden, the screw sent me to put the hoes and mattocks back in the shed. I put the tools down, opened the shed door and turned around to face Mulcahy and two of his pals standing alongside the door, out of sight of the screws.

'You're a fuckin' mongrel dog, Glasheen. I was a Legacy kid.'

'And aren't you a credit to them.'

They came at me. I went straight down, curled up, tried to cover my head. They kicked me hard, in the thigh, in the stomach, in the head. Then one of them fell on top of me and the kicking stopped.

There was a cracking noise and another one fell. I got out from under the body, stood up. Les Newcombe was swinging a mattock at Mulcahy, who was backing off fast. The other two were trying to get to their feet but they were dazed and bleeding. I booted the one nearest me, picked up a hoe and stood alongside Les.

Mulcahy smiled and said, 'No harm done, fellers. It's over.'

Les said, 'At him, Bill.'

'No, let it go,' I said.

Les shook his head, rushed Mulcahy, hit him in the stomach and then the chest with the handle of the mattock. That was the end of Mulcahy for the day.

Afterwards, Mulcahy and his mates explained their injuries— two broken ribs in Mulcahy's case, cuts and bruises for the others—by saying they'd tripped over a hoe. I had no more trouble with them.

When I thanked Les later for coming to the rescue he said forget it, I'd have done the same for him. I wasn't so sure about that, but I let it pass.

I said, 'I don't know what would have happened if you hadn't shown. You really went off.'

'You think I was hard on them?'

'No criticism, Les. But I mean, Mulcahy had given up when you hit him that last time.'

'I'd have broken his arms as well if I'd had more time.' He saw my look, shook his head and said, 'You haven't quite got the hang of things in here yet, have you? All right, picture this: you're at a pub and someone's dirty on you, he says to you step outside. What do you do?'

'Depends. Maybe go out and fight, maybe slip away. Or just ignore it.'

He shook his head again. 'What you do is this: you pick up the heaviest thing to hand and hit the bastard real hard with it. You don't wait. Every second you hesitate, the other bloke's position gets stronger and yours gets weaker. That goes double in here. This is Rafferty's rules, not Queensberry's. You hit fast, hit hard.'

No one visited me. No one replied to my letters. The daily routine ground on. Any break that didn't involve personal injury was a big treat. Like when some squareheads from the Billy Graham Crusade, which was in town that month, came around and spoke to us.

I went along, same reason as everyone else, it was something to do. The speakers were earnest young Americans. They all wore the same suit, had their hair cut short. The prisoners gigged the shit out of them. But at the end, when they called on members of the audience to come forward and 'decide for Christ', about sixty blokes did so.

I whispered to Jim, 'Do they know something I don't?'

'Decide for Christ, you get a packet of biscuits,' he said, and stood up and joined the queue.

The next week the Salvos came out and put on a show-singing, sermonising and silver band. The star of their show was one Cyril Cathcart, 'the Man with the World's Smallest Organ'. A harmonica player, as it turned out.

Then one day a screw came to the cell. 'You've got a visitor,' he said. 'Come on, quick smart.'

He took me to an interview room. Sidoti was there, smoking a cigarette. He told the screw there was no need for him to hang about, he'd be OK.

When we were alone he said quietly, 'I told you we'd get quits.'

'Go root your boot.'

'Heard from your mate Slaney?'

I said nothing.

'Maybe you backed the wrong horse there, eh?' He watched me for a few moments. 'You don't know what I'm talking about, do you? Brother Slaney is under investigation. He won't be around much longer, and in the meantime he won't be sticking his neck out on your behalf, regardless of what deals you think you've made.'

'Fuck you *and* your donkey.'

'Now, now, don't be like that. I'm the only friend you've got at the moment.'

'Then get me out.'

'You've been sentenced by the court, I can't just override that. Especially not without a good reason.'

'Such as what?'

'Look, I'm not going to piss around. I know for certain that Slaney looked into the Ray Waters business and that the trail led him to you, and it was all connected with the J. Farren Price robbery. I don't know all the details but they're not that important.'

I didn't reply.

'So, the way for you to get out of here, and go on living afterwards, is to give me what you were going to give Slaney.'

'What if I was to say there's nothing to be had?'

'This isn't my opening gambit. This is your last chance. If I don't get the money, it's back to the original plan, eliminate Bill Glasheen, cop killer. Hey, don't think that'll break my heart. If you're not helping me, you're in my way. After you've gone I'll be free to track down that J. Farren Price loot at my leisure.'

'Go stick your head up your arse.'

He put his hands out, palms up. 'All right, that's how you want it. So be it. Farewell, William.'

Later that day I was called up to the office. The screw had a file open. He glanced at me and continued to leaf through it. He didn't offer me a seat.

'You haven't got a trade, have you, Glasheen?'

'I'm a businessman.'

He ignored that and continued. 'You're going to be given a chance to learn something useful while you're in custody.' He made an entry on a form in front of him. 'Do you know where Oberon is?'

'One hundred and eleven miles west of Sydney by road. Mean elevation of three thousand, six hundred and fifty one feet, principal industries are farming and timber, population approximately three thousand—'

He put his pen down and his face turned red. 'Think you're smart, do you?'

'It just slipped out.'

'See how smart you are after a month or two of forestry work.'

'Thanks all the same, but I'd rather stay here.'

'You'll go where you're bloody well sent.'

'Did somebody outside the jail have a hand in this?'

He hesitated and lowered his eyes for a fraction of a second. 'It wasn't our idea, I can tell you that.'

'I don't want to go.'

He shook his head. 'It's not up to you.' He stood up. 'You leave right now. The officer's waiting. You can pick up your personal property on your way out.'

That was how they transferred you within the jail system, without warning, so you had no time to stage a sickie or any other trick if it happened to be not to your liking.

Oberon was a small farming town high on a plateau on the other side of the Blue Mountains. The camp was in the bush twenty miles out of town, rugged and remote, surrounded by a cyclone fence. We got there at eight o'clock at night, well after dinner. We weren't fed.

They issued me with a rough woollen coat and an old army jumper. I was assigned to one of a number of wooden huts, like *Stalag 17*. There were six people to a hut. The beds had thin straw mattresses, you could have as many blankets as you wanted but they told me five was the best number—more than that didn't make you any warmer.

The first morning they got us up before dawn. I was put with a work crew and driven in a truck out to a pine plantation. We were set to work in teams, either walking up and down the rows pruning off the lower straggly branches, or bashing the suckers which sprang up where they'd clear-felled the scrub. I was with the pruning group. They sent us off, two men to each row, while the screws strolled along a hundred or so yards behind. If you kept it down you could talk while you worked.

It was a weird kind of forest. The sun filtered only weakly through the pine branches. There was no undergrowth, bar the eucalypt suckers, no insects or small animals, hardly any birds, and the thick layer of pine needles absorbed most of the sound. But there were mushrooms growing among the fallen pine needles, and a couple of the blokes collected them in a sweater.

We worked through the rows of pines all morning, snipping off lower branches. No one worked that hard and the screws didn't seem to care. At lunchtime we went back down the hill to where the trucks were parked. One of the prisoners, an Aboriginal bloke, had stayed behind to cook lunch. Although the bush seemed lifeless, he had managed somehow to get hold of a couple of rabbits and they were cooking on a spit when we got back.

The work continued in the afternoon and finished up at four o'clock. The evening meal was better than at Long Bay, except for the bread, which was old stuff from the Oberon bakery. There was home brew available for a price, some of the prisoners had crystal sets, and there was even an SP bookie. After tea it was absolutely quiet, no cars, no trucks, nothing.

The inmates were all small fry like me, low-security, short-term prisoners or first offenders. Except for one, a bloke named Hector Rackley. He was a big, ugly-looking bloke with long arms. His teeth were all missing, apart from one either side of his face, which made him look like a vampire. His eyes were wide set, with big staring pupils, and his skin was always under a film of sweat, like he was highly excited, or had just come in from exercise. At meal times he sat alone, muttering to himself.

One night I saw him jump a bloke who passed too close to him. He punched the Christ out of the poor bastard before the screws got to him. The guards thought it was a great hoot. No action was taken. Two days later I got up for a piss after lights out. Something was going on behind the admin hut. I walked over, quietly. Three screws and Rackley were working a prisoner over, taking turns belting him. Rackley saw me. I started walking away but Rackley was fast on his feet. He grabbed me, spun me round, and in half a second I was on the deck with Rackley's knee in my back, my arm twisted behind me.

'What are you going to do now, goose?' He pushed my arm a bit further up my back. 'I'll tell you: you're not going to do anything, are you? Mind your own business in future, understand?' He let go of me.

The next day one of the prisoners, a kid from Deniliquin, was absent. Later we got word he was in hospital with a punctured lung. I never found out the reason for the flogging, if there was one.

I asked the blokes in my hut how come a psycho like Rackley was in low security. No one really knew, but they said the word on Rackley was he was an ex-cop and he still had some influence outside.

In my third week I was put with a different pruning crew, partnered with Rackley. We were sent off to work a seemingly endless pine row, in a plantation where the young pines stretched away to the horizon. I tried not to meet his eye, and kept as great a distance between us as possible. But I was more or less forced into communication with him. He'd talk incessantly for an hour or two, then suddenly go quiet and brood for a while, then start off talking again. Sometimes he just mumbled to himself. Even though I didn't particularly want to know, I found out a fair bit about him.

He'd served in New Guinea during the war, then become a cop afterwards. He'd been in the bush at Dubbo and Cobar, and in Sydney. He bragged about bashing bodgies, dagoes and Abos and rooting the women.

That afternoon I said, 'You're telling this to the wrong bloke. I'd rather not know about it, thanks all the same.' He paused for a couple of seconds and then carried on like I hadn't said anything. I tried to ignore him as best I could.

Every day was like that, he'd talk, then go quiet, and then talk some more. His favourite topic was killing, how many people he'd killed, how he'd done it and how much he'd enjoyed it. There were seven Japs he knew he'd killed in New Guinea. Five of them he shot, one he bludgeoned to death, and the other he'd reckoned he'd strangled, which was his personal favourite. As a cop he'd shot a bloke in Dubbo, for which he'd been commended. There were some others he'd 'done' as well, but he wouldn't be commended for those he said because 'no bastard will ever find them'.

Once he'd sketched in the broad outlines of the killings he'd committed, he got down to details—how you crack a skull, where you put your thumbs when you're strangling a bloke, how easy it is to gouge out an eye. One thing he said stayed with me. He said the first person you kill, that's a really big deal, but the ones after that don't mean anything much. Just like having a shit, he said.

Chapter 11

The Indian summer lasted right through June and into July. I remained partnered with Rackley on the pruning crew.

One day he asked me if I ever did any fishing. I said yeah, sometimes. He took on a sly look, said he'd show me something later.

Mid-afternoon he put his saw down and said to follow him. We walked down the hill about a quarter of a mile.

'Will the screws miss us?' I said.

He ignored me. We kept walking.

At the bottom of the hill was a creek which formed the border of this part of the forest. On the other side was thick eucalypt scrub. We walked along the edge of the stream for two hundred yards, disturbing four or five large snakes lazing on the bank, and even a wombat.

Rackley told me to wait while he walked back into the forest a little way. He returned with a hessian sack, from which he pulled two sticks wound with fishing line, a jar and a mattock blade. He went to the water's edge and dug into the mud under a tuft of grass.

'Here y'are, grab these!' He dropped a couple of large grey worms in my hand. 'Put them in the jar.'

He went to another tuft and did the same. When we had a dozen or so worms he gestured to continue down the track.

Another ten minutes' walking brought us into a narrow section of valley where we came upon a large elongated pool. It curved around for a hundred yards or so, about thirty yards wide in the middle. It was still and deep, but I could hear water gurgling out at the other end where the stream continued down the valley.

Rackley signalled not to make any noise. He whispered, 'Bait up a hook and see if you can cast it over near that rock,' pointing to a large granite outcrop on the opposite bank.

I did as he said. The line sank and I sat on my haunches. Rackley moved along another five yards and did the same. Flies were thick, and a bad smell wafted my way every so often, but after less than two minutes I got a big bite on the line. Rackley called out at almost the same instant and we pulled in a large brown trout each.

'What do you think of that, eh?' he said.

'Never seen anything like it!'

He made a fire and we cooked them on the spot.

As we sat there eating the fish the flies were so bad they almost drove us away. I finished the fish, washed my greasy hands in the water. The rotten smell came again.

'Can you smell that?' I said.

He grinned, nodding, and said, 'Follow me. I'll show you something.'

We skirted around the end of the pool, and stepping carefully on rocks we crossed over to the other side.

'I suppose we're technically out of the prison now,' I said.

'Who cares?'

We worked our way to the granite outcrop opposite where we'd been fishing. The pool cut back into a little shady bay behind the rock, where gum trees overhung the water. The smell and the flies got much worse. Rackley stopped at the water's edge and pointed in front of him, smiling. A rope was hanging down from a branch of a tree with something attached to the end of it. Rackley picked up a stick and snared the rope, pulled it towards him. He lifted the thing on the end, held it up so I could see.

It was a pig's head. He nudged it with the stick so that it swung around on the rope. Its open mouth and eye sockets were swarming with flies and big fat maggots, which dropped steadily into the water below.

'Berley,' he said.

When the head was facing us, Rackley reached over and tapped its snout and said, 'Hey Porky, say hello to your Uncle Bill!'

That afternoon I asked a screw to put me somewhere else. He said what did I mean, most blokes want the forest job. What about the other jobs, I said. There was nothing vacant in the kitchen or laundry, he said, but there might be something coming up in the trout hatchery soon. I told him I'd take that. He said all right, he'd keep me in mind. Meanwhile, I was to stay with forestry.

It turned cold that night, and over the next week winter set in in earnest. One morning I woke up shivering. There was a layer of ice on the blanket where my breath had condensed and frozen. Snow had drifted in under the door of the hut. It was wet and cold out in the pine forest, and the dark mood even got to Rackley, who shut up for once.

It was still snowing when they marshalled us into the trucks to go to work. When I lined up with the forestry crew one of the warders said, 'Where do you think you're going, Glasheen?'

'The forestry.'

He shook his head. 'You're with the hatchery crew today. Wait over there with the other truck.'

As I walked away he said, 'Have fun.'

We were driven for about twenty minutes, then were set down outside a shed on a river, maybe the same river I'd been at the day before, for all I knew. There was a couple of inches of snow on the ground.

Near the river stood a series of concrete tanks with chicken wire on top. They gave us each a pair of nail-clippers, a net, a tin bucket and a bottle of liquid.

A ranger said to me, 'Hey, you! Have you done this before?'

I shook my head.

'I'll show you.'

The screws disappeared inside the shed to sit around the fire. The ranger told me to follow him. He went over to the concrete tank, lifted the chicken wire back. Water was pumping through the tank, creating a permanent whirlpool. The ranger filled the bucket with water, put it down at his feet. Then he took the net and scooped out a dozen or so little fish and tipped them into the bucket. He did it twice more, and when there were thirty or so fingerlings in the bucket he took it over and put it beside another tank.

'Sit down here,' he said.

He poured a capful of the liquid into the bucket. 'That slows them down a bit. Don't use too much, though, or else they all die. All right, now reach in and grab one.'

I did. The water was icy, so cold that it hurt. Even with the dope in the water the fish weren't easy to catch. I remembered what Shirley Hill had prophesied months before about the hand reaching into the icy depths for the elusive quarry. I shuddered.

I finally got hold of a fingerling, two inches long.

'Hold it by the tail and flip it over, that's right. Now use the clippers to snip that fin there, the top right. Each year it's a different fin, you see, so later on we can monitor their growth rates. If you're still here next year, for example, you'll be clipping the top lefthand fin, all the way through the six lateral fins. Be careful, don't scratch its belly with the clippers. Now put it back in the bucket.'

I dropped it in.

'For God's sake, do it carefully! When you've done them all, tip the bucket slowly, hear me, *slowly* into this tank, and get another batch of fingerlings from over there. Always remember to replace that chicken wire or else the birds will get the fish.'

After a few minutes my hands were so cold that I could scarcely grab any fish at all. After ten minutes my arms were numb and I was shivering all over. I poured a little more of the dope into the water. It slowed the little bastards down all right—half a dozen floated up to the surface dead. I was clipping the remaining live fingerlings when the ranger came by.

'I told you not to use too much of that stuff! Don't you listen? Look what you've done!'

At midday they called a stop for lunch. I put my hands in front of the fire. As they warmed up and the feeling returned, they ached worse than ever. I said to one of the blokes, 'This is shitting me to tears. I'm going to see the screw, get a different job.'

'You'd be lucky.'

'What do you mean?'

'This is the all-time shit job. That's why it's easy to get. It's harder to get out of. Unless you've got influence.'

Sure enough, when I asked the screw he said no deal.

Each day working at the hatchery was the same. The cold water made my arms ache until they went numb. Then I'd shiver all day sitting at my bucket. By the third day the skin on my hands was so dry that deep fissures opened in the cracks. I tried wrapping my hands up at night, but any movement would open the fissures. I continued to clip the fish as best I could. Sometimes to amuse myself I'd snip patterns in a fish's tail fin, or cut out my own minute initials. Let the gigs monitor that, I thought.

After two weeks of standing in the cold I'd developed a racking cough. At lunchtime I approached the screw, told him the work was making me sick. He said I should have thought of that when I stole the money from the Legacy kiddies.

The trucks were late that day, didn't get there until nearly five o'clock, when it was getting dark. The screws came out and marshalled us into the trucks. The rangers had long gone.

I was the last into the truck. Just as they were closing up the back, I said, 'Cripes, I left my sweater over there. Can I go back and get it?'

'No. It's too late.'

The other screw said, 'No, he better have it. If the silly cunt freezes to death the blame will be on us.'

I ran back, picked up the sweater and went over to the first tank, removed the housebrick and pulled the chicken wire back. I did the same at the other tanks, just moving the wire enough to allow a bird sufficient space to get in and out again.

The screw called out to me, 'Hurry up, Glasheen.'

'Go ahead without me if you like, I'll make my own way back.'

'Not bloody likely.'

I looked up to the trees, said, '*Bon appétit*,' and scooted back to the truck.

Next morning two thirds of the fingerlings had been taken by the birds. Everyone except the rangers thought it was a gas. No one accused me of anything, they were too grateful. That was the end of hatchery work for a while.

I was put back on forestry, working with Rackley again. The intermittent snow had turned into misty rain and fog. Working in the forest, that old song kept running through my head. 'In the pines, in the pines, where the sun never shines, I shivered the whole night through.'

Rackley was just the same. If I thought he'd told me all there was to tell about bashings, rape and murder, I was wrong. He had plenty left. But he was acting strange, even by his standards.

One bitterly cold, grey, windy Monday, Rackley was silent all morning, then after lunch he said, 'Let's go fishing.'

'A bit cold, isn't it? There won't be any maggots now on that pig's head, and this weather will have put the fish off the bite.'

'Come on, we'll have a go anyway.' He looked at me, waiting.

'No, I think I'll give it a miss, thanks all the same.'

He walked over to me, clamped his hand around my neck. 'Come *now*. You're going to keep me company.'

We walked over the hill into the bush. There was a howling westerly blowing, whipping up what felt like sharp bits of ice crystal. Although I had my overcoat on, my eyes were streaming and I was freezing cold. But Rackley seemed oblivious, wearing just a thin sweater over his shirt. He was talking now, rabbiting on about how he'd asked his contacts outside to get him some better fishing tackle, some new hooks and some good German line, and how he'd have it any day now.

We were approaching the pool. I stopped and said, 'Why have you dragged me out here?'

He shook his head, said, 'Why didn't you play ball with them when they asked you?'

'Play ball with who?'

He shook his head again, walked off the track and reached under a large tree stump. He brought out a bag, carried it over, dusted it off and dropped it at his feet. It wasn't the same bag he'd had last time. He bent over to tip out the contents. Ropes, copper wire, potato sacks, what looked like lumps of rolled up lead flashings, an axe handle and a machete.

'What kind of fish were you thinking of going after, exactly?'

Rackley muttered, 'You need it spelled out for you?' He started sorting the ropes and sacks.

'Rackley, do you want money? We can work out a deal.' He just shook his head again.

I grabbed him on the shoulder, said, 'Hey, Rackley, stop this!' He stood up and punched me hard on the side of the head. I fell over, then backed away on my knees. He went on sorting out his stuff.

I said again, 'Rackley, this is crazy.' He didn't answer me.

I stood up and kept backing away.

Rackley said, 'Don't you go running away, now. That'd just be silly.'

I took a few more steps backwards. I looked at the grey sky and the treetops thrashing about in the wind, at the miles of bush going into the distance. I was about to die and there wasn't a soul any-where to help me. I bent over and vomited, stood up then vomited again.

Rackley was twenty yards away. He had the sacks laid out on the ground with the lead to one side, and the wire and ropes on the other. He picked up the machete and stood up. 'Come here,' he said.

I stood still.

He grinned. 'Now, don't try to run. You know I'm a lot faster than you.'

I turned around and sprinted into the bush, ran like crazy for a few minutes. I stopped and listened for him, but I couldn't hear anything above the wind. I kept running for another hundred yards, then heard something and stopped dead.

Rackley was calling out not all that far away. 'Glasheen! Where are you? Come on out. If I don't do this now, it'll be tomorrow or the next day. So come on, let's get it over with. I'll make it quick.'

I started running again, this time heading up the slope, trying to get back to the work crew in the next valley. But my sense of direction was messed up. Somehow I'd run in a circle. I came out the other side of the clearing where Rackley had his stuff laid out. I stopped, looked around. He wasn't there. I walked over, picked up the axe handle, gave it a swing.

I stood still, catching my breath. I was shaking badly. I walked slowly, quietly along the track, back up the hill. The path climbed steadily for a couple of hundred yards, then went into a dip. On instinct, I stopped at the edge of the gully and left the track. I stepped carefully through the scrub, trying to circle around the hollow. Then I saw Rackley a few feet in front of me, facing away towards the track. He was hunched over, holding the machete.

I stopped dead still, unsure what to do. Rackley looked quickly from side to side, as though he'd sensed my presence. He started to turn round. I ran the last few feet at him, swung the axe handle hard at the back of his head. Rackley dodged sideways quicker than I thought anyone could. He missed the worst of the blow, but still copped a solid knock on the side of his skull. He dropped the machete and fell to his knees. But no further. He swayed a bit, then shook his head, looked up at me.

I skipped back a few feet, still holding the axe handle. I said, 'I'm going back over the hill, Rackley. Forget about this. It's not going to happen. Just forget about it.'

He grinned, bent down and picked up the machete again. I rushed forward and hit him hard. He grunted, folding over to protect himself. Then I hit him again and it was like I'd switched off an electric light. He sagged, went completely limp. I waited a moment then reached down and felt his wrist for a pulse. Whatever it was that had made his blood pump and his muscles and reflexes work wasn't there any more.

I breathed deeply for a minute or two, then felt again for a pulse, just to be sure. I sat down. The wind was screaming in the treetops, and blood was rushing almost as loudly in my own head. I looked around at the bush, at the green of the trees, the sharp outline of the dark tops against the sky, at the leaf litter at my feet, at my own hands, and at the body of Hector Rackley. The corpse looked weird, out of place. I stood up, feeling light, almost warm. Alive. Rackley had said the first one you killed was a big deal.

I stood there for a while, trying to get my mind on the job in front of me. I thought, Should I get the screws, try to tell them what had happened? Even if I explained the extenuating circumstances, I'd still be looking at murder, or manslaughter at the very least.

I walked back down the hill, back to the stuff Rackley had laid out on the ground, and tried to recreate in my own mind what his plan had been. I scouted around the edge of the pool, feeling the depth with a long tree branch. Sure enough, about twenty-five yards along there was a rock overhang where the current had cut into the hillside. The water was too deep there for me to touch the bottom with the stick.

I went back to the body, dragged it down the hill and laid it on the sacks. I threaded the ropes and wire through the lead weights, put some rocks in for good measure, placed the axe handle on top and tied it all up in a big bundle.

I tried to drag the package up to the overhang, but it was too heavy and awkward. So I undid it all and dragged just the body. Then I got the ropes, lead and stones, tied it all together again and rolled it into the water.

It made a big splash, sunk down three feet and stopped. I poked the branch at it. The body had fallen onto a submerged stump, would fall no further. It was still clearly visible, facing up at the sky. I took my clothes off and got into the water. It was so cold I thought I was going to pass out. I swam over to the body, tried to get a foothold on the mossy stump. My feet eventually found a notch on the slippery surface, which allowed me to stand up. I took the stick from the rock above me, then dived as deep as I could. Reaching down with the stick, I could just touch bottom, some fifteen feet below. Deep enough. I perched on the stump again, and carefully as I could manoeuvred the body off and let it drop into the water. It disappeared completely.

I got out of the pool, dressed, smoothed over the tracks where I'd dragged the body. There was some dried blood where Rackley had fallen. I scraped up the dirt and threw it away, chucked the knife and the remaining sacks into the pool, and ran back up the hill and down the other side to where we were supposed to be working.

I ran all the way and the bitter wind dried the wet patches on my clothes. I got to the row where we had been sucker bashing and less than ten minutes later two screws arrived.

'There you are. Where's the other bloke?'

'He, ah, he . . .' I looked back over the hill. 'He shot through.'

'Bloody hell!' The screw ran up to the top of the hill.

The other said, 'When? How long ago?'

'About half an hour.'

He looked hard at me and said, 'What did you do about stopping him?' He nodded like he'd figured it all out. 'You were going to piss off too, weren't you? Don't bother to deny it. Why did you come back? Was it the good tucker the abo cooks?' He laughed.

The other screw came back down the hill. 'He's bloody gone all right. Jesus, there'll be trouble over this. Well, we better get back and raise the hue and cry. It's a job for the coppers now.'

Two detectives came out from Bathurst. They questioned me for fifteen minutes. Where had Rackley gone? What had he said when he pissed off? Why hadn't I gone with him? How was he getting away? Was anyone else involved? I said I didn't know. He just left, I said. One of them knew him personally, knew what a psycho he was, and it didn't even seem to cross his mind that I might have had a hand in things. There was a road less than a mile away and they figured he'd either had someone pick him up or had hitch-hiked out of the district.

I went back to work at forestry next day, but now they had me with the abo at the base camp, looking after the fire, helping with lunch.

Two days later, in the middle of the day, a screw drove out and said, 'Which one is Glasheen?'

I answered and he said, 'You've got a visitor.'

'I don't want to see him. I'll stay here.'

He shook his head. 'He said you might say that. He said to tell you if you make him come all the way out here, it'll only be worse.

138

That was his message.'

He drove me back to the camp. I knew that by now Rheinberger and Sidoti might have suspicions about what really had become of Rackley. It wouldn't take much detecting to find the body.

But the visitor was Fred Slaney.

When he saw me he said, 'Jesus, you'd be a mug, getting yourself put in the slot. How are you going to get me my money sitting around here wasting time?'

'I tried to contact you.'

'Yeah. I've been busy with other matters. Have you got my money?'

'How could I? I've been busy with other matters too.'

'That's not much good to me, is it?'

'What do you expect?'

'My money, that's what. But you're in luck. I'm going to be understanding. You can have an extension. Until the end of September.'

'I still have three months left to serve.'

'No, you don't.'

He threw a folded up piece of paper across the table to me. I opened it and read it. It was from the court, seemed to say I'd been granted bail.

'How'd this come about?' I said.

'You've been given appeal bail. It applies to the period during which you're waiting for your appeal to come up at the district court.'

'Appeal?'

'You've appealed against the severity of your original sentence, which you should have done yourself back in April. With no priors, bail is more or less automatic. Your brief should have told you that. You'll go up before the district court sometime in the next few months. You should get off. Anyway, you're free to go.'

I shook my head. 'I can't show my face outside. There'll be people after me.'

'Who? Sidoti and the other bloke?'

'You know about them?'

'Upstarts. They've gotten a little big for their britches. They'll be sorted out soon enough.'

'I heard you were . . .'

'Being investigated by the internal affairs cunts? Don't get your hopes up, feller. It's nothing.'

'So when can I go?'

'Now. The paperwork has been done. They're ready to let you go. I can drop you in Oberon and you can catch the Sydney train from there.'

Slaney pulled up outside the Oberon railway station. Before I got out he said, I'm going to be busy for a while. I may not see you between now and the settle-up date. I'm not going to repeat myself on this, so you get it straight now: I'm counting on that money, and when the time comes there's to be no "wait till next week" or any of that. Let me down, you're dead. And if I can't find you I'll kill one of your relatives or friends. You clear on that?'

'Yeah.'

'All right. You're a free man. Have fun.'

Chapter 12

I'd missed the passenger train for that day. The next went out at eleven the following morning, according to the station assistant. He said there was a mail train came through on the main line at five a.m. but I'd have to get to Sodwalls, or Tarana, or even Lithgow if I wanted to be on that.

I hitched a ride from Oberon, two hours later walked into the bar of the Station Hotel in Lithgow for a drink. I had all of thirty bob in my pocket, earnings from my hard labour. The blokes in the bar copped a look at my army greatcoat and jail-issue daks.

I had three whiskies then a couple of beers. After an hour a bloke came over, struck up a conversation, asked me if I'd been out on the forestry camp. I told him yeah. He said his brother had been there last year.

'Good to be free?'

I said, 'Oh yeah, sure,' but I was lying. I wasn't free.

'I see in the paper a bloke did a bolt from there.'

'That's right,' I said. 'What did it say?'

'Said he was considered dangerous. Last I saw, they still hadn't found him. The brother said it doesn't happen much from there, blokes taking off like that.'

'I suppose not.'

'Where are you off to now?'

'Back to Sydney.'

He nodded and opened his wallet, took out a ten-pound note and held it out to me.

'What's that for?'

'Take it, as a loan, buy yourself a feed, get a room and that.'

'Thanks, but that's all right, pal.'

'No, go on, take it. When the brother got out he had nothing. You can pay me when you get on your feet. Send it to me care of the pub.'

I found a second-hand shop, bought an old leather jacket for a quid, left the greatcoat there and went back to the pub. The good samaritan had left.

I booked a room, ate a counter meal, got pissed and went to bed. I asked them to wake me at four a.m. They gave me an alarm clock. In the morning the whole town was under a thick layer of fog and coal smoke, and it was as cold as it had ever been in Oberon. There was a coal fire burning in the waiting room at the station. A couple of bundles of Sydney newspapers had been left on the platform. I took a paper from each bundle. It started to snow as the train pulled in.

I read all the important stuff. Eddie Fisher and Elizabeth Taylor had been divorced, Col Joye had a hit record, Lee Gordon had surfaced again, Sal Mineo had been in town and two chicks who won a date with him said he didn't even try to kiss them goodnight. An American named George Adamski was out here telling how he'd been abducted by flying saucers, taken for a spin around the moon, and how he'd played table tennis on Saturn with the spacemen.

A former SP bookie named Bob Askin was the new state opposition leader, and Arthur Calwell had taken over leadership of the federal ALP. Some chow seamen on a ship berthed at Woolloomooloo had been pinched with a haul of watches and sex drugs, and St George were blitzing the Rugby League comp.

There was a picture of Jack Davey in Hollywood with Jayne Mansfield. She was wearing a dress made from pure Australian wool. The article said Davey was halfway through his promotional tour on behalf of the Wool Board, and quoted him saying he'd already lined up some tremendous talent for his forthcoming 'Wool Show'.

It was raining hard when I hit Sydney. The train edged in the last mile to Central Station. I looked out the window at the rain, mist, steam and factory smoke, at the black and brown sawtooth roofs at Eveleigh, the factory walls at Redfern, the acres of train tracks, the sheds, the big curved corrugated-iron roof over the Central Steam platform. It looked pretty good to me.

I went straight across Railway Square to the Great Southern and had a couple of drinks. Then I took a cab up to my flat in East Sydney. I went up the back stairs, opened the door and walked into the wrong flat. Different furniture, different everything.

A bloke came out of the kitchen in a singlet. 'Who are you?' he said.

'I live here,' I said lamely.

'No, you bloody well don't!'

The landlord was apologetic. He'd held on for three weeks, he said, even though there'd been no rent paid. Then when he heard I'd gone to jail, he started to wonder. How did he know I was in jail? I asked. The policemen who came around told him. Where are my things? I said. The policemen took them. They told Sam they'd make sure I got them, and told him to throw the rest away. St Vincent de Paul came and took some of it.

What about my car? I said. Sam didn't know. It had gone from outside at about that time. There is something here, though, he said. Some things that were left, and some mail. He went inside and came back with a bundle. I took it with me.

I went to the Manning Building. The lock on the office door had been changed. I squinted through the keyhole. The room was empty.

I went round the corner to the post box. The key still worked. The box was crammed with mail and there was another note from the counter staff asking me to please clear the box. Most of the letters were shit. There were three separate letters from Uncle Dick. The latest was two weeks old. It was short. For God's sake, contact him immediately, it said.

There were some postal notes there as well, totalling twelve quid.

I cashed them and went back to the Great Southern, ordered

another scotch and stationed myself at the phone.

First I rang the agent who handled the Manning Building and got the same story as with the landlord at my flat. Sidoti had been around, cancelled the lease and arranged for everything to be carted away. Then I rang the real estate agent at Newport. He said there'd been no action with the weekender. I told him I'd ring in three weeks' time.

I had another drink and considered my options. I went back to the Manning Building and knocked on Mr Ling's door. No answer. I tried again and Number One Son opened up. He shook his head, said, 'Not today!'

I said, 'Where's Mr Ling?'

He just said, 'Not here. Wait.' He closed the door, returned a moment later and offered me a fortune cookie. It read *You have beware of many dragon*.

I put my bundle in a locker at Central Station and took the tram to Maroubra Beach. I got out at the top of Malabar Road and walked the half-mile round to the Ocean View Hotel.

Neither Molly nor Laurie were serving in the bar. I asked the barmaid if they were upstairs. She said who? I said Laurie, the publican. She said oh, the *old* publican. He's gone, she said, been out for nearly two months. She didn't know where he'd gone to. The new publican would be here later, I could ask him.

I tried ringing Max at Perkal Towers, got no answer, I put through a call to Buena Vista House. They wouldn't tell me whether Max was still a patient there. I said to the nurse if he is there, tell him to write to me at the post office box.

I went back to town, collected my bundle and booked into the Aranui Lodge in Elizabeth Street. I paid for two weeks. They gave me a room on the second floor, right on the wedge-shaped corner of Wentworth and Elizabeth Streets. There was a toilet down the hall with a sign saying 'Will gentlemen please learn to use the toilets.'

I bought a bottle of Australian brandy and settled in. There was quite a lot of carousing during the night, radios playing; blokes coughing, hawking, swearing. Next door was a feller who played a record incessantly on a portable player, sounded like Johnny Cash singing 'Don't Take Your Guns To Town' in German.

I undid the bundle my old landlord had given me. A shirt, three paperbacks, T. Whitney Ulmer's *The Business of Life* and some letters. I opened the Ulmer book, thinking, Give me a preachment for *this* situation, you old mongrel. It said *Take stock*.

There was a letter from Del telling me she was engaged to be married to someone called Tony Hennessy. There was a parcel from America, a book called *Your Bible and You*. A printed note inside said 'Compliments of Little Richard Penniman', and handwritten on it was 'Billy, I very much hope you read this, best wishes, R.' I chucked it in the bin.

The following day the new publican at the Ocean View Hotel told me Laurie had moved on, up the Central Coast somewhere. He had a caravan park.

'He was going bad, right?' I said.

He shook his head. 'Who told you that? From what I know he did pretty well out of this place. I bloody well paid him enough for the licence, I know that.'

There was a bloke at Paddington named Barry, a mate of Kevin Simmonds, whose place we'd used for the whack-up after the bowling club robbery. I rang him, asked if he'd seen Kevin lately. Are you serious? he said. Kevin's in jail, in Long Bay. Got done a month ago.

He'd gone to Brisbane for a rest, Barry said, then he came back, was laying low at Barry's place. One day he slipped up the street to buy some groceries. A CIB copper spotted him, chased and caught him. He copped eight years for an armed hold-up at the Rose Bay Commonwealth Bank and another seven for an earlier armed rob. Cumulative. Fifteen years total.

I headed out to Teddy Rallis' place at Burwood. A sign in the front yard said 'Saw Doctor'. Teddy's brother was living there now. He wouldn't tell me where Ted was, except to say that Ted had left town, permanently.

'What's going on?' I asked him.

The brother shrugged, said Ted had apparently felt it was a good time to make a start somewhere else, he didn't feel Sydney had a great deal more to offer him.

I asked did it concern Fred Slaney? The brother shrugged again and said he couldn't say. But with Ted it could be anything.

So it was back to the city for me, to take stock, like the book said. A line from a song kept going through my mind: 'I feel like a stranger in my own home town.'

I put through a reverse-charge trunk call to Adelaide, to Uncle Dick.

'Bill, thank Christ you've rung. Where the hell have you been?'

'Out of town.'

'Why are you ringing reverse charge? You haven't gone bad, have you?'

'Actually I am having the tiniest bit of a rough trot right at the moment.'

'I knew it. I've been trying for months to contact you. Your phone's disconnected and everything. What's happening over there?'

'There've been complications.'

'Well, there've been some bloody complications down here as well. I need that five hundred quid.'

'Oh.'

'Don't tell me you haven't got it.'

'I'm strapped.'

'Didn't I teach you anything? Haven't you got some emergency money somewhere?'

'I'm that stiff, I'm *flyblown*.'

It took the wind out of his sails. It turned out Dick had broken two of his own rules, pay your taxes and don't send obscene publications through the post. He'd been diddling his taxes for years, and as sales of his marriage instruction manuals had dropped off he'd started including a booklet with each order, *Love Secrets of the Kama Sutra*. In it was a drawing of some Indian carving that Dick had copied out of a book at the library. A bloke and chick wrapped around each other, their hands all over each other's privates.

A Country Party member of state parliament, a Methodist lay

preacher, had found the publication in his fourteen-year-old son's bedroom, had raised it in parliament. The matter was referred to the Minister for Posts and Telegraph. The Tax Department got involved as well. End result was, Dick was facing half a dozen charges, including fraud (for the nerve tonic), tax evasion, and various breaches of the Postal Act. The Tax Department was prepared to drop the charges if all back taxes were paid immediately. Dick had been advised that the other stuff could be contested in court, but he'd need a skilled brief.

There was a bloke down there, could straighten things out behind the scenes, but he wanted money up front. The five hundred wouldn't fix everything, but it would clear the tax debt and keep the brief onside so Dick could get an adjournment while he raised the rest of the money.

I told him sit tight, I was on the job. I'd be in touch, I wouldn't let him down. He said all right, but I could tell he didn't believe a word of it.

I went to the Great Southern for a little more stocktaking. The crowd in the front bar picked up at lunchtime and people started putting zacks in the jukebox. Some of the songs were new to me: 'Personality' by Lloyd Price, and a rock'n'roll version of 'Mona Lisa', and something called 'Bongo Rock'. Christ, I thought, maybe Max was right about the future of the bongos.

The lunch crowd disappeared but I continued taking stock. The afternoon drunks, mainly shift workers from the markets, kept feeding the jukebox. I sort of lost track of time, listening to the same few records playing over and over.

Mid-afternoon a record was playing that sounded familiar. I tuned in: steel guitar, some nasal, Aussie-style hillbilly singing, a singalong chorus, 'Talking the blues to myself, Get another bottle down off the shelf . . .'

I went over to the jukebox: B-11 was playing, 'Talking the Blues' by Sandy Garufi and the Prairielanders, on the W&G label. The flip was called 'Harmony House Boogie'. The song finished. I put in a zack and played it again.

No doubt about it. It was me, with Max and the gang singing along, the thing we'd recorded at Harmony House when we'd been too cranked up on reefers and dexes to go home. I played the flipside. It was the jam version of 'Jumping with Symphony Sid'. I played the A side again.

'Good song that one, eh boss?' A feller at the bar. His mates were singing along with it.

'You like it?' I said.

He nodded. 'Right up there with Slim Dusty.'

I tried to get a look at the composer credit as the record spun around. It was hard to read, but it looked like Glasheen written there after the title. And two other names.

I turned to the bloke at the bar. 'Do you ever hear this one on the radio?'

'Where've you been? They flog the thing noon and night.'

'Like a hit record sort of thing?'

'Yeah. A hit record.'

I went down the road to Eric Andersen's, looked through the record bins. Sure enough, there it was. I took it to the counter, asked the lass to play it. She put it on the turntable behind the counter. It boomed out through the store.

'What do you think of that song, love? Like it?' I said.

'My dad really likes it. I think Fabian is just the *best*, though.'

I went to every record shop in the city, had them play 'Talking the Blues'. At Harry Landis' I made the mistake of telling the kid behind the counter that I was the singer on it. He said, is that right, and yawned.

I rang Lee Gordon. A bloke I didn't know answered the phone, told me Lee wasn't available. I said to tell him it was Billy Glasheen. He said he's still unavailable.

I was paid up at the Aranui Lodge but I was spending my remaining few quid at a rate that would have me penniless by the end of the week. I checked Ulmer. It said *Adjust to change. Dance with circumstance.* I made a decision there and then to stop drinking spirits for the time being, switch to wine.

I kept trying to get through to Lee Gordon. If Gordon was

travelling well, which according to what I was reading in the papers he was, then he was theoretically biteable for virtually any amount, maybe even the whole nine grand I needed for Slaney. But I never got past the front desk.

Another week passed, my hard-earneds dwindled. I made adjustments, lowered my expectations. For breakfast I'd hit Mason's Cafe in Elizabeth Street, where the derelicts poured metho into their cups of tea. The proprietor was a Greek bloke, called himself the working man's friend, even though the patrons were all down-and-outs and ex-thugs.

I scabbed as many free meals as I could. St Vincent de Paul were good for a feed every few days, so too the Sydney City Mission. There was St Barnabas's on Sundays, if you could stand the hymn singing and the sermon, and there was the Harbour Lights Hostel for Homeless Men.

I filled in time doing the rounds of Haymarket pubs: the Chamberlain or the Newmarket, the Covent Gardens, the Evening Star, the Palace, or the West End. But when funds were low it was the Penfolds Wine Bar in Pitt Street, better known as the Rocket Range.

It was the cheapest dive in all of Sydney, frequented solely by down-and-outs, the 'men with broken hearts' as Hank Williams called them. There were different theories about how the name Rocket Range came about—that it referred to drunks flying out the front door, or that it had something to do with men and women going in, getting stuck into the fortified wines and then lighting up like sky rockets.

Behind the bar there was a noticeboard with pension cheques waiting to be collected. Old whores would proposition drunken old codgers. People would fight for no reason, glass each other, kick and gouge. Islanders, Chinamen, American and African Negroes, most of them off boats, would hang out down there, so too would squareheads running out of money at the end of a binge. It was a place of plummeting expectations. Once you got used to it, it wasn't so bad.

Chapter 13

When my money ran right out I resorted to casual labouring at Darling Harbour goods yard. Me and Henry, a Samoan bloke from the Rocket Range, turned up at six-thirty at the main office in Goulburn Street. We were sent over to South Shed with a bunch of semi-derros and ex-cons to load open train trucks. The cargo was kegs of beer. The overseer tapped a keg at nine o'clock, by lunchtime we were rotten. No one seemed to care. We got paid at the end of the day, two quid. I asked if there'd be work the next day. The overseer was incoherent, the bloke in the pay office said they wouldn't know until then, but it was worth a try.

Next day we came back, went through the same routine, got pissed by midday on draught beer. This is all right, I said to Henry. If I'd known this is what working life is like I'd have got a job sooner. Henry pinched a bottle of wine out of a crate that day, put it in his bag, got stopped at the gate on the way out. The railway cops took him out the back, gave him a flogging then called the real cops. He went to jail the next day. The rule seemed to be you could consume anything you wanted inside the yard, but no takeaways. I didn't go back to the rail after that.

At Em McQuillan's gym up in Wilson Street, Newtown, they paid you a quid to go four rounds sparring with a real boxer. I hadn't had any twang for months now, so I thought why not.

McQuillan said, yeah, what did want? I said I'd do a round or two for a pound or two. He looked me over and said you ever boxed before? I said a bit. He looked doubtful. We want a sparring partner, not a punching bag. I told him I'd be fine, don't worry. He said all right, get togged up.

He put me up against a Yugoslav kid. He told me not to hit him too hard, he wanted no marks, no damage, but keep throwing punches and keep moving around. Sparring partners are like sexual partners, he said, a bit of interesting movement helps a lot. Four rounds for your twenty bob, is that understood? No risk, I said.

So me and the Yugoslav kid danced around a bit. I jabbed at him, he at me. Connecting punches ran at about ten to one, his favour. He was genuinely fast and I was genuinely slow.

At the end of the first round my head was ringing. Halfway through the second round, I was puffing so hard my chest ached. Sweat ran down into my eyes. The second hand on the big clock was moving at a tenth of the correct speed. I got to the end of the round, flopped down on the stool. Ern had some words with the kid, then came over to me and said, 'You okay to go on, son?'

'Got him right where I want him,' I said

I limped through the next round. The pain in my chest got worse but I kept at it, dancing around, trying to dodge the kid. He was a local favourite, and the hangers-on had gathered to watch. Go on, Drago, give it to him, they said.

The kid was fast all right, but lazy with his guard. I threw a hard right at him, which got him square, knocked him sideways, made him cranky. Twenty seconds to go he knocked me down, sprawling under the ropes. A bloke helped me up saying you've nearly got him, killer, now finish him off. My nose was bleeding.

Afterwards, sitting there trying to regain my breath, I got a coughing spasm. Ern came over, said, 'Not too fond of getting hit are you? Still, you didn't do that bad, all up. Any time you want to earn a quid, we'll have you, but not while you've got that cough. You'll be giving it to our boxers.' He gave me a complimentary ticket to the Stadium fights that Saturday night.

I gave up trying to get through to Lee Gordon on the phone and instead turned up at his Rushcutters Bay office. I was still wearing the leather jacket I'd bought in Lithgow, strides the St Vincent de Paul people had given me, and prison-issue boots. I'd kept my washing and shaving up though, and was keeping my clothes clean.

The bloke in the front office tried to shoo me away. I told him I was a friend of Lee's. He said yeah, sure, write him a letter. He looked rough enough to be trouble, so I reined in my temper. I tried to explain that I'd road-managed the Little Richard Big Show, chauffeured Johnny Ray around, procured reefers for Lionel Hampton and got cocaine for Sammy Davis Jnr. He said yeah, thanks. Now piss off.

The same bloke was in the office the following day, then again the day after that. On the fourth visit a new dogsbody was in place. He was talking on the phone when I entered, something about the Wanganui Elvis', whoever that was. I told him Lee was expecting me. He was dubious but he said wait here, and disappeared. He came back a few minutes later and gave me two ten-quid notes.

'Mr Gordon said to give you that. Off you go now.'

'Hang on. Did you tell him who it was? Glasheen, did you tell him that?'

'Yeah. He said that should hold you until the orphans' pool fills up with coins again. Now nick off, and don't come back.'

Returning to the Aranui Lodge after a heart starter at the Vanity Fair next day, I spotted two suited blokes in the lobby and froze. I'd acquired the hobo's habit of automatic terror at the sight of cops. I turned around, went back down the street and nipped into the lane.

I waited there for five minutes. The two cops came out the front door. Sidoti and Rheinberger. They got in their car and drove away. Inside, my room was messed up, my things all over the floor. I checked out of there, moved into the Cosy Private Hotel. I stayed there for five days, then relocated to the Central Residential and after that the People's Palace.

My possessions had been whittled down to a suitcase and a cardboard box. I kept on the move, never stayed anywhere more than five nights.

That year there was a record cold snap. Winter in Sydney is pretty mild generally, and frosts are rare. By nine o'clock most days, unless there's a wind blowing, you could sunbathe if you wanted.

The cold seemed to hang longer around the shadowy back streets of Surry Hills, the Haymarket and Darlinghurst. It felt less like an absence of heat and more like a positive force emanating from the bricks, doorways and vacant lots of downtown.

I was still in the habit of rising early from when I was in the slot, and as the dives I was staying in weren't conducive to gracious living, I cleared out as soon as I got up. The pain in my chest persisted, and was sharpest first thing in the morning. A couple of drinks took the edge off it. The cough came on at night when I lay down, and my only cure was to stay up as long as I could.

One night I fell asleep drunk near the Railway Institute in Chalmers Street. I woke up freezing at two in the morning, too late to get a room. I walked around for a while dodging the paddy-wagons prowling the empty streets. It started to rain. I tried to sleep in the doorway of a gardener's shed in Prince Alfred Park, but the rain blew in.

I started walking again, came to a hole in the fence beside the railway line. I went in, crossed a few of the twenty or so tracks. There was a little fibro and iron shack next to the tracks, under the brick colonnades between Central and Redfern stations. There was no lock on the door. I went in. It was a kind of smoko room for the fettlers, with a kero heater, a kettle and teapot, a table and a couple of chairs. I closed the door behind me and lit the heater. The windows had been painted out, I guessed to keep the bosses from peeking in, springing the workers having a bludge. I hoped it would keep the railway cops from seeing the glow of the fire. I got warm, made a cup of tea, then grabbed a couple of hours' sleep.

An early train woke me, scared the shit out of me. I tidied up, crossed the tracks back to the park. After that I went there every few nights. If the fettlers knew a freeloader was using their smoko room, they didn't seem to care. There was always kero for the fire and tea for the billy.

One night I found the shed padlocked, and thereafter if I had nowhere to stay I'd spend the night going around the world in eighty days—buying a train ticket and riding the city circle trains all night, or riding out to the marshalling yards at Emu Plains or Auburn, then back again.

In the daytime I kept on the move. There were a couple of spots that caught the sun early in the day, like the low brick wall outside the main entrance to the electric trains at Central Station, but it was in view of the demons. There were other places—doorways and loading docks of deserted buildings, the back walls of the rag-trade factories and workshops around the Surry Hills district. Special little nooks and corners. You could pick them by the broken brown glass, or empty port bottles still in the paper bags, the smell of piss and damp concrete, sometimes dried bloodstains and spew—the markers of the deadbeats' daily circuit.

Hobo Mecca was Belmore Park, right opposite the Manning Building. People slept there, sunned themselves, drank their port and sherry. The wallopers cruised through in a wagon every couple of hours, arresting two or three people each time, until they got their quota for the day. Pension days were worst, when the uniformed blokes arrested chats, took their few quid off them in the Central cells.

I was reduced to pinching milk money, and one time I hoisted a transistor radio from Elliotts. I listened to it back in my room, heard 'Talking the Blues' played over and over. Another time, when I hadn't eaten for a day and a half, I walked past a bloke in George Street eating fish and chips out of newspaper. They smelled so good I knocked him down, sprinted away with the bag. I wolfed the food skulking behind the rotunda in Belmore Park.

I teamed up for a while with an old bloke named Charles who tried to teach me the ins and outs of bludging. The idea was you went up to a mark, asked them to loan you a bob or two for a pie, or for the tram fare down to Repat. You had to pick a certain type of person and play them right, he said. Be polite but pitiable. First bloke I asked made a face so I told him fuck you, you zube, and hit him. Charles said he didn't think I quite had the knack of public relations.

The Christians trolled for converts among the lowlifes. They'd get a few, too. One of the regular faces around the traps would suddenly disappear, then turn up later in clean clothes singing hymns down at the Domain. A few God-botherers hung around sweeping up, washing dishes, whatever, just for something to do. Like Smallgoods Bob. A rough-looking bloke, long scar on the side of his neck, another dividing his eyebrow, but a man of apparently sober habits. He was a bouncer and sometime cook at the City Mission. But unlike the others he didn't talk any religion, and absented himself when the hymn singing started.

I asked him once what he was doing there. 'I just like to do my bit', he said. 'It helps me remember where I came from'.

One cold morning in early August I was in the Rocket Range warding off the chill when a hobo behind me started a boozy tirade.

'"Who has woe? Who has sorrow? Who has complaining? Who has wounds without cause? Who has redness of eyes?" Friends, I quote the good book, Proverbs, chapter twenty-three, verse twenty-nine.'

Here we go, I thought.

The voice continued. 'The holy text provides us with the answer to its own question in the very next verse: 'Those who tarry long over wine, and those who take mixed wine." And so, my good friends, I believe I will have a glass of Penfolds Invalid Port. Inn keeper, kindly hit me with your finest!'

The bloke had moved up next to me at the bar. He slapped a two-bob piece on the counter and picked up the glass the barman poured him. I put my head down, tried to read my paper.

Out of the corner of my eye I could see him hold up his glass and peer into it. He said, '"Do not look at wine when it sparkles in the cup and goes down smoothly. At the last it bites like a serpent, and stings like an adder."'

He drank it down and ordered another. One of the old whores sidled up to him. She was wearing an overcoat and a South Sydney beanie and mittens. He glanced at her, bowed and said, '"Your eyes will see strange things and your mind utter perverse things. You will be like one who lies down in the midst of the sea, like one who lies on top of a mast."'

I snuck a look at him. Big feller in a shabby suit.

'Lend us a quid, can you?' I said.

He held his gaze at the ceiling. '"Wine is a mocker, strong drink a brawler; and whoever is led astray by it is not wise."'

Then he turned to face me. 'By the Jesus, could it be Bill Glasheen?'

'How's things, Murray?'

We got up to date over a few muscats. He'd gone to the pisspot clinic, left and stayed sober for a month. Then he had just the one, then another. He hadn't been back to work, was surviving on a Repat pension and the remnants of his savings, living in a residential at the Rocks. He asked me how my business was going. I told him it had gone, everything had gone. He sought no explanation.

I told him how I'd poached a bit of his business. He said how so? I told him about my inquiry agent gig, about Rodney Irving, his missing wife. He was mildly interested. Yeah, I said, he gave me a fifty-quid advance. Murray nodded, said it was high. I said that's nothing, he offered five hundred if I found her.

Murray put his drink down, looked at me. 'Who did you say this chap was?'

'Like I told you. A blower, returned man, ex-prisoner of war.'

'A rogue?'

I shook my head. 'A squarehead, I'd say. Shot nerves but a gent.'

'And what about the woman?'

'Long-term de facto. She'd been in the biz with him. Nice-looking, in the photo. I never got close enough to find out any more.' I told him how I'd had a bit of a look for her but she'd well and truly shot through. Murray made me tell him what I'd done, step by step.

When I finished he said, 'Was that all?'

'What more could I do?'

Murray started counting on his fingers. 'You could've tried the electoral rolls, the Department of Motor Transport, the post-office, the Tax Department, the gas company, the electric, all that stuff—under her name, her maiden name, her mother's maiden name, her middle name. Did you do any of that?'

I told him no.

'Then you go back to the friends and find out who had it in for her, who her enemies are. They'll give her up, if they can, long before her friends will.'

'The friends were all up front with me.'

Murray waved his hand. 'They were pissing in your pocket, Bill. You should have heavied the poof, at least.'

He returned to his drink. After a little time he said, 'You think that offer might still be going? The five hundred quid?'

'It was still current last Anzac Day. He might have found her by now, though. What are you thinking?'

He lowered his voice, leaned closer. 'Find out if the offer is still good. If we can't track this woman down in a week or two, I'd be very surprised. You look like you could use a few quid, and Jesus, I know I could.'

Rodney's daughter Pauline answered when I rang that night. No, she said, Rodney wasn't at home. I told her how he'd told me he was going into hospital and wanted me to persist with the inquiries concerning the whereabouts of Fay Small.

That's right, she said, and he had been disappointed when I took the retainer and then didn't so much as pay him the courtesy of a progress report. Well, other things intervened, I said. Would want me to continue the search? She said I should ask him. Why didn't I ring back after tea, he'd be home by then.

I did and he was. He sounded the same as ever. I asked how the treatment had gone. Good as gold, he said. I told him I was sorry I hadn't been in touch. He said that was okay, did I have any news? I said not really, I'd been sidetracked by other matters which couldn't be put off. But now I was in a position to concentrate full-time on the search for Fay Small, provided the offer still stood. He said good for you, yes, the offer is still open. More than ever he wanted to make contact with her. So I got him to give me Fay's middle name and her mother's maiden name, her date of birth.

I tramped down to Murray's room in the Rocks. He was too rotten to make any sense at all. I wrote it all down for him, left it on the dresser, left him there in his stupor.

When next I saw Murray, at the Chamberlain, he'd made inquiries with the public authorities. Fay Small wasn't anywhere under her own name, nor her mother's, not in Sydney anyway. He said it was time to start knocking on doors. Like whose? I asked him. Leave it to me, he said.

'Billy, old son, when we find her, we'll split the take between us, is that agreed?'

'The five hundred?'

'Yeah, five hundred.' He looked down at his drink. 'Or whatever.'

'What do you mean?'

'When we find her, this Irving chap may be prepared to pay a little more to know her location.'

'He's a nerve case with one foot in the grave as it is.'

Murray just shrugged.

'Anyway,' I said, 'that's assuming we find her.'

'Oh, we'll find her all right.'

But that day Murray got too pissed to do anything, and at four o'clock I put him in a cab back to his room.

In his sober moments, Murray covered the same ground I had, but he asked smarter questions. He spoke to the bookshop assistant Michael Keogh, and to Fay Small's other friends. He roneoed off a little note with the address of my post office box on it, which he circulated to all and sundry. He rang a contact in the Commonwealth Bank, gave him my name too.

There was nothing much for me to do. Murray would go out each day and do his investigating, then we'd meet at night, and if he was still sober he'd report the day's events.

On the third day he said, 'Did Irving tell you he'd hired other snoops as well as you?'

'What do you mean?'

'There are other agents on the trail. Michael Keogh got a visit from a bloke and so did the friend at Kenso, but from a different mob.'

'Do we know who these people were?'

He nodded. 'Yeah, they both left cards. Licensed agents. I know them. Mugs and mountebanks. They're no real worry to us.'

'But who are they working for, then?'

Murray looked at me, surprised. 'Irving, of course. He can offer the sponduliks as many times as he likes, he only has to pay out once. But don't worry, if anyone gets that money it'll be us.'

'Seems like long odds. I wish I could be more use.'

Murray slapped me on the back. 'Drink up and be sanguine, William. I've got a few tricks in the bag. We'll get a result very soon, and then you'll be the busy one, mark my words.'

Murray disappeared again. After hearing nothing for a week I went looking. He'd checked out of his residential that morning. No one had seen him at the Rocket Range or at any of the other watering holes for at least three days.

I rang the alky hospital. They said they'd never heard of him. Then I rang the Central Street police station, asked if they knew anything of Murray Liddicoat. What's he done? they asked. Nothing, I said, but he may have been picked up drunk, or vagged. No record here, mate, the cop said. I did the same with Regent Street and Phillip Street, and got the same result. Which might just have meant the coppers on the desk couldn't be bothered looking through the charge book. I saw Smallgoods Bob at the City Mission. Yes, he knew Murray, but no, he hadn't seen him.

I checked my post box. Two enquiries about the betting system, one complaint about the hillbilly guitar tutor, two postal notes to the value of twelve pounds and a letter from Fay Small. It said:

Dear Mr Glasheen

I understand that you wish to make contact with me. That may be arranged, but I am most anxious that Rodney Irving (and his associates) remain ignorant of my whereabouts.

If you want us to meet, it will have to be in Melbourne. I will be at the Galleon Coffee Shop in St Kilda, at one p.m. on Tuesday 18th August. If you tell Mr Irving about this communication, or if you are not alone at that time and place, then I will not come forward. There will be a table reserved in my name. Tell the waiter you're to meet me. If nothing is amiss, I'll approach you.

Yours sincerely

Mrs. F. Small

That was Sunday night, August the 16th. First thing next day I cashed the postal notes. I bought an overnight ticket to Melbourne on the Spirit of Progress, went to Elliotts and bought a second-hand port, put some things in the bag and left my other suitcase in a locker at the People's Palace. I had lunch at the Oceanic, then went to the Great Southern to have a few drinks and listen to the jukebox until the train went at six.

Late in the afternoon a bloke came over and said, 'Hey, pal, you like that country and western rock'n'roll music, don't you? I remember you used to play that song, 'Talking the Blues". Right?'

I told him yeah and he said, 'Well, there's a new one out, it's tremendous. It'll be on in a tick. It's going to be a big hit, this one, you wait.'

'What about "Talking the Blues"?'

'A bit old hat. Wait till you hear this new one. This is it now.'

It was primitive, even by hillbilly standards. A dying stockman telling his last wishes to his mates.

'Are you serious?' I said.

'Just listen to it!'

'What's he saying?'

'"Tie me kangaroo down, sport." Good, isn't it?'

'What's that he's singing, "let my abos go loose, Bruce"? You can't be serious.'

He looked hurt. 'Well I think it's got a real old Aussie bush flavour to it.'

I bought a bottle of brandy and boarded the train.

Chapter 14

The sky was blue when I got off at Spencer Street Station, but it was colder than Sydney. I left my bag in a locker and walked through morning peak-hour city streets. I went into a cafe in Bourke Street and had a mixed grill, found a pub and downed a couple of sherries, then at ten o'clock took a tram to St Kilda.

The waitress at the Galleon looked askance at me, not that it was that fancy a place. I told her I was expecting to meet Mrs Small. She directed me to a seat at the back. I ordered a coffee and waited.

She didn't show. I had another coffee at eleven-thirty, then at a quarter to twelve I paid the bill and left. I walked outside, looked up and down the street, wondered what I should do. I turned back to where I'd got off the tram.

A voice behind me said, 'Excuse me, are you Mr Glasheen?' I turned around.

She was tall, nearly my height, and my age. Sunglasses, almost black hair, blue houndstooth suit.

'It's Bill, call me Bill,' I said.

She took off her sunglasses, said, 'Fay.' She had dark brown eyes and her gaze was dead level.

'I thought you weren't going to show,' I said.

'Well, here I am.' She smiled a little.

I wasn't sure what I should do—strong arm her, take her to a phone, call Rodney Irving, hold her till he got there. Or follow her to where she lived, then call Irving. I gave up trying to figure.

'What happens now?' I said.

'Let's eat. Maybe we can work something out.'

We walked around the corner, towards the water. Luna Park was shut up for the winter, there were white caps out on Port Phillip Bay. We went into another cafe, sat down and ordered sandwiches. 'Rodney wants you to come back to Sydney,' I said. She nodded and took a bite of her sandwich.

I went on. 'He hasn't been well. He told me about his nerve trouble, how it drove you away. But now he's getting treatment. He's been in hospital. He wants you to know that.' She nodded again, kept eating, looking at me.

'What else did he tell you?'

'Oh, enough for me to get the picture.' I stopped talking, coughed for a few seconds.

'Are you all right?' she said.

I pointed to the clock on the wall. 'I normally have an aperitif at this time of day. Must be the break in routine.'

'If I'd wanted to make contact with Rodney, I would have. But I contacted you.'

'Yeah. So?'

'So, I have a deal to put to you. Want to hear it?'

I shrugged, trying to look as though I couldn't give a continental either way.

She went on, 'I'll recompense you for your trouble. You go back to Sydney, wait a couple of weeks, then contact Rodney and give him a message.'

'What would that be?'

'That I've gone.'

'And do I tell him where to?'

'What you do is present him with evidence that I'm in one place, when really I'll be somewhere else.'

'You really won't give him another chance? He's really cut up.'

She laughed. It was a good sound, and a good look. 'You don't really believe that's what this is all about, do you?' She picked up the bill, opened her purse and got out ten bob, left it on the table. 'How much is Rodney paying you?'

'He's paid me fifty pounds so far, but he promised five hundred if I found you.'

'I'll give you a thousand. Do you want to meet here tomorrow, say one o'clock?' She stood up. 'You don't have to answer yet. Just think about it.' I stood up, turned around to get my jacket off the back of the chair, and when I turned around again she was gone.

I went back to the city, collected my port and took the tram back to St Kilda. I booked into a shithole in Eildon Street, the Sunset Lodge, where the foyer smelled of piss. Felt right at home. I lay down and slept for a couple of hours, woke up and it was dark.

I had a tub and a shave, went out at seven o'clock to find a pub. The two nearby were both closed. I walked around in the cold for a while, then ended up back at the bay front, near Luna Park and a big old 1930s movie house. Across the road was a milk bar with four or five motorbikes and a couple of cabs parked out front. A jukebox was playing 'Personality'. I went in, asked the Greek behind the counter where I could find a pub. He pointed to his watch, said the pubs were all closed. Did he know where I could get a drink? He pointed upwards with his finger, whatever that was supposed to mean. I ordered a steak sandwich and a coffee and sat down in a booth. He brought over the food.

A bunch of bodgies were hanging around the jukebox, playing records. When someone punched in 'Tie Me Kangaroo Down Sport' I left.

There was a doorway next to the milk bar and some stairs going up. A little sign said Club Katherina. I went up the stairs.

Inside there were musicians setting up to play and a small crowd—uni types in tweed coats with leather elbow patches, a few Beats. The place had a counter but no bar, no bottles of booze to be seen. I sidled across, leaned over and asked the girl if they served alcohol. She said no, what did I want? I said brandy. She said sit down, she'd bring me a coffee.

The coffee had a good nip of brandy in it. The band started playing. They were okay, but serious, like the crowd. I had a couple more sly brandies then left.

Outside I could smell the salt water on the wind, hear seagulls squawking in the darkness. The bodgies had gone home, but there were a couple of taxis parked at the milk bar. The street was deserted, no trams, hardly any cars. I walked back to my hotel.

I didn't wake till eleven o'clock the next day. I showered, dressed and left the hotel. Walking along the street, I felt pretty good. I had a think about why that should be. I could find no special reason, except that I was out of Sydney and I was looking forward to meeting Fay Small again.

I got to the cafe, she wasn't there. I sat down, ordered a glass of water. She arrived ten minutes later. She smiled and sat down.

'How are you?' she said.

'All right. What's the real truth about Rodney Irving?'

'You haven't worked it out?'

'I'm a slow learner. Let's play twenty questions. First question, is Rodney really an ex-prisoner of war?'

'Oh yes, he's that all right.'

'Does he really have nerve trouble?'

'Well, yes, he does. Worse than he probably let on to you.'

'Okay. Is it true that he loves you and wants you back?'

'He wants me back all right.' She pointed at my pack of cigarettes on the table, I nodded, she took one, I lit it. She inhaled and said, 'But not because he loves me.'

'Okay, he doesn't love you, then why does he . . . ? Is there money involved?'

'Congratulations. You win the kewpie doll.'

I didn't say anything for a minute or two. She waited for me, calmly smoking her cig. I cast around in my mind for any real proof that Rodney Irving had been on the up and up. Of course, I could find none.

I said, 'So you tell me then, what's Rodney's caper?'

'The first thing you have to realise about Rodney Irving is he's a salesman, every bit of him, all the time. It's like a religion. And he's the best. Second thing about him is, as far as he's concerned everything is a contest. He's out to win. He's got this insight about the people he meets—what they're about, what they want. And he uses that. He knows how to give a mug the thing he wants.'

The waitress came to our table, asked if we were ready to order. Fay stubbed her cig, said she'd have espresso and raisin toast. I said the same for me.

When the waitress had cleared out I said, 'He didn't give me much. A little bit of money.'

'And a story.' She looked at me, waited.

'What do you mean?'

'I don't know what Rod said to you, but my guess is you came away with some idea about a decent old digger pining for the woman who left him. He would've been careful not to blame her, though, probably took the blame himself—let the listener do the dirty work.'

'But money's at the root of this business?'

She nodded slowly. 'I took some money. Actually, a lot of money. He wants it back.'

'Is it his?'

She tilted her head, raised her shoulders. 'We stole it from someone else. Then I stole it from him.'

'You were lovers?'

'Until he took up with Pauline.'

'His daughter?'

'That's a good one. She's not his daughter.'

'How much money?'

The waitress arrived and put the coffee and toast on the table, slapped down a bill and left. Fay put a spoonful of sugar in her coffee, stirred it and said, 'Twenty thousand pounds.' She took a bite of raisin toast and chewed slowly.

I said, 'Call me old-fashioned, but in my book, if he helped steal it, then he has a right to half of it.'

Fay put the toast down. 'I was his partner. He broke faith with me when he tried to cut me out. That meant all bets were off. You think it's cold-blooded? It is, but I don't have anyone looking after me or my interests. I've got to do that for myself. That's the beginning and the end of the moral question here.'

She took a sip of coffee. 'My life's taken a new turn and I'm going with it. Are you prepared to help me?'

'Why are you still here? If I had that much dough and someone was on my hammer, I wouldn't be hanging around. I don't get it.'

'I've been away already. I came back to arrange the transfer of the money out of the country. There are things to be done in order to take it out safely, without arousing suspicion. As soon as that's completed, I'll be off.'

'Why did you make contact with me?'

'That was a last-minute change in plan, after your friend Murray went and saw Michael Keogh.'

'You've been in contact with Keogh?'

'That's right. We're old friends. Platonic, of course. Michael's as camp as a row of tents. He's been keeping me posted on what's happening in Sydney.'

'And how did Murray's visit change things?'

'He frightened the life out of poor Michael. He told him to tell me that if I didn't get in touch with you, he'd run ads in the papers in every city, with my picture, offering a reward. But he said he was open to negotiation.'

'The old fox!'

'I weighed the risk of trying to dodge you completely against the chance of doing a deal. Then it occurred to me that I could use this. From what I heard about Murray, I was pretty sure he'd be open to offers.'

'But instead of Murray you got me, a rock-solid paragon of virtue.'

'I got a down-at-heel bloke in a leather jacket.'

'Why don't you go back to Sydney, give Rodney, say, half the money, get him off your back?'

'Things don't work that way with him.'

'Are you scared of him?'

'He has a way of knowing what people are thinking and what they're going to do. Yes, I'm scared of him.'

'I was a goose. Rodney played me, without even trying.'

'Don't feel bad. He's conned smarter people than you.'

'No, that's okay. I learned something. I can see the technique now. I've got an uncle does the same thing, but not as well. The thing is, Fay, I see *your* technique at work, too.'

She gave a slow, easy smile. 'And that is?'

'You admit to all charges, disarm the other party with honesty.'

'Is that so bad?'

'Well,' I said, 'it's loads more fun being conned by you than by Rodney Irving, or my uncle.'

'Well, that rather leaves me with nothing to say.' She took another cigarette.

'I'm going to try the candid method myself. Here goes: Why don't you come back to Sydney with me?'

She looked at me evenly. 'Why?'

I thought for a moment. 'It feels good meeting you each day, having a cup of coffee with you. I want to know what happens next. Come back to Sydney, we'll front Irving together, have it out once and for all. I'll be on your side.'

She shook her head, smiled, put her hand on mine. 'You're not really made for this game, are you? Where are you staying?'

I told her. She said she'd be in touch and then took off.

I didn't see her for the next two days. I began thinking about how I might get back to Sydney. Then on the fourth there was a message for me at the Sunset Lodge telling me to meet her at a cafe in South Yarra.

We didn't talk about swindling Rodney Irving, not straight off. Instead I asked about her, where she was from and how she'd taken up with Irving. She told me she'd come from New Zealand, a town called Cromwell. She'd been married at eighteen, to a bloke twenty-one. He was killed at the end of the war in a truck crash in New Guinea, after the fighting had finished. She was an only child, and both her parents had died within four years of the end of the war. Her only known relation was a cousin in South Africa.

She'd come to Australia in 1946, lived in Brisbane for a while, then moved to Sydney. That's where she'd met and fallen in love with Rodney Irving.

'I'd never met anyone like Rodney before,' she said. 'My first husband was a nice boy from the same town as me. Rodney Irving had a kind of . . . I don't know what you call it, it was more than charm. He'd been through that terrible experience as a prisoner of the Japanese. Things happened to those men, you know, that no one will ever understand. Some of them were saints, or heroes or whatever, but some of them, my God. Rodney developed some kind of intuition. It's scary. He can find weaknesses in people they don't know themselves. That's what he works on. Their deep down point of weakness is his strength. Rod's idea is you give the mark a little bit of what he wants in order to get a whole lot of what you want.'

'What did he give you?'

'Showed me how to trust my own intuition. We went to work together. In those years after the war, people seemed so confused. And used to being told what to do. Sort of tough and gullible at the same time.'

'Yeah, I remember.'

'Everything we did we got away with, like it was meant to happen that way. Rodney always said the rules were for mugs, people like us were meant to make our own. And that's what we did. It was easy. It was like everyone else was half asleep. That's what Rodney gave me. He awakened me.'

'Tell me, did you ever have, you know, scruples, about taking money from mugs?'

She looked down. 'My outlook was, as long as Rodney and I were true to each other, then deep down we were all right. We could be thieves, but still keep faith.'

'What about these attacks of his?'

'What he told you was true, more or less. The attacks usually start with a flare-up of his old malaria, but then turn into something else. He goes without sleep for days on end. He goes into rages, smashes things. Sometimes it's the opposite: he broods, he won't talk at all for weeks at a stretch. Then he accuses people of plotting against him. Other times he just disappears.'

'So how did you come by all this money?'

She explained how there were all sorts of ways to boost the take in the small magazine game. The checker, which was what she'd been, knew more than anyone what was going on. In her case, she not only checked but invoiced as well. So sometimes she'd double invoice clients, especially poorly organised companies. If they paid up, great. If they queried it, no trouble, the complaint stopped with her anyway. That alone was worth nearly a thousand a year. She could also ring up and confirm ads that had never been placed, or confirm quarter-page ads as full page, all that sort of stuff. Sometimes they'd sell the same space twice, which is another neat trick of the trade.

She said, 'Rodney does well on what he makes legitimately, for God's sake. Like when the Health Department started a staff newsletter, Victory Press took it on. Rodney rang all the Chinese restaurants, selling ads. They got the message: buy ad space or get a visit from the inspectors. The next month he hit the Greek restaurants.'

'And to think,' I said, 'just a little while ago I was considering running into a bank with a gun.'

'Trade union magazines,' Fay went on, 'are a goldmine. Rodney could hint to a businessman that an advert in their magazine would avert strike action. After Rodney had worked on him, the mug would feel privileged for the chance to buy. This was nothing Rodney could be called to account for.'

'You made twenty thousand pounds that way?'

'We saved nearly all the money we made from the double selling and from multiple invoicing. Then we finished up at Victory with a flourish. Rodney pulled all the stops out, sold over two hundred pages worth of advertising in the one magazine, all paid for up front, special deal for cash. I checked and invoiced them all, then did the rounds collecting the cash.'

'So what's so hot about that?'

'The magazine only ran to twenty pages.'

'Why didn't Victory Press bring charges against you and Rodney?'

'They have too much to hide. They quietly fixed up everyone who complained. Nearly went broke.'

'There wasn't a trace of hostility towards you or Rodney when I visited Victory,' I said. 'The bloke said they were holding your holiday pay for you.'

'Yeah, well, they're all salesmen.'

Finally, after lunch, she said, 'I've organised the transfer. I need your answer: will you help me deal with Rodney Irving?'

'I've done a bit of thinking,' I said. 'Like you, I'm out for myself. It's all I can afford to be right now. Yeah, I'll do the rort for you. I'll go back to Sydney, give Rodney Irving a bum steer. What address do you want me to pass on to him?'

She shook her head. 'It's not that simple. Rodney's too smart. He'll pick a lie. You'll have to work for this. It's the only way.'

'What do I do?'

She ran her foot up the inside of my thigh. 'Why don't you bring your things around to my hotel and we can discuss it there?'

'You going to throw me a charity fuck?'

'Would that be so bad?'

'Charity's my favourite virtue.'

Some time late in the night, I was lying awake. The wind and rain were pelting against the window. Fay was warm and naked next to me, asleep. I took in the smell of her body, ran my finger up the soft skin on the inside of her arm, her breasts. Outside the window a quarter-moon was setting over the bay. Could it get better than this? In the morning we had breakfast together in the dining room.

'So what am I supposed to tell Irving?'

'You work it out. Think like a private eye. You're down here to trick me, remember. What would you do to get the upper hand? Think low, think unscrupulous.'

'It's hard. I trust you now.'

'Pretend you don't. We've got parts to play in this. Yours is desperado, mine is heartless, self-seeking bitch.'

'Well, no one's perfect. I want to meet up with you again. Afterwards.'

'One thing at a time. But whatever happens, keep faith with me, deep down.'

'First charity, now faith. What next?'

'Keep your fingers crossed.'

That night, when Fay had fallen asleep, I got out of bed, walked quietly across the room. Her handbag was on a chair. I picked it up, carried it into the bathroom.

I shut the door, turned on the light, went through the bag. Mainly women's stuff, plus a sealed envelope addressed to Mrs Zita King in Johannesburg. I copied down the address on the back of a packet of cigs, put the envelope back. I turned out the light, tiptoed back through the room, returned the bag to the chair.

I got into bed and Fay murmured, 'You're doing fine.'

Next morning she was gone. I don't know how she got dressed, packed and out of the room without waking me, but she had. She'd left one suitcase in the hotel room. Inside were papers, ledger books, lists of names and addresses. Meant nothing to me.

I went downstairs to the reception desk, asked if Mrs Small was still around. The bloke gave me a funny look, said she'd checked out early this morning. But there was a letter for me. He handed me a large envelope with 'Mr Small' written on it.

I took it back to the hotel room, opened it. It contained a bundle of money and a note:

Dear Bill

Sorry to leave like this but I was always going to move on, as you knew. To complete the business we discussed there's something you must do. It involves Michael Keogh. He lives in a flat in Kirribilli. You can find the address in the phone book. In exactly two weeks' time, go there after nine o'clock and break in. There are stairs at the back, and you can get in the kitchen window without being seen. It's up to you to work out what to do once you're inside. Sorry to be so mysterious but this is the best way. I have every faith in you.

I hope we meet again sometime.

Love

Fay

PS: As for the stuff in the bag, you may as well have it. Maybe your uncle will find it amusing. Don't keep this letter.

The money was in ten-pound notes, a hundred of them. I had a closer look at the stuff in the suitcase, tipped it all out on the floor. There were old magazines, bowling-club newsletters, exercise books, notebooks with faded entries. It looked for all the world like a load of rubbish. I put it all back in the suitcase.

I stayed another night, tried to figure out how I could follow Fay, but I was no better a sleuth now than I had been six months before. She could be out of the country by now on a bodgie passport.

When I went to check out the bloke on the front desk told me the room was already paid up until the following morning. I stayed another night, but Fay didn't come back.

I went into the city, bought some new strides, an overcoat, and some good shoes. I left the prison-issue shoes in the shop. I gave the leather jacket to a bodgie in Bourke Street. He said crazy, dad.

Uncle Dick's phone had been disconnected, so next day, a Thursday, I took the overnight train to Adelaide, booked into the Sportsmen's Hotel. I had his address as a block of flats in Hindley Street. I went there, got no answer. The landlord told me Dick didn't live there any more. Where was he now? I asked. The man shook his head, pursed his lips, said he wouldn't know. I said look, I'm his nephew, has he gone to jail? That was possible, he sniffed. Where? He didn't know.

I found Dick in Adelaide Jail. He was in low security and was allowed visitors. He'd always looked after his appearance and threaded himself out pretty well, but when they brought him out to the visitors' room he was wearing a faded blue boilersuit. He had lost weight, but his hair was still dark, slicked back. Even thought the thin mo he used to sport in the old days was gone, he still looked every inch a lurk man.

He looked me up and down, finally said, 'You took your bloody time getting here.'

'I was held up.' I gestured around the room. 'In circumstances not unlike this.'

He shook his head. 'How the hell did you let that happen?'

'It's a long story. But that's all behind me, or will be as soon as I front my appeal. They sent me to Long Bay, then Oberon—'

'Yeah, yeah. You can tell me all about it later. Do you have any money?'

'A little.'

'Good.' He asked the screw if he could borrow a pencil and paper. The bloke obliged happily.

'A co-operative screw?' I said.

'Got to know how to handle them.' Dick wrote a name and a phone number on the paper, handed it to me. 'Contact this bloke, tell him who you are. If he wants money, give it to him. Can you manage three hundred quid?'

I told him I could.

'All right, off you go. Get me out of this joint, Bill. I'm relying on you.'

That afternoon I met Dick's brief. I gave him two hundred and fifty quid. He said he'd set the wheels moving. I asked why this couldn't have been done before. He said Dick's credit in Adelaide had been poor of late, and favours like this required cash money, in advance.

He said it was too late to spring him that day, we'd have to wait until Monday. I said if he was sure Dick would be out on Monday, I'd piss off, ring from Sydney next week. He said he couldn't foresee any problem, smiling, patting the pocket which held the money I'd given him.

I gave him another hundred, told him to give it to Dick as soon as he'd sprung him. 'There's one more thing. I want to leave some . . . papers with you for safe keeping, to pass on to Dick.'

'Certainly.'

I wrote a note for Dick explaining that Fay's suitcase had come into my possession as a result of a complicated transaction. I said I couldn't make any sense of it, but maybe he could have a look at it when he got a chance.

I caught a TAA aeroplane back to Sydney that afternoon. The taxi driver at Mascot said where to, buddy? I said the Astra, Bondi, thinking what the hell, I can afford it. I told him to go via the city so I could pick up my suitcase at the People's Palace. He said you're the boss.

By the time we made Bondi the fare was over thirty shillings. The driver was apologetic. He said it's a long way from the People's Palace to the Astra. I said mate, the difference is only a few bob, and gave him a five-shilling tip.

I asked for a room with a view. The receptionist smiled, politely enquired how long I'd be staying. I said a few days. She gave me a key and said I might be interested to know that the hotel had recently placed a television set in the lounge for the pleasure of patrons. I told her good-o and went downstairs.

Bandstand was on. The studio audience was more high-tone than on Six O'Clock Rock, the boys wore coats and ties, the girls all wore frocks, and the artists didn't chew gum. The singers mimed, so the only bum notes were the ones already on the recording. It was dull stuff and I started to nod off, sitting in the leather arm-chair of the Astra lounge.

Near the end of the show Brian Henderson announced an act that had never appeared on Bandstand before, Sandy Garufi and the Prairielanders singing their recent smash hit, 'Talking the Blues'.

That woke me up quick enough. The camera panned across to the group, and a pretty unprepossessing bunch they were. Six blokes in suits, with straw cowboy hats. The steel guitar started off and the leader, strumming an acoustic guitar, half recited, half sang the words: 'There's no one I can talk to, they've all got troubles of their own . . .'

It was my voice all right. Sandy and the boys were miming it, badly. Sandy would open his mouth a half-second after the vocal, or would finish early. For the break, the camera zoomed in on the steel-guitar player, bent over his instrument. A beatnik with a goat-ee. He looked up and smiled at the camera.

It was Max Perkal.

Chapter 15

Next day I banged on Max's door. He opened up, looked blankly at me for a second or two, then said, 'Bill?'

'The same. How are you, Max?'

'Fit and well, brother, fit and well. You look awful.'

'You should've seen me a month ago.'

We had a drink together. Max seemed well enough, and he wasn't promising me riches beyond my wildest dreams, which was a relief. I asked him if he remembered me visiting him, and what he'd said to me. He got sheepish.

'I was all mixed up in the head. I might've carried on a bit. I wasn't a well man. Disregard everything I said.'

'So how are you now?'

'Saner than I've ever been.'

'Hmm. How did they fix you?'

'They give you dope to put you to sleep, then more dope to wake you up. It's not bad, actually. After a while of that, regular habits and shit, you start to come good. They talk to you, give you more pills. The doctors were good fellers, except for one jerk who tried to tell me it was the bennies and dexes that had sent me around the twist in the first place.'

'Get out!'

'Yeah. What a flip. I told him they were the only things keeping me sane.'

'So, Max,' I said, 'what's the story with the record on the radio? *My* record.'

'Well, yeah, you *sang* it.'

'And wrote it, and played guitar. What happened there?'

'I had to sell a share in it to Tex Morton.'

'I didn't even know it had been made into a record.'

Max grinned and said, 'Well, that "Kiss Crazy" was doing nothing—'

'I could've told you that.'

'And Tex heard your song, which was on a demonstration tape I made up. He thought it had potential. So in return for a share, he paid to have it pressed, did a deal with the record company.'

'You did all this from the rathouse?'

'It was kind of therapy.'

'So how do Sandy Garufi and the Prairielanders come into it?'

'Well, you weren't around, so Tex and I thought I'd better find someone to take the rap, so we asked Sandy and he said yeah, sure. He learned the words and that.'

'His miming is bloody rough.'

'You should hear him sing it! Anyway, that's the story. We paid Sandy and the boys fifty quid. They're happy. They're getting more gigs than they ever got before.'

'And now it's a hit record! Have we made any money?'

'Oh yeah, we'll make something all right.'

'I noticed you'd given yourself a composer credit as well. Not that I mind, so long as there's a whack-up for me. A good one. I need it badly.'

'So what's been happening with you? Somebody said they saw you pissed in Belmore Park, swearing at passers-by.'

'Fuck 'em. They probably had it coming.'

'Somebody else said you'd been in jail for stealing piggy-banks from an orphanage or something.'

'I was set up. A couple of coppers framed me, then when I was in the slot they destroyed what was left of the business, took the stock.'

'That's too bad.'

'But that's nothing compared to my real worry.'

'Which is?'

'Fred Slaney is standing over me for ten thousand pounds. For the Waters thing.'

For a moment I thought the news was going to snap his string, but then he said, 'You better tell me the whole thing.'

I did. Max just shook his head the whole time I talked, muttering, 'Well I'll be fucked!' once in a while.

'So how long before the payment falls due?'

'End of the month.'

'And you're cashed up now?'

'I'm nine grand short.'

'Oh. Where are you staying?'

'The Astra.'

'You can move in here. Lani and me are shacked up together now, so you can have her old flat. Any plans on how to raise that money?'

'For starters, I was hoping the royalties from "Talking the Blues" might help cover it.'

'Well, maybe. But those music business accountants are pretty slow to settle up. You won't see a zack for months.'

Dick's lawyer reported that the old boy had been sprung from the go-slow. He was unable to give me a phone number, or even an address, as Dick had seen fit to leave Adelaide almost immediately after his release.

'Where?'

'I understand that he and a lady friend are presently holidaying somewhere by the sea. He was, of course, extremely relieved and grateful that you were able to come to his aid when you did.'

'Fabulous. What about the suitcase I left?'

'It's still here. Your uncle said something about dealing with first things first.'

'Who was this woman?'

'As I understand it, an old friend of your uncle's. I don't know the name.'

'Tell him to ring me when you hear from him.' I left the number.

On my third day at Perkal Towers, Teddy Rallis' brother came around. He said Ted had wanted me to know that just because he'd racked off, he didn't mean to leave me to front Fred Slaney alone.

I said, 'How does Ted know about all that?'

He handed me a note. 'He explains it all there.'

I read it. It was circumspect, used initials rather than full names. Laurie O'Brien had given him the mail. Ted took Slaney's involvement as a signal that his days of earning a living in Sydney were over. He advised me to watch my step, maybe consider relocating.

I read the letter and folded it up. The brother was still standing there at the door.

'I'm sorry, mate. Come in. Would you like a drink or something?'

'No, I've got to piss off. There's something else, though. Ted told me to give you this.' He reached into his jacket pocket, pulled out an envelope and handed it to me.

'What's this?'

'To help with the Slaney problem. Two thousand quid. Ted says you're on your own after this. He's right out of it now, and won't be back. Good luck.' He walked off.

I called the Newport estate agent, asked him if there was any progress. He said he was very glad I'd called. There'd been an offer of fifteen hundred pounds. What were my instructions? I told him don't go below seventeen-fifty.

On the night Fay Small had stipulated, I went to the flat in Kirribilli rented by Michael Keogh. I took a large screwdriver and easily broke in through the kitchen window, just as Fay said I would.

The flat was neat, with modern furniture and framed prints on the walls. I didn't know what I was supposed to be doing there. I walked from room to room. Even though it was a set-up, I was nervous. I wiped down everything I touched. My fingerprints were on file now.

I looked around, found nothing out of the ordinary except some physical culture photos hidden away at the back of the sideboard.

I went to the kitchen, had a look in the rubbish bin.

Sitting right on top was an opened air-mail envelope with

Keogh's address written in Fay's hand. There was a return address on the back, in Islington, London. It had been franked a week before. I took it.

A figure approached out of the shadows, walking towards the flats, as I was walking away. Michael Keogh didn't slow down as he passed, but said quietly, 'Well done. Hunky dory.'

Next day I rang Rodney Irving. Had I turned anything up? he asked. I told him, yeah, possibly. He said would I come over and give him a report.

I took the ferry to Manly, sat inside to keep out of the cold westerly that was raging down Sydney Harbour. I hopped a cab from the wharf up to Irving's pad in Lauderdale Avenue.

He met me at the door. He looked at me closely for a few seconds, then welcomed me in.

'How have you been?' he said.

'Oh, just fair. I'm all right now. Yourself?'

'You know, back from a spell. Much improved.'

I sat down. He poured a drink for both of us, said cheers. 'So, what do you have?'

'I found Fay Small.'

He nodded. 'You did?'

My turn to nod. He held back, but I wanted him to ask me, rather than me volunteer anything.

'Did you speak to her?'

'Yes. She contacted me.'

Something in his face changed. 'Why did she do that?'

'My partner put the word around that unless she came forward within a week we'd run her picture in the newspapers, offer a reward. She wrote to me, said to meet her in Melbourne. I did.'

'She was calling the shots.'

'Yeah, pretty much.'

'And she's gone now?'

'Yeah.'

'Do you know where?'

'I think I do.'

'So, where is she?'

'There's things to work out first.'

'Did Fay fuck you?'

I didn't answer.

He pressed his lips together. 'All right. She would've told you how she pinched my money?'

'Yeah, she did.'

'She's *very* good. You married?'

I shook my head.

'I'll give you some advice,' he said, speaking softly, maybe sadly. 'The secret with women is to get rid of them when you've had enough. But fix them up first. Don't stint with the money. It may cost you, but then you're free to move on. I was slow off the mark with Fay.' He poured us both another drink.

After a while he said, 'How much are you trying for?'

'If you want her address, you'll give me a thousand quid.'

He laughed. 'How much did Fay give you?'

'Not enough to let you off the hook.'

'What did she get for her money?'

'A head start.'

'Our deal was for five hundred pounds. How do I know your information is worth a thousand?'

'You'll have to trust me.'

'I read about you in the paper.'

'Yeah, ain't I'm a dog. You want what I've got or not?'

'Show me.'

I handed him the address in South Africa I'd written down.

'How did you get this?'

'I went through her handbag when she was asleep.'

Rodney laughed, shook his head. 'She had a lend of you. It's a red herring.'

'Yeah, that's what I thought, too. What do you think of this then?' I gave him the envelope I'd taken from Keogh's flat.

He inspected it closely, the handwriting, the date. 'How did you get this?'

'Michael Keogh's flat, last night. That was in the rubbish. If you're quick off the mark, you could catch her in London.'

He looked at me for a long time. 'Sorry, mate. This is shit. As you well know.'

I walked over to him, grabbed his shirt front and hit him. He fell to the ground.

'I need that thousand. Badly. If I have to wring your decrepit neck, I'll do it. You get me?'

'You'd hit a sick man?'

'I'd steal zacks from orphans.'

Irving got to his feet. He went out and returned with a bundle of notes. Somehow he'd recovered his composure. He wasn't angry, or scared. He held up the money. 'If I pay you, by rights that would mean you're still working for me.'

I looked at him, said nothing.

'I'm serious,' he went on. 'I want you onside. You're the only one who got a result.'

'I'm not working for you. I'm self-employed.' I snatched the money out of his hand, walked to the door.

Before I went out I said to him, 'Tell me something. What's the real reason you knocked on that door at the Manning Building back then? Were you really looking for Murray Liddicoat?'

'No, I was after you.' He got to his feet. 'You had just the right sort of . . . well, instability. Strangely enough, I always felt if anyone was going to come through, it'd be you.'

Outside the wind had dropped. Dark blue clouds hung in the late-afternoon light. It was five o'clock. I walked back down the hill to Manly. I saw no reason not to pop into the Manly Pacific Hotel for a quick drink before I took the ferry back to the city.

The front bar was busy, spirits were high. Behind the bar a long banner urged 'SEAGULLS TO WIN, 1959'. The local Rugby League team had surprised everyone by defeating Western Suburbs in the final the previous Saturday, and this coming Saturday they were to face St George in the grand final.

At six o'clock there was a stir as a bunch of blokes came in, headed for the bar. There was much slapping of backs, shaking of hands and general wishing of good luck. The Manly-Warringah forwards.

They took up position at the bar, near me. A rowdy, rough-looking lot. The bloke next to me asked for a light. I obliged, asked him how he felt about the game coming up on Saturday.

'Very bloody confident. The team's never been better.'

Having been out of action, I didn't know the new players around that season. I knew this bloke, though, everyone did. Greenie Kingston, big, mean second-rower for Manly. I finished my drink, wished him well, shook hands and took off.

The real estate bloke called me next afternoon, said the party up there had amended his offer to seventeen-fifty. I said good-o. He said get a solicitor, you can exchange contracts this week. I asked him how long before I got my brass. He said well, you know, the customary period is ninety days from exchange of contracts.

So I rang Abe, my favourite loan shark. I hadn't spoken to him in years. He said he was glad to hear from me, how were things? I told him pretty fair. He asked what he could do for me. I explained the situation, how I needed some money. He said how much? I told him about seventeen hundred. He hesitated.

I said, 'What's the problem?'

'There's no problem. But will you be able to make it good? I've been hearing some strange things about you.'

'Half-truths and inventions. There's some lying bastards about, that's for sure.'

'That may be, but they're saying you're a bit of a risk, that you spend too much time at the Chows', that you've been drinking at the Rocket Range.'

'I was just rounding out my life experience a little.'

'And there was something about you stealing small change from crippled kids.'

'Listen, Abe. I'm not going to beg. I'm on the good foot. I've got this house sale coming through. I just need some oscar for a short period. If you can stake me, good. If not, see you later.'

'Now, now, don't get like that. Cripes, what the hell, we go back, don't we? All right, drop over, we'll sort something out.'

I met Abe at Livio's, a strip joint up at the Cross. He was with 'Last Card' Louis Benedetto. There were two strippers on the stage, moving around in a bored sort of way to some recorded honking tenor-sax music. There was no one else in the joint.

I shook hands with Abe and Louis. Abe told me to go to the bar and pour myself a drink. I did.

The girls were down to bras and panties. Abe called out, 'Give them a bit of a jiggle, girls.' To me he said, 'They're practising a new routine called the Lure of Lesbos. You know, it's kind of classical.'

I sat down with my drink.

Abe said, 'So Bill, you need an advance?'

I nodded. 'Seventeen hundred.'

He nodded slowly. 'So, you'd give me back two and a half grand in three months' time. You understand that?'

'Yeah, whatever the regular thing is.'

'Louis, would you give the cash to Billy.' Louis reached into his jacket, handed me an envelope.

'But please don't let this slide. I'd hate to have to send someone around to job you.'

The two girls on stage were completely naked now but appeared to be successfully resisting the lure of Lesbos. Abe called to them, 'Come on, Sherri, give Elaine a kiss and a cuddle, will you.' One of the girls put her arm round the shoulder of the other, fondled her breast.

I got up to leave and Abe said, 'Why don't you hang around, watch Sherri and Elaine commit unnatural acts?'

I told him I had to be going. I shook hands and said goodbye, just as two tough-looking blokes came in. They hung back respectfully. Out of the corner of my eye, I could see one of them staring at me. I walked past and copped a good look at him. It was the lunkhead who'd chased me away from Lee Gordon's office. He stared, trying to place me. Back then I was sick and broke, wearing a worn-out leather jacket.

I smiled and said, 'How's it going, champ?' and shaped up to him, made a few sparring movements.

'Good, thanks.' He smiled back, confused.

Max came downstairs on Friday morning and gave me another five hundred quid, for the Save Billy Glasheen Fund. I asked him where the hell he got it from. Being in the rathouse, he said, the rent from the flats had had a chance to build up.

I put it with the other money and it made an attractive pile on the kitchen table.

Max scratched his chin. 'How much have you got there?'

'About six thousand.'

'Not enough.'

'But getting closer.'

'You're having a bit of a good run with money right now, aren't you. Like you're attracting money to you?'

'Hmm. So?'

'Don't get defensive. I'm speaking as a friend. Just that, you're having a good run all right.' He looked at me, putting on a sad-wise face. 'But if you don't mind me saying it, you don't *look* like a winner, new clothes notwithstanding.'

'Christ, what is this?'

'You're still under a cloud.'

'Jesus, spare me the psychology.'

'Let me finish. I have a suggestion about how to get right.'

'I'm not *not* right! Oh, Jesus. Okay, you're pitching something, Max. Out with it.'

'You need of a symbolic victory to get the bad luck and trouble out of your system.'

'Okay, that's enough! Whatever you're about to say next, I don't want to hear it.'

'What sort of attitude is that? You don't even know what I was about to say.'

'You were about to tell me to put it on a racehorse. Forget it. I'm not taking any sort of punt with that money.'

'All right. Understood. But think of the times in the past we've made a killing. I mean a profit. What was different?'

'We were lucky.'

'What else was different?'

I thought about 1952 when we'd rorted an SP bookie for thousands of quid by means of well-organised Mandrake broadcast. 'We knew the result in advance,' I said.

'So what would you say if I told you I had some very, *very* good information?'

'I'd say stick it up your arse. I'd be out of trouble now if I hadn't blown my money on a sure thing at Randwick.'

'How so?'

'The Boot put me on to a ring-in. I put three thousand quid down with Homer Smith. The horse got beat, I ended up without my fare home. Until the race is run and you've collected the money, nothing is that sure.'

'Ah, but that's the horse races, in which anything can happen. There's no ethics there. Forget the gallopers, turn your mind to a field of endeavour conducted fairly and above board, where decency, courage, skill and manly honesty prevail.'

'Nothing's coming to me...'

'I'm talking about the Rugby League. Obviously.'

'You're suggesting a punt on the *footy*?'

'Who's going to win tomorrow?'

St George had won the premiership three years on the trot, and they'd gone through the whole season undefeated. The old-timers were saying they'd never seen a fitter, more cohesive team. Saints' star players were household names: Reg Gasnier, Johnny Riley, Johnny Raper, Norm Provan. Up against Manly-Warringah, no contest.

I said, 'Like every single person in Sydney, I'd say that St George are odds-on favourites by a long, long way.'

Max nodded, eager. 'What start would you give them?'

'At least ten points. No, fifteen. Yeah, St George to win by fifteen points.'

Max smiled. 'All right. Here's what you do.' He picked up the money on the table. 'Put this cash on Manly, all right? Manly. But do it today. The bookies will give them a twelve-and-a-half, maybe fifteen-point start.'

I took the money out of Max's hand, put it down on the table and patted him on the back.

'Yeah, right.'

'No need to patronise me. The fact is, Manly have a real chance, and if they do get beat, it won't be by anything like fifteen points.'

'Spare me!'

'I have information.'

'Like what?'

'Like this.' He moved closer, as if he was worried about being overheard. 'Gasnier and Riley won't be playing tomorrow.'

'Terrific.' I picked up the newspaper, sat down and started looking for the comics.

'It's true. The word hasn't got out yet, but it will. They're not fit. The head-start the bookies were offering will shorten to near zero once the news gets about. But there's more.'

'Fair dinkum?'

'Darcy Lawler has five hundred quid riding on Manly.'

I put the paper aside. No one likes referees much, in any sport, least of all in Rugby League. But Lawler was in a class of his own. A humble barber Monday to Friday, on the weekends he was the code's leading referee. Around town they said Lawler sometimes took more than just a sporting interest in the game, and was not averse to using his position to protect his investments. And, of course, he was the ref for tomorrow's grand final.

'How do you know all this?'

'St George's team doctor is a mate of mine. He owes me a couple of favours. He called me this morning to tell me Gasnier and Riley won't be playing, to give me a chance to get a bet on before it was announced.'

'And how about this alleged bet of Lawler's?'

'I went to his shop this morning, got myself a haircut. You never know what you'll hear in a barber shop, especially his. Anyway, while I'm there the phone rings. Darcy answers it. He turns up the radio so I can't hear anything. But I catch the names Gasnier and Riley. I knew what that meant. Someone was giving him the mail on those two. He thanks the caller, then makes a call of his own.

He turns away from me, away from the radio, talks quietly into the phone. I jerried right away he was talking to a bookie. I craned enough to hear him say five hundred on Manly.'

I thought about it. Bookies didn't offer odds as such on footy matches. If you won, you doubled your money, that was the best you could bet. But in lieu of odds, bookies would give the less favoured team a points start. Saints might still win the big game all right, but not by fifteen points. It wasn't a bad bet anyway, but with Gasnier and Riley out and Lawler reffing, no denying, it was good punting value. But so had Strictly Taboo been.

'Forget it. Too much at stake.'

'But it's good, you know it is.'

'If I had a lazy spot or two, maybe. But my life's riding on it. Nope.'

'But you haven't got enough to pay the cop off, have you?'

'I'm near enough to strike a deal with him.'

'You hope. Listen, deep down you know this bet is for you, I can tell you do. It's meant to be. You know it, and I know you know it.' Max placed himself in front of me. In his right hand was T. W. Ulmer's book of preachments. 'Consult the book.'

I looked at him. He held it out. 'Go on. If you get a clear message, go ahead. If it urges caution, or doesn't relate, then forget it.'

I took the book from him, opened it.

'Well, what does it say?'

I read aloud. *The weary sailor beholds the humble seagull. Land is near.'*

I looked at Max. He was nodding, grinning, waiting for me to speak. I said, 'You'd say seagull equals Manly-Warringah. Therefore, we place the bet. Right?'

'How clear do you want it, for Christ's sake?'

'I'll put a thousand on it.'

Max shook his head. 'No, you'll fuck it up for all of us if you're not fully committed.'

'What?'

'Fate has tapped on your door, offered you a big chance, maybe the biggest you'll ever get, and your response is to say you're prepared to risk spare change. Forget it. I don't want any jonahs in on this bet, it's too good. If you want in, it's all or nothing. If you can't see what this means, fine. Hang on to your money. I was wrong about you.'

He walked over to the door, stopped and said, 'A bloke out of jail like you, maybe you could get a job in a stove factory or something. You're a bright feller, and who knows, someone might die and you could end up with the foreman's job. That way, in three or four lifetimes you might get out of debt with the copper. Hey, here's an idea: each payday you could buy a five-bob lottery ticket—who knows what could happen, eh?'

They say a mug is someone who repeats the same mistake and expects a different result, and by that definition I qualified. But Max hadn't been there when Slaney had offed the little bloke at the Blues Point building site, hadn't seen how easy it had been for him.

'You think I've lost my nerve? You're right, I have. I'll put a grand on it. If you don't want that, leave me right out. Good luck, pal.'

Max gave a big sigh and said, 'All right. Give me the thou'.'

He left to put the bet on and I went to the pub for the afternoon.

As it turned out, Max was playing a Hawaiian show at the Harbord Diggers Club that very night, right there in the beating heart of Manly-Warringah territory. Lovely Lani was performing her Tahitian fire dance. I took a cab over at nine o'clock to see the act and cop some free smorgasbord.

I saw Max at the bar.

'The bookie take the bet?' I asked.

He looked left and right, tapped the side of his nose. 'The cat's in the bag, the bag's in the river.'

I watched the show, played the pokies, got drunker. At eleven o'clock, the Manly-Warringah team arrived. The patrons at the Diggers cheered the lads, local heroes. They bought them drinks, wished them well.

Max pegged them at the back of the room, led the band into 'The Hawaiian War Chant', announcing this number was for the next Rugby League premiers of New South Wales, the mighty

Manly-Warringah Seagulls. A huge cheer went up. Lani shook everything she had, and after the song the lads toasted her and Max. The beer flowed.

I said to Max during the break, 'Aren't they supposed to get blind *after* the game?'

'They're pros. They could run on pissed tomorrow and still do all right.'

The Manly coach and a few of the players came over to our table and introduced themselves, trying to cop a close-up of Lani's cleavage.

Handshakes all round. I said to the coach, Ken Arthurson, 'So, the team going to do it tomorrow, Ken?'

'They're tremendously fit. Put your money on them.'

He handed out complimentaries to the game, told us to come around for a victory drink afterwards.

Lani and the band returned to the stage and I got talking to a blonde girl named Sharon. I bought us both a drink, then another.

We went out to the snooker room and I got into a game of pool with some of the Manly team. In the third game I had a fantastic run. Balls were dropping into the pocket at a great rate and I was striding around the table like Eddie Charlton. Sharon was laughing and clapping and looking better with each drink.

Lani came in with Kingston. She had finished her part of the show and they were buddying up in a big way. She was smiling, leaning against him, giving playful little slaps.

I lined up for a shot, pulled the cue back sharply, at the instant that Kingston took a step. The butt of the cue caught him square the face. I felt something crack. Kingston cried out and his hand shot up to cover his eye. He took a staggering step backwards.

'Jesus! I'm sorry, sport,' I said. 'Are you all right?'

He took his hand away, wincing.

'It's nothing,' he said, but his eye was half-closed, and his cheek was swelling up.

Lani said, 'Maybe I can kiss it better.'

Next morning I woke up crook in bed, fully dressed, with no

memory of getting home. I got to my feet, felt in my coat pocket for cigs, pulled out a crumpled pair of panties. I shook them and sand fell out.

I put coffee on, took a headache powder, lit a smoke, tried to reconstruct the previous night. A picture was flashing in my mind's eye of Max grinning, nodding, saying something over and over to me. Another picture: Sharon, on the beach.

I threw water over my face, went back to the kitchen. More pictures: seagulls in the dark, fumbling with a bra, some giggling and some panting. Good associations with that memory. Then another picture: Max saying, 'You'll thank me for this later.' Bad associations with this one. Real bad.

I went to the sideboard, opened it. My money was gone. My insides turned to water.

No one answered the door upstairs at Max's. His car was gone from outside. I went back and showered, had another headache powder. Other bits and pieces came back to me. Max and Kingston gigging me, saying I had no ticker. Sharon leaning all over me, saying she was sure that couldn't be true. Me saying, '*Have* the effing money, then!'

I sat there for half an hour, head pounding, hands shaking. I smoked three or four cigs. I tried Max's place again. No one.

Unless Max showed up and called off the bet, it appeared that for better or worse I had six thousand quid riding on Manly-Warringah. Never drink on an empty stomach.

Down at the local for a hair of the dog, I read the morning paper. Sure enough, Gasnier and Riley were out of the game. Norm Provan's young brother Peter had been brought in from reserves. The two teams were now rated even. OK, maybe, just maybe.

Back to Perkal Towers, still no Max and Lani. I opened the Ulmer book. The preachment said, *There are no real certainties upon which one may count. Be not afraid to act, to take matters into your own hands, trusting that the forces of the universe will look favourably upon the man of courage.*

Chapter 16

At two o'clock I headed off to the Sydney Cricket Ground. I flashed my comp ticket, went into the Brewongle stand. I half watched the reserve-grade match, then at two-thirty made my way to the Manly-Warringah dressing room.

I said hello to Arthurson at the door.

He said, 'G'day, Tige,' without much feeling, shook hands, and drew heavily on his cig.

'What's the mail?' I said. 'Plunge the rent money on Manly to win?'

He dropped his cig, stubbed it out with his toe. 'Depends how understanding your landlord is.' He walked off, lighting another one.

I looked around the dressing room. Players were sitting, slumped, smoking. A couple were half-heartedly limbering up. I could smell liniment, aftershave and stale alcohol. A lot of stale alcohol. I took a closer look. Pale skin, bloodshot eyes, discarded Bex powders lying around. They didn't look like winners.

Greenie Kingston was sitting down, frowning and massaging his forehead. He looked at me blankly. His face was puffy, his eyes bleary and unfocused.

'How you feeling, champ, ready to clean them up?' I said.

He looked at me a second longer, nodded and said, 'You!' He put a hand carefully to the side of his face and turned away.

All right, I thought. It doesn't matter if they lose, as long as they lose by less than twelve points. I tried to light a smoke, but my shaking hand put the match out. *No real certainties. Take matters into your own hands*, the preachment said.

Time to act.

I made my way over to where big jugs of orange juice were sitting on a table. With my back to the room, I emptied half a bottle of bennies into a jug, swilled it around to dissolve the pills, waited a minute, then did a circuit of the players.

'Here you are, boys,' I said, 'drink up! It'll give you energy.' A couple of the blokes said no thanks, dig, but I made a friendly nuisance of myself until nearly everyone had taken a drink. I gave a cup to one of the kids hanging around, told him to take it over to Kingston.

Over the next five minutes I watched the team spirit begin to lift. I got another jug of juice, stirred in some more pills and did another round. 'Fruit juice for energy!' I said.

Kingston was sitting with his head in his hands. This won't do, I thought. I moved over nearer him and said, 'Come on, Greenie. Look lively there, son. This isn't the under-fifteens.'

He looked at me, his mouth hanging open, his face reddening.

I pushed. 'But look mate, if you're not up to it, maybe you could get a game of soccer with the reffos down at the Marks Field.'

Kingston stood up, clenched his fists. He wasn't exactly breathing fire yet but he was looking better. I kept stirring the possum. 'What's the matter, you're not frightened of Harry Bath, are you, Greenie? Is that it?'

Somebody near me said, 'Give it a rest, lad. Greenie will rip you apart if you keep that up.'

'What, this bloke? Look at him, he's too slow and stupid.'

Kingston took a swing at me, which missed. A couple of teammates told him to forget it, don't let the arsehole bother you.

I headed for the door, ran into Arthurson coming in. He looked around. Players were shouting, yahooing, laughing, running on the spot, bobbing around. Kingston was sparring.

Arthurson said, 'You lot came good in a hurry!'

Ugly, bald-headed Roy Bull called out, 'Hey Ken, we' re going to fair dinkum *fuck* St George.'

I watched the teams take the field from under the scoreboard. Manly looked ready for battle, so did Saints. Darcy Lawler blew his whistle and Manly kicked off.

They were ready for battle all right, but not for football. Kingston ran across the field, away from the play, straight up to Harry Bath and belted him. Bath hit him back. Lawler ignored it. Two minutes later Saints' captain Ken Kearney shoved his elbow into Kingston's face. Lawler cautioned him. Then a Manly player head-butted Saints' Peter Provan and broke his nose. Bath and Kingston took turns stepping on each other's heads every chance they got.

I chain smoked. A quarter of an hour in and the match had slipped completely out of hand. Every tackle involved a biff, and players were hitting each other all over the field, whether they were in the play or not. But the object of special attention was Greenie Kingston's face. Every time he was tackled, it got a working over. All of it was ignored by Lawler and the touch judges.

I did some quick sums. A hundred or so bennies, divided among thirteen people, about seven each. Too many.

But Manly plugged on and Kingston got the ball over the line. The try was disallowed. Saints' winger Eddie Lumsden scored after fifteen minutes, and kicked the goal as well. Five-nil. Not long after, he scored again, converted that too. Big Norm Provan scored next, and that too was converted. By half-time the score was fifteen to nil.

The second half was worse. Lawler made a half-hearted attempt to regain control, cautioned a few players, but it was too late. Manly crossed the line twice more, but both tries were disallowed. Lumsden scored another try for Saints, converted again, bringing the score to twenty-nil. Manly ran out of what little playing spirit they'd had. There was plenty of meanness left in them though, and through the second half the brawling continued more or less continuously. People around me on the hill were saying they'd never seen a game like it.

Then in the middle of the paddock, right in front of the ref, Kingston walked up to Harry Bath and king hit him. Bath hit him back. They stood there slugging it out until they were separated.

Lawler sent them both off.

The game finished ten minutes later, Saints up twenty to nil. Seven players needed medical attention. There were broken bones, cuts and bruises, dislocated limbs.

The crowd streamed out of the ground. The sky had clouded over, it was getting dark quickly. I sat in the dirt among the chip packets, cigarette butts and newspapers, my head on my knees. Kids were walking around picking up drink bottles for the tuppence deposit. The cleaning crew had started up at the other end of the hill.

It was cold now, but I didn't care. I'd let myself be conned by a mug punter in a porkpie hat fresh from the bughouse. Slaney could come and shoot me right now. I wouldn't even run.

I don't know how long I sat there. One of the clean-up crew called out come on, matey, they're locking up now.

He came over, looked into my face and said, 'Cheer up, mate, it was only a game.'

I walked home to Bondi Junction, strangely numb but still revving on the tail end of the bennies. The whole block of flats was in darkness. I fried a couple of eggs and a tomato for dinner, opened a bottle of beer. At eight o'clock I headed out the door with a view to getting mindlessly drunk. I heard a toilet flushing somewhere in the building.

I went upstairs, tried Max's door. It was open. I went in, turned on the light. Max blinked, didn't say anything, just looked at me in a funny way. His hair was cut really short, in a very bad crewcut.

'You took the rest of my money and bet with it?' I said.

He nodded.

'Did you go to the game?'

He shook his head.

'Listen to the radio?'

He shook his head again.

'You know the result?'

In a croaky voice he whispered, 'What was it?'

'St George. Twenty to bollocking-fucking nil!'

He looked at me for ten seconds or so, then sighed. He slowly stood up, walked over to the window, opened it and let fly with a Tarzan yodel. Then he turned to me, his eyes impossibly wide, and said, 'Yes.' He slapped his hands to his forehead, he dropped to his knees, closed his eyes and waved his two fists in the air. 'I knew it!'

'Settle down,' I said.

He turned to me. '"If the fool persists in his folly, he will become wise."'

'What?'

'Blake.'

'Who?'

'A beatnik from the last century.'

He was pacing the room now. 'Yeah, a drink. Grouse idea.' He went to the sideboard, opened it up, got out the brandy, poured two big glasses, offered me one.

'Cheers, comrade!'

'You're going rats again.' I said, and pushed the drink away.

He put his hand on my shoulder. 'I did something without telling you.'

I looked at him, waited.

'I switched the bet.'

'Come again?'

'I withdrew the earlier bet, put everything, your money, my money, Lani's money, all on St George.'

My heart did something strange.

'Why?'

'I had a feeling.'

'A *feeling*?'

'A dream, really. About your book of oracles. The book was open on the table there. I walked up to it. I had this feeling that it was of vital importance I read the preachment. So I go to the table, see.' Max was acting out the dream now. 'I can see there's printing there, but I can't read it.'

I nodded.

'But as I stared, the letters slowly became clear, and eventually I could read them. The words read *The saints are in heaven*.'

'And?'

'That's it.'

'You changed the bet based on *that*?'

'Well, yeah. That and the fact that Darcy Lawler had switched *his* bet to Saints.'

I picked up the drink. 'This is moving too fast for me. Darcy changed his bet? How did you know that?'

'Well, I was pretty certain what the dream meant, right?'

'Who wouldn't be?'

'But I thought a bit of corroboration wouldn't hurt. So I went back to Darcy's barber shop, got another haircut.'

'Natch.'

'Darce wasn't there this morning, the big day. There was another barber on. He didn't know me from Adam. I talked to him, strolled around the shop, got myself over near the phone, and when he wasn't looking I grabbed the notepad there, slipped it in my pocket. Written on it was "St George £500".'

'You're telling me Darcy Lawler leaves his betting intentions there for everyone to see?'

'Not for *everyone* to see. I had to rub the top sheet with a lead pencil—you know, like they do in the detective books. I've still got it. See it for yourself.'

He dug in his trouser pockets, handed me a crumpled sheet of paper.

I carefully flattened it out. It had been rubbed with a soft lead pencil all right, and sure enough there were figures and letters there. All over it, in fact—it was completely covered with semi-legible impressions, all written over one another.

'Where does it say "St George £500"?' I said.

Max pointed to a corner of the page. 'There. Can't you see it?'

I looked again at the smudgy paper. 'I can see what looks like "M-W" down here, and I think "5" right next to it, and here it says "l lb sausages", and this looks like "ring Mum", and "Californian Poppy, 4 doz." But, no, I'm fucked if I make out "St George £500."'

He took the scrap back from me. 'Use your eyes. Look, there! Can't you bloody well see it?'

'Max, it's not there.'

He shrugged. 'Well, I can see it. It doesn't matter whether the cat is black or white, as long as it catches mice.'

'Blake?'

'Some Chinese bloke.'

I put my drink down, put my head in my hands. 'I'm getting too old for this.'

Max said, 'When you're in the bughouse all these jokers come around and talk to you, see, and ask you how you feel about a whole lot of shit.'

'They tell you how to bet?'

'They talk about inferiority complexes and stuff like that. About how you can use self-confidence to overcome it. How when you're confident, you get better results in everything.'

'Yeah?'

'Yeah. And how the opposite is true, if you expect the worst it'll probably happen. So last night, before I went to bed, after you'd given me the rest of your money, I did this confidence exercise.'

'Confidence trick, more like.'

He ignored the comment. 'I wrote on a piece of paper "I win, I win, I win". Then I pictured myself collecting our winnings to-day. See, this is what the doctors told me, I had to drive out these deep-seated expectations of failure. So I wrote that shit, imagined it coming true, and went to sleep on it. Then I had that dream. It was fair dinkum weird. But I knew what it meant.'

'Who did you place the bet with?'

Max gave me his shithouse-rat smile. 'Homer Smith. Who else?' At two to one. Twelve big fucking thousand pounds coming to you, my friend. I said you'd thank me later.'

I said, 'Where do you collect?'

'City Tatts. Tonight. After the trots. You want to come along?'

'My oath.'

I left Max standing in the middle of his living room, juggling oranges and whistling a be-bop version of 'The Man on the Flying Trapeze,' and went up to the Teagardens, sank a couple with a bloke who'd barracked for Manly.

'It was too bad,' he said. 'With fairer refereeing, and if Kingston had been fit, they really might have had a chance.'

I said, 'What do you mean, if Kingston had been fit?'

'Didn't you hear?' he said. 'He went on with a fractured cheekbone. Apparently some clown hit him with a pool cue last night. Somehow the St George blokes found out. Jesus, they gave him a punishing, didn't they?'

I went into City Tatts at ten o' clock, waited till they threw me out at three in the morning. There was no Max, no Homer Smith.

Max wasn't back at Perkal Towers and he didn't come in all night. I didn't hear his phone ring once. There was no sign of him next morning, nor all that day.

Sunday evening I made some phone calls, got Homer Smith's address at Centennial Park.

I took a cab over there, found a closed-up, empty house. I walked around the back. There was a window broken. I let myself in. Nothing, no one.

Monday, still no Max. When he hadn't turned up by ten o'clock I put some things in a bag, caught a bus to Central, went to the West End Hotel. There was a bloke in the back bar, an SP bookie named Frank. I had a quick word with him, he gave me an address in Sussex Street. I walked down there, knocked on the door, told them what Frank had told me to say, handed over thirty quid and was given a pistol and half a dozen bullets.

I went back to Central Station, took a train to Cronulla. I found a real estate agent near the station, told them I was an artist, come out here to paint bush scenes, and I wanted to rent a furnished holiday cabin up the river, somewhere I wouldn't be disturbed. They showed me a list of what they had.

There was a fibro shack on the other side of Port Hacking, behind Maianbar Spit, a mile upriver from Bundeena. The only access was by water. A little runabout came with the house. I paid them a month's rent, gave them a bodgie name, received the keys, and motored up the river.

I checked around the house. It would be a long, tough walk in overland, and to get in by water you had to boat into the narrow little bay. From the front room of the cabin I had a clear view of the approach.

On Wednesday I boated down to Bundeena and rang Perkal Towers from the public phone. Lani said she still hadn't seen Max, and there had been a break-in on Monday night. Somebody had got into the downstairs flat, my flat, left the door hanging half off its hinges. She was frightened.

I sat there watching the tide come in and go out. No boat other than mine came into the bay the whole time. I let my beard grow.

I rang Lani every other day. On day five she told me my flat had been rumbled again. And a bloke had been around asking about me. New Australian feller, didn't leave a name but said I'd know who it was, and that he was looking forward to catching up with me. And there was a letter from Long Bay Jail.

I told her to open it, read it to me. It was from Les Newcombe. He'd heard I was out and about. Could I get a few cartons of cigs to him? 'Cartons of cigs' meant money. I told her thanks, and was there anything else.

'Yeah,' she said, a call from Jack Davey, of all people. He said get in touch with him.'

No answer at Davey's place. I still had *The Wonder Book of Australiana*, but now it was redundant. I knew that bludger inside out.

Next morning, Saturday, I shaved my beard into a Dizzy Gillespie goatee, cleaned up as best I could. I put on a sports jacket, stuck the gun in my belt and took the little boat across to Cronulla. I left it at the boatshed, took a train to Central.

From there I walked across Belmore Park, past the Manning Building, around to the dog-leg lane at the back. I knocked on the Chinaman's door. The bloke who answered shook his head at me.

I said, 'Mr Ling knows me.' I pointed at myself. 'Old friend.'

He called back over his shoulder to someone inside.

Number One Son came out. 'It's you,' he said. 'What do you want?'

'I want to come in and have a pipe.'

He shook his head. 'All finish.'

'Where's Mr Ling?'

'Gone. He is old man. Too many pipes.'

'Hmm. Is there anywhere else I can go?'

He smiled. 'Not my business. Very bad. Wait.'

He walked away, came back carrying a bowl of fortune cookies. 'Please take.'

I took a cookie, unfolded the message inside. It said, *Almost people know have friends are surprise.* The kid was looking at me, smiling, eager for my response.

I shook my head, said, 'Getting closer.'

His smile left. He nodded soberly.

I rang Jack Davey's place from a public phone in Surry Hills. His housekeeper said he wasn't there. I told her that he'd been trying to get in touch with me.

'Well, of course, Mr Davey is in St Vincents Hospital. You knew that, didn't you?'

'How come?'

'It's been in the papers. He's in having tests.'

'Tests for what?'

'I'm sorry, I don't know.'

She gave me the number in his room, but when I tried it was continuously engaged.

The hospital room was packed with radio and television people, well-wishers, hangers-on. Davey was sitting up in bed, looking thin and grey, but smiling. I manoeuvred through the mob, shook hands. Davey stared at me a second, then said, 'Turning beatnik on us, Bill?'

'Yeah, it's the coming thing. How was America?'

'Fabulous. I met Marilyn Monroe. She was mighty.'

The sister came in, called out above the racket that this wouldn't do, everyone would have to leave the room immediately. Eventually they did.

When the room was empty Davey said to me, 'Let's play some

cards.' We played pontoon for a while, substituting matches for pound notes, and after ten minutes I was well ahead.

'So how's the new quiz show coming along then? I've got those facts and figures well and truly licked.'

'You mean the Wool Show?'

'What else would I be talking about?'

'Yeah. Well, we're still working on it, but I wouldn't hold my breath.'

'What do you mean?'

'I don't think it's going to be ready in time.'

'In time for what?'

'I'm getting the wind-up from my producer.'

'Eh?'

'I've got cancer of the lung.'

'But I've learned that frigging book backwards.'

'Awfully sorry, but it wasn't my idea, I can assure you.'

'You don't seem that crook,' I said.

'I won't be going home again.'

'Sorry. I didn't know.'

'Yeah, it's a pisser all right. But if you were scripting this, you'd have to say this is the right time for me to bail.'

'Bullshit. You're at the peak of your career!'

'I'm last week's winner. Television just doesn't work for me, not like it does for Bob Dyer and those mugs.'

'They're no competition for you.'

'The truth is, I'm not competition for them. You know when my best time was? The Depression. A crowd of battlers in a crummy auditorium, me telling blue jokes, handing out prizes of five or ten quid, or a year's supply of soap powder. Nowadays you turn on the box and some apprentice gasfitter from down the road is a rock'n'roll singer earning more than Bob Menzies. And a sight more than me.'

'Don't worry about it. You'll hit your stride with the TV caper sooner or later, get amongst that big money.'

'No, it's just not my game, I know that. Young dickhead producers walking around calling me daddy-o, it gives me the shits. And there's something else about this television I've noticed, it's turning people skittish. The old radio shows were for laughs. But these TV shows are all about winning, about getting the Morris Minor, or being the brainiest bloke in the country.'

'I suppose so. That so bad?'

'I tell you, the way it's going, soon every bastard will want a new car, no one will want to go to work. Where will that leave you and me? Anyway, I'm sorry you wasted your time with that book.'

'Forget it. It was character forming.'

'I'll leave instructions with my accountant, tell him when he finally sorts everything out to make sure you get that twelve hundred.'

'Thousand.'

'Whatever.'

From Taylor Square I took the tram out to Long Bay Jail, arrived ten minutes before visiting time finished. I gave them a false name, but the screw standing guard in the visiting room, a bloke named Swatridge, recognised me. I handed him a five-quid note, told him I had a few things to discuss with Les. He took the note. I went and sat at the long table with steel mesh running down the centre of it.

Les came in and sat on the opposite side of the mesh. He asked how I was, how Oberon had been. Crook, I told him.

'I've got a few bob for you. Do I hand it over?'

He shook his head, called out to the screw. 'What's the best pub around here, Mr Swatridge, still the Pagewood Rex?'

'Yeah, the Rex, no fear. Thinking of popping out for one, are you?'

'Yeah, I might.' He turned back to me, spoke quietly. 'You can see Swatridge at the Rex, after five. He's there every day. Give the brass to him. He'll take a tax on it, but there's no way around that. Thanks, Bill, I knew you'd be staunch.'

'How's Kev?'

Les hesitated. 'Oh, all right. You hear what he copped?'

'Fifteen years.'

'Grim, eh?'

'How about old Jim, is he out yet?'

'Walked three weeks ago. Probably writing dud checks even as we speak.'

A bell rang. The screw said, 'Time's up.'

I stood up. 'Well, keep your chin up, Les. If you need anything write to me at Bondi.'

'Yeah, thanks. I'll do that.'

I met Swatridge at six o'clock in the front bar at the Pagewood Rex. I gave him fifty quid and asked how. much tax he'd take. He said ten quid. So I gave him another ten, said make sure Les gets the whole fifty. I gave him two cartons of cigs, said give those to him too.

DAVEY FUNERAL

SYDNEY, Thursday. Two thousand mourners crowded St Andrew's Cathedral, and another ten thousand stood in pouring rain today to pay their last tributes to Jack Davey.

Amongst the invited mourners were many prominent members of the commercial world, show business and the sporting fraternity.

In his oration, the Dean of Sydney said Jack Davey had become more than a household word, he was a friend to literally millions of people. 'His support for many good causes and charities is well known,' he said.

Tears were abundant when the hymn ' Rock Of Ages' was played over loudspeakers.

Although Davey was not a Catholic, a number of women were seen to kneel and bless themselves as the coffin was carried past.

(*Daily Mirror*, October 8, 1959)

Chapter 17

Another five days at Port Hacking and I was half nuts. I drank brandy, listened to the radio and stared out the window. I kept the loaded gun near me at all times, ready for Slaney, Sidoti, or anyone else who might turn up.

On Thursday night I tuned into a program called *Accent on Trad*. Some hokey jazz band was playing. I was too lazy or too smashed to switch to another station. The band played a blues, and after that a ragged version of 'When The Saints Go Marching In'. Then they got their piano player to sing 'Bill Bailey'.

Listening to the raspy, tuneless singing, I got the idea it was Max. It may have been booze and cabin fever playing with my mind, but it sounded to me like he was singing, 'Won't you come home, Bill Glasheen, won't you come home? I got our cash from Homer Smith.'

Next morning I rang Perkal Towers. Max answered. He told me come back, all is forgiven. I said what about the cash, do you have it? He said it had taken some doing but, yeah, he had our money.

I took the train back to the city, with the gun stuck in the waistband of my trousers, under my jacket. I took a cab out to Bondi, had him stop a hundred yards from Perkal Towers. I looked hard but I couldn't spot anyone hanging around outside, so I went on in. The door to my flat was right off the hinges, leaning up against the frame. Inside the flat was a mess, the mattress turned over, clothes pulled out. I went upstairs to Max's place.

Lani was in the hallway on a ladder, tacking up ribbons and

party balloons. There was a woman in the living room giving directions to a bloke who was hammering some kind of South Sea Island native masks onto the wall. In the other room a bloke was setting up a trestle table.

Max was walking around overseeing the operation, smoking a cigar. He shook hands with a wide grin, but made a sign for me to watch what I said.

'I suppose you know about old Jack Davey, then?' he said.

'Yeah. I missed the funeral.'

Max nodded solemnly. 'We won't see his like again, that's for certain.'

'What's with all the activity?'

'I'm throwing a bash tomorrow night. A wake for Jack, and a send off for Sabrina.'

'I didn't know you knew her,' I said.

'I've been trying to get her to dance with the Hawaiian Review. She wouldn't be in it. Now she's going back to England. So tomorrow night's going to be the party of the season. Invite anyone you like.'

'You got the you-know-what?'

Max looked around, said, 'Let's go in here.'

In the privacy of the bedroom he told me the whole saga. The night of the grand final, after I'd gone off to the pub, Max had had another of his flashes of insight. He'd decided not to wait to meet up with Homer at City Tatts, but instead went straight to Harold Park trots, where Homer was supposed to be swinging the bag. But he wasn't there. So Max went to his home at Centennial Park, found it empty. He broke in, saw everything gone. While he was there Homer himself arrived. Max jumped him.

The mongrel begged Max to go easy on him, said how he was just a frail sick old man, and he didn't have the money. Max sat down and Homer tried to brain him with a cricket bat. Max gave him a bit of a shake and finally got the truth out of him.

Homer had been planning his retirement for some time. He'd had the removalists in that afternoon to take his stuff up to Nambucca Heads where he had a pad. He'd just come back one last time to check he hadn't forgotten anything.

He'd decided the money he owed us, and Christ knows what other money he was holding would be better off with him, to help his retirement. Max told him bugger your retirement, give me the money. Homer said he didn't have it.

While this was going on, there was a knock at the door and Homer nearly shat himself. The caller eventually went away, but Max jerried there'd likely be other angry punters on Homer's hammer. He dragged him across the road to Centennial Park, told him he'd throttle him there and then if he didn't come good with the money. Homer wheedled, told Max that it was tied up, he would have to send it to him later. Max asked him how tied up. Homer said in real estate, investment blocks in Nambucca Heads.

Max, full to the eyeballs with yippee beans, drove Homer straight up to Nambucca Heads that night, knowing that the moment he let the old buzzard out of his sight that'd be the end of it. He camped on the lounge at Homer's pad in Nambucca, shadowed him to the bank on Monday, then to the estate agents, got him to put his investment blocks on the market.

Max hung around Nambucca while all that went through. By the time he thought to get a message through to Perkal Towers, Lani had already left. To help fill in time, Max got himself a gig at the local RSL. Turned out pretty good for him, he said, staying at Homer's classy pad on the river, earning a good bob, throwing *après*-gig parties, generally playing the celebrity.

Homer gradually wigged that Max wasn't going to leave without the money. So one day he presented Max with the whole lot, sixteen thousand pounds, even though the land still hadn't been sold. Christ knows where he'd got it, Max said, but he had it sure enough.

When Max finished I said, 'So let's get it straight: you have the money with you right now, in cash?'

'Sure do. Plus I took a little more, sort of penalty rates.'

'Okay. Give.'

Max reached under the bed, pulled out an Ansett Airlines bag. He tipped it upside down on the floor. Bundles of ten-pound notes, maybe a hundred of them, fell out. Max counted out my share, twelve thousand plus another thousand, said, 'Interest,' and passed it across to me. I looked at it a long time.

Max said, 'What's the matter?'

'I was just thinking, each one of these,' I held up a bundle, 'really does have a meaning all its own.'

'Brother, isn't that the truth?'

When I went downstairs with the bag, Constable Sidoti was in the lobby, his back to me, inspecting the hinges on my busted front door. I took the gun out, held it just inside my jacket and continued slowly down the stairs.

Sidoti glanced around at me and then turned back to the door. 'If you use slightly bigger screws, this door will go straight back on, I think. You shouldn't even need to reset the hinges. I can do it for you right now if you've got any tools handy.'

I stood there like a galah wondering what to do.

Sidoti said, 'I'm fair dinkum. Do you want me to fix this door for you?'

'What do you want?'

He leaned the door back up against the frame, brushed off his hands. 'What I want is to start again with you, see if we can get on the good foot. I know it must sound like a funny thing to say, but I think I handled this all wrong, right from the start.'

'You're dead right there.'

He nodded. 'I was wrong to have come on so strong at the beginning. Because of that, we've been in opposition to each other ever since, when really we could have accomplished a lot more working together.'

'Why don't you just go away and never come back?'

'I mean what I say. I want us to be friends. Think about it. And while you're thinking, there's something you should know about Slaney.'

'What?'

'Been quite a while since you've seen him, hasn't it?'

I didn't answer.

'That's because he's gone.'

'You said that once before.'

'This time it's true. He's gone and he won't be back. Ask around if you like. And with Slaney gone, you, my friend, are in need of allies.'

'You framed me. You wrecked my business. You had me harassed. You stole my car and even my personal possessions. So get fucked.'

He spread his hands out. 'Well, in fairness, the harassment was also a spontaneous expression of rank-and-file police feeling. But I take your point just the same. Give us a chance to demonstrate our bona fides. For starters we'll replace your car. How would that be?'

'Don't bother.'

'Wait till we get your car back, at least.'

After he left, I got tools and rehung the front door. I found some preserving jars upstairs, cut up an old raincoat, counted out nine thousand pounds, and wrapped it up in three separate parcels, put each of them in a jar. After the sun had gone down I went into the back yard and buried the first jar in the garden behind the laundry shed. Then I walked over to Cooper Park, buried another jar in thick bush in a gully there behind a large Moreton Bay fig. I buried the last jar deep in a sand bunker at the Royal Sydney Golf Club.

Abe's loan was good for three months but I figured I might save myself some interest by repaying him early. So I rang him Saturday morning, said I was ready to get square. He told me I could come down to his office straight away.

The goon showed me in, then stood off to one side. Abe was at his desk, talking on the phone. He gestured for me to help myself to a drink from the bottle sitting on the cabinet. I did that and then sat down.

Abe was arguing with somebody, apparently about a milk-bar pinball machine which wasn't returning what it should have been.

He hung up, smiled and said, 'Well, Bill. Here you are.'

I reached into my jacket pocket, handed him a stack of money. 'There you go,' I said, 'two thousand pounds.' I flashed what I hoped was a winning smile.

Abe shook his head and said, 'Where's the rest?'

'I'm paying you back before time, so I figured a discount was in order. That's seventeen hundred principal, plus three hundred interest.'

He looked sourly at me. 'If you wanted charity you should have gone to the Smith Family. Twenty-five hundred pounds.'

'Christ, that's not really fair.'

'Maybe you should lodge a complaint with the Loan Shark Control Board Ethics Committee.'

I glanced at the heavy. He grinned and gave me a little wave. I gave Abe the rest of the money. He smiled, thanked me, reached over and patted me on the shoulder.

Then I said, 'Have you heard anything about Detective Sergeant Fred Slaney recently?'

He was silent for a second or two. 'Why do you ask?'

'I'd rather not say. I just need to know where he is.'

'Slaney's in trouble.'

'How so?'

'They've got it in for him. They've prepared a dossier which goes back to when Adam was a lad. According to this document, take just about any rort that's happened in Sydney over the last twenty years, accuse Slaney of being involved and you'd be right more times than you'd be wrong.'

'That the truth?'

'Probably. The way I hear it, the anti-Slaney mob have got people snookered away ready to testify against him. Abortionists, pros, burglars, so on. All willing to swear that in return for pay-offs, Slaney gave them the green light.'

'What'll happen?'

'Well, you wouldn't want both the coppers and the underworld against you. But then, when was the last time a senior cop got the sack in this town?'

'Where's Slaney now?'

'Who knows? As I understand it, he was told by the higher-ups to make himself scarce for a while.'

'Okay, Abe. Thanks.'

'Anything for an old friend.'

There was already a pretty good crowd upstairs when I arrived at Max's flat at ten o'clock. Max had bought new furniture, the sharp-looking, laminated stuff, and the crew at the party sort of matched it, all angles.

The living room was decorated like a South Sea Island beach hut, with carved tikis on the walls, straw mats on the floor, shit like that. The lights were dim. The Judge, wearing a set of Mickey Mouse ears, was playing Latin bebop on the old Beale piano and Lachie was tapping a conga drum. Twenty or so people were dancing. I went over to the bar, poured a beer. The combo took a break, someone put a record on the stereogram. Lachie joined me at the bar.

'How you going, baby? Haven't seen you for ages. Dig a reefer?'

'Gee, it's been a while. Yeah, all right.'

We passed it back and forth. It hit me like a cricket bat to the skull.

Lachie grinned. 'Killer weed, eh?' He went back to the drums.

I hung there for a while, watching the people dance, silhouetted against the low lights. A Jerry Lee Lewis record was playing, 'The End Of The Road'.

Johnny O'Keefe came over, speeding fit to blow his top. We shook hands, I asked him what he was up to. He said he was going to America next month, that he was going to kill them over there, no risk.

While O'Keefe was raving at me I spotted a girl across the room. She had her hair done in a short urchin cut and was wearing matador pants and a striped top, bopping to 'Breathless'. I poured a glass of champagne, wished O'Keefe luck and made my way through the crowd towards the good-looking girl.

When I got to her she was half turned away from me, dancing in the near dark.

'Hi,' I said. 'my name's Bill.'

She turned around to face me. 'Yeah, oddly enough, I hadn't

forgotten your name.'

'*Trish*. How are you? You look mighty. Here, I brought you a drink.'

'Thanks. How have you been? Sorry I never returned your book.'

'What book?'

'*The Outsider*.'

'Eh?'

'Remember, the French existentialists, about whom you're so crazy?'

'Oh yeah, them.'

'You never actually read it, did you?'

'Yes I did, really. Great stuff, for sure. Up there with Mickey Spillane.'

'Really? Who wrote it then?'

'Alan MacCoo, Alvin Kamoose, no, Alfred Magoo . . . er, something like that.'

'Albert Camus.'

'It was on the tip of my tongue.'

'So, what's with the goatee?'

'I'm going beatnik. What do you think?'

'You look like Mandrake the Magician.'

The band started playing again and Trish cha-cha'd off into the crowd.

'Good to see you, Trish.' I poured another drink and moved on.

Max was in the kitchen raving to Greenie Kingston, telling him what tactics they should have used against Saints. Kingston looked my way. He registered confusion for a second or two, then his face darkened. I kept moving, into the next room.

A female voice behind me said, 'The Evil One dogs your steps. Blackness engulfs you.'

I turned around. 'Oh, hi Shirl. How's things?'

Shirley Hill was dressed like a crazed gypsy. 'I mean it. Vibrations. Not good. Do you carry a talisman of any sort?'

I held up my glass of scotch. 'Only this.'

She reached into her handbag, took out a tiny dark-blue medicine bottle with a cork stopper, handed it to me. 'Have this. It will help to avert evil.'

'What the hell is it?'

'It's a mixture. Very strong magical properties: black cat's urine, bile from a dead goat, Chinese herbs, golden mushrooms. And so on. It will keep evil at bay. Up to a point.'

I held it out to her. 'I'm not really a believer.'

'Doesn't matter.' She started dancing away towards the living room. 'Just keep it on your person.'

Out in the crowded hallway Sabrina was talking to two young reporters, who were writing in notebooks. 'Hang around Sydney for too long,' she was saying, 'and you become part of the furniture.'

'How about romance, Sabby. Any Aussie fellows win your heart?'

She grinned. 'That's been a big disappointment. All these supposed rugged bronzed Aussies. Too shy to say boo. So, no. No romance, fellers. Yet.'

'Yet? Doesn't leave much time, does it?'

Sabrina looked around the room and said, 'The night's still young.'

A tap on my shoulder, and a young voice said, 'G'day, Mr Glasheen. Tremendous party, eh?'

Young bloke in a thin tie, a sharp crease in his strides, and well-shined Julius Marlows. 'Paul,' he said, 'Paul Keating. Remember me? Peakhurst School of Arts. I was helping Max.'

'Oh yeah, too right. Cripes, you've got taller. How's it going, pal? How did you go with those dances of yours, Croydon skating rink wasn't it?'

'Yeah. I followed Mr Perk . . . Max's advice. Stick with Italian clothes and American music, you can't go wrong, he said.'

'So you made a bob or two?'

'Yeah. I paid the band five quid, sweetened up the by-laws in-spectors with free grog, promised the head louts a couple of quid at the end of the night if there were no fights. It worked out pretty well.'

'I'm glad to hear it, buddy. You going to stay with the promotion caper?'

'I see it more as a stepping stone. You know what Max says? He

215

reckons if you can run a suburban dance, then you can run anything. Like maybe a small business, or even stand for the Jaycees or the local council or something like that.'

'Yeah, well I'd take anything he told me with a big grain of salt. But best of luck.'

'Good to see you again, Mr Glasheen.' He picked up a champagne bottle. 'Like a drink?'

'Why not? Thanks, Phil.'

The kid split. I downed the drink, maybe a little too quickly, because the floor suddenly lurched up at me. I steadied myself, climbed onto a stool, popped a couple of dexes.

I sat there for a while, waiting for the spinning to slow down. A voice called out, 'Hey, you're that bloke!'

A big, putty-nosed guy. I knew the face: the yellow Hawaiian shirt feller who'd hounded me at the Manning Building. I stood up.

'You're the one sold me the betting system. I recognise you all right, even with that beard.' He closed in on me, breathing heavily. 'Why did you run away from me, why didn't you answer my letters?'

I reached behind my back, picked a champagne bottle off the table. The bloke put his hand out and smiled. 'Stan Wolgast is the name, do you remember me?'

I put the bottle down, shook hands, nodded.

'Well, I'm bloody glad I finally caught up with you. It gives me a chance to express my thanks.'

'Eh?'

'You changed my life.'

'That's all right, don't mention it.' Head case, I thought. Best humour the fucker.

'You don't really remember me, do you?'

'Yeah, you're the bloke who . . . chased me.'

'I mean before that, when I wrote to you. I bought the Excelsior Betting System from you.'

'Is that right?'

'Yeah. At first the results weren't so good. I was pretty discouraged, actually. That's when I wrote to you. You sent me back a letter, do you remember?'

'Refresh my memory.'

'Well, you wrote back saying to persevere, that a splendid result was just around the corner. Remember?'

'Oh, yeah. Right. Well, I'm glad to hear that changed your life. Listen, sport, I've got to be going. Nice to talk to you.'

He stood there grinning. 'So I kept following the instructions, just like you said, applying the formula and that. Then the system started paying off. So I gave up my job at the markets.'

'Why did you do that?'

He laughed and playfully punched me on the shoulder. 'Crikey, Bill, I didn't need it any more. I decided to buy a hotel license up north. I had money rolling in by then.'

'How much?'

'Oh, it was just over five thousand quid. Of course, it's a lot more now.'

'Fair dinkum?'

'But I don't need to tell you about that, eh?'

'No, I suppose not. So, Stan, you started making money and then, er, took a trip to Hawaii, did you?'

'Jingies, you're a clever bloke. I did just that!' He shook his head, still grinning. 'When I started winning big, at first I thought I should give you a grand or two, to show my appreciation. You know, for good luck. But then I thought, strike me lucky, what need would *he* of all people have for it?'

I laughed weakly.

'But I wanted to thank you, just the same. I tried at the time, slipped the girl at the post office a fiver to give me your address, so I could at least shake your hand. But you ran away and I couldn't catch you. Then last Thursday night I was at the Nambucca Heads rissole, I saw this bloke playing the Hawaiian guitar, tremendous he was. I had a yarn with him, told him how much I liked the instrument and asked him would he give me some lessons if I paid him. He said he was too busy but he told me I could send away for a book, gave me an address. It was the same address I'd sent to for the betting system. Well, you can imagine my delight when he told me he knew you. He said I could probably even meet you. Anyway, to cut a long story short, here I am. So, Bill, I'd just like to say thanks. And any time you're up Nambucca Heads way, call into the Big Flathead Hotel-Motel. We'll put you up, the deluxe suite. That offer stands for your entire lifetime.'

Stan Wolgast pumped my hand again, slapped me on the back, said, 'Well, good to meet you. This is a terrific party, eh? *Sabrina's* here! Anyway, cheers, Bill.'

'Yeah, aloha.'

He wandered off and I poured myself a large scotch. I was leaning against the door when someone came through it.

Les Newcombe, wild-eyed, grubby and dishevelled.

'Thank Christ you're here. I've been knocking on your door downstairs. I heard the noise, thought you might be up here.'

I stared at him stupidly. 'They let you out?'

'We let ourselves out.'

'We?'

'Kev and me. You haven't read the papers then?'

'Not today. Jesus H, you mean you're on the run? What are you doing *here*?'

'Remember you said if I needed anything—'

'Yeah, yeah. I said *write* me. You better not let this mob in here see you.' I pulled the door to behind me. 'Where's Kev?'

'Outside.'

'Bloody hell. Come downstairs to my flat. Bring Kev, keep out of sight.'

I went downstairs and opened up. Kev and Les came in. They cleaned up, had a cup of tea, then told me what happened.

They'd slipped out of the jail the day before. Kev had worked out a way. The jacks sealed off the whole Malabar-La Perouse peninsula, so they buried themselves for the day in sand in Botany Cemetery, then at night they stole some clothes, got away. They'd been hiding out all that day at the Sydney Showground, listening to the news on a transistor.

'So what are you going to do now?' I asked them.

Les said, 'First thing, we're going to get armed up.'

'How?'

Les looked to Kevin then said, 'You'll love this, Bill. We're going to knock over the armory at Emu Plains Prison. Tonight.'

'You're going to break *into* a prison?'

'Yeah. Funny, eh?'

'Hilarious.'

'Then, once we're tooled up, we're going to do some armed robs, get some dough together. Later on we'll buy passports, go overseas.'

I nodded slowly. 'And you're here because . . . ?'

'We need a car and a driver who's in the know. So Bill, you want to get with the strength, make some real money?'

'No way. I'm not up to it.'

'Oh, come on, don't be weak. You're good on the job, Three of us together, we'll clean up.'

'You're welcome to rest up here for a while, but you can't stay. Understand? There's a party upstairs, press blokes are everywhere. Johnny O'Keefe and Sabrina are swanning around somewhere.'

'Sabrina? Top sort. I'd love to meet her. It's been a long while between drinks, too,' said Kevin.

'Yeah. Well, the thing is, the coppers will probably be here soon, over the racket. Do you want some money?'

Les said, 'We need *big* money.'

Outside I could hear cars pulling up. Smooth, well-tuned motors. We all looked at each other. A car door slammed. Maybe more party guests. Then another door, and what might have been the squawk of a police two-way.

'Make yourselves scarce. Use the back door. I'll delay them. Good luck, fellers. And *please*, don't come back.'

I went into the lobby, out to the front door. Half a dozen coppers, surfer boy Constable Rheinberger among them, were walking up the path. Leading them was a tall, beaky bloke with wire-rim glasses. He flashed his badge at me: Detective Sergeant Ray Kelly.

'Party a bit noisy is it, gents? I'll ask them to turn it down a bit.'

Kelly said, 'Are you Glasheen?'

I nodded.

'You're in flat two, right?'

'Yeah.'

He pointed. 'Inside.' He turned to the uniformed blokes and said, 'You two come with me.' To Rheinberger and another feller he said, 'Have a look around the back.'

Kelly and the two uniformed cops followed me into the flat. He gestured for me to sit down on the couch while they searched. He came back into the lounge room, put his gun away. Rheinberger and the other cop came in the back way, reported that they'd found no one outside. Kelly told them all to wait in the lobby.

He got himself a bottle of beer from the fridge, carefully wiped an already clean glass with his hanky and poured himself a beer.

'Yeah, go ahead, help yourself,' I said.

He took a sip. 'Where are your mates?'

'Who?'

'Newcombe and Simmonds.'

'Who are they?'

'The blokes you robbed the Belrose Bowling Club with last March. The blokes you visited at Long Bay last week.'

'Belrose Bowling Club?'

He sighed. 'We have the fingerprints on file from the original investigation—Newcombe, Simmonds and another, at the time un-identified. Then we find that you visited Newcombe last week, and while there you were heard to ask after Simmonds. You, Glasheen, are right at the dead centre of this investigation, and I use the word advisedly. So where are they?'

'I don't know.'

'Have they been here?'

'Sure. We're throwing a big welcome home party for them right now. Why don't you fellers down tools and pop in for a while? We can all have a jolly old drink together.'

Kelly walked over, stopped an inch away. At six foot three or four, he was nearly a half-foot taller than me. He took off his specs, grabbed hold of my left ear and twisted it slowly round. It hurt like crazy. I stood dead still and stared back at him, doing my best not to wince.

'Do you have any idea how hard I could make things for you?'

'Yeah. I think I do.'

'Then I'll ask you again. Have Newcombe and Simmonds been here?'

I thought to hell with it, my acting the hero couldn't do Les and Kev any good at this stage, nor could any information I had really do them any harm. 'They were here. Uninvited,' I said, 'but they're long gone. I don't know where. I knew nothing about the jail break,' I added.

Kelly let go of my ear, walked out and told one of the cops to get on the radio, get more cars into the area. He came back in and said, 'You're in a lot of trouble. You understand that?'

'What's new?'

'If Newcombe and Simmonds come back, you're to get in touch with me. Whose place is that upstairs?'

'The landlord's. A bloke named Perkal.'

He went to the door. 'You, Freshwater.'

'Rheinberger, sir.'

'You come upstairs with us. You two go around, watch the back door. The rest of you wait out in the street. All right, let's have a look.'

Two half-drunk girls came down the stairs, dancer friends of Max's. One of them said to me who are your friends, Bill? No one you want to know, I told her.

Kelly, Rheinberger and I went upstairs. I went in first. There was a smell of reefer in the air, but it was a safe bet neither of the cops would recognise it. The band had moved to the next room and was playing rockabilly. Kelly and Rheinberger looked around.

No one in the crowd seemed to notice anything much, but those party-goers who'd had any sort of experience with crime—and there were a few of them there—froze right up. The cops started moving slowly about the room, looking hard at guilty faces.

I poured myself a big drink and squeezed through the doorway into the crowded dance room. Over the PA I heard a voice say, 'Here's one I wrote myself called "Beat the Devil". I hope you like it.' The voice was familiar.

The bassist played a run that started up high and worked all the

221

way down the neck. When it got to the last note the drummer hit the crash cymbal while the guitarist blasted away up top. Hitsville. The crowd exploded into a shrieking mass, vibrating wildly under the dim lights.

The singer did a hiccupping, mumbling Presley-style 'a-well-uh-well-uh' thing. A girl screamed.

'Me and my friend in a hopped-up Ford, we beat the Devil and outran the law . . .'

I pushed through the crowd, towards the band. A semi-circle of clapping rock'n'rollers had formed, including Beatnik Trish, Sabrina and Shirley Hill. I copped a look at the combination. Max was on electric guitar, Les Newcombe on drums, and Kevin Simmonds was out front singing. Les and Kev were wearing sports jackets, both of them mine.

'Car on fire when we hit the straight, but here comes the devil doing eighty-eight . . .'

I looked around, fast, and saw Rheinberger enter the room on the other side. Kevin kept right on singing.

'I was going pretty fast, lookin' behind, up jumped the devil do-ing ninety-nine . . .'

Rheinberger glanced at the band. Nothing seemed to register. He gave a bit of a sneer, then turned his attention to the row of women dancing in formation. He nodded his head, grinning, started tapping his foot.

Kevin raved on.

'I said, Look out Mabel, and I gave it the gun, here comes Satan doing a hundred and one . . .'

Rheinberger was sort of dancing with the girls now, uninvited. I moved away, back out through the crowd, but ran into Kelly.

He shouted out to me above the racket, 'Where's that other bloke got to?'

I nodded my head in the direction of the band. Kelly looked over, shook his head, pushed through the crowd. He reached out, tapped Rheinberger hard on the shoulder, gestured to him to come outside. On the way back he pointed at me to join them.

In the hallway Kelly said to me, 'I expect your co-operation. I'm going to leave Freshwater here—'

'Rheinberger, sir.'

'In case your pals return. Meanwhile if you hear anything at all about those two, then I want to hear it too, understand?' To Rheinberger he said, 'We'll send someone to get you in an hour or so. I doubt they'll come back here, but you never know. You know what to do if they show?'

'Yes, sir.'

Just then, one of the uniforms came running up the stairs. 'Mr Kelly, there's a report in. They've just been sighted in Double Bay.' Kelly took off.

I went to the kitchen and poured a calming draught. I sat at the table, had a couple more. Then I sort of drifted off. People came and went.

Max, a drink in his hand, smoking a cigar, shook me awake. 'Those mates of yours! Whoa! Those cats are real gone. You should've told me about them?'

'Mates of mine?'

'That's what they said. That Kevin. See how the chicks reacted? Baby, we'll get them in the studio and onto the dance circuit. Star material, if ever I saw it.'

'They've got commitments. Where'd they get to?'

'Last I saw, Kevin was talking to Sabrina. I don't know where the other bloke is.'

I went out of the kitchen. There were people kissing in corners, swallowing pills, smoking reefers, drinking the free piss. Others were pairing off and melting away to the back yard or the parked cars for a quick one.

Shirley Hill was dancing alone in the centre of the living room, eyes closed, swaying and waving her arms around, smiling to herself, while a bearded kid played bongos on the floor. Rheinberger was there, hitting the booze. He saw me and moved up, stood grinning for a few seconds. 'Hey, sorry about your front door.'

I didn't answer him.

'Good party, eh? All these good-looking sheilas. And how about the set on that girl over there, eh? Listen, Bill, you're probably not a bad bloke underneath it all.'

'Thanks awfully.'

'And like Sidoti says, there's no need for us to be enemies.' He dropped his voice. 'I was sort of wondering, ah, you know . . . Well, I'm a broad-minded bloke, and all these tarts here, I was thinking, if I could get hold of some of that sex drug stuff you beatniks get into . . .'

'Eh?'

'Just between you and me, I wouldn't mind trying some of it. Just once. If you could sort of see your way clear to . . . well, you know., it would help us to bury the hatchet.' He grinned, waiting.

'Never touch the stuff. I've got to go.'

Rheinberger grabbed my coat lapels and said, 'I asked you nicely, didn't I? Huh?'

'Get your hands off me.'

'Sorry. I didn't mean to be pushy.' He patted my jacket, down to the side pocket where Shirley's talisman was. Before I could stop him he'd whipped the little bottle out.

'What's this then?'

'A good-luck charm.'

He held the dark bottle up, gave it a shake. 'Oh yeah? I think this is dope.'

'Don't be a flip.'

He unscrewed the cap, smiled. 'I saw that druggy sheila pass it to you. It's a drug, all right.'

'No.'

'Here's cheers,' he said, and drank it down. He made a face. 'Phew. That'd kill a brown dog.' He took a slug of his booze, wiped his mouth. 'Now, just let me at those sheilas.'

I went into the next room, got a reefer from Lachie, went outside to smoke it in peace. I stumbled back inside. There was a drunk passed out on the couch, another in the hallway, a couple having a root in the bathroom.

The door to the spare bedroom opened. Kevin came out of the darkened room arm in arm with Sabrina. The strap of Sabrina's frock had slipped down over her shoulder, a breast had broken free and she was barefoot. She snuggled into Kevin.

Kevin, smiling, said, 'Hey, Billy, old pal! Did you see us playing with the band before? Are we stars or what?'

I said, 'Make yourself scarce, there are cops all over the place.'

'They've all gone. I saw them leave.'

'Not all of them. There's this bloke named—'

'Hey you, Simmonds!' Rheinberger was standing at the end of the hallway, wild-eyed, his tie undone, swaying, waving a gun at us. 'Yeah, I recognise you now. Stand aside, Glasheen. You, sweetheart,' he waved his gun at Sabrina, 'you go back in there, close the door.' She did.

'Feel like a little game, do you, Simmonds? I'll give you a three-second start. See how good you are.'

Kev looked from Rheinberger to me, then back down the hall at the front door.

Rheinberger lifted the gun, took careful aim at Kevin's head, said, 'One, two . . .' then he started giggling. He kept the gun up for ten, twenty seconds, as he dissolved into uncontrolled laughter. Then he dropped the gun, stopped laughing and started singing, 'Who's the leader of the gang that's made for you and me . . .'

Kevin straightened up, looked at me. 'What's with him?'

'M-I-C-K-E-Y-M-O-U-S-E!' Rheinberger started doing a jig.

I shrugged my shoulders.

Rheinberger stopped dancing, started laughing again. Then he looked at us, his eyes staring wide. He pointed his finger in the air and said, 'The Great Googa-Mooga.' Then he vomited on the floor, turned and went into the toilet, locked the door behind him.

Shirley Hill came into the hallway, walked up to me and said quietly, 'I told you it would avert evil.'

'Bloody hell,' said Kev.

Sabrina popped her head out of the doorway, grabbed Kev's hand and the two of them retired back into the bedroom.

I went into the kitchen, found a half-full bottle of Cutty. I put it under my arm and went downstairs to my flat. I locked the door behind me, thinking fuck the lot of them, they can sort themselves out. My bedroom door was open, and Les Newcombe and Beatnik

Trish were on my bed. I went back to my lounge room, lay down on the couch with the bottle.

I woke up later as Trish was tiptoeing through the lounge room, carrying her shoes.

I sat up. 'Where's Les?'

She said, 'Oh, you're awake. He left half an hour ago.'

'What time is it?'

'About four o'clock.' She started for the door.

'Hey, didn't you say bodgie was passé?'

'Les is a fugitive.'

'So?'

'Like that guy in the book. The Outsider. Living for the moment, beyond the standards of the crummy bankrupt society which imprisoned him.'

'I've been to prison too!'

'So I heard. Stealing money from spastic children, wasn't it?'

When I came to the next afternoon, I was sick, sober and sorry. I went upstairs looking for a heart starter. All I could find was a stale bottle of beer. I drank it anyway.

Max, Lani and a couple of others were finishing the clean-up. No one knew what had become of the two young blokes who sang the rock'n'roll so well, nor of the cop who'd been sick in the toilet for three hours, talking to people who weren't there.

The helpers split, and Max and Lani dragged their suitcases out into the hallway.

They were off to Hayman Island, Max said, to play a two-month engagement at some new hotel up there. The deal included free accommodation. His plan was to play music, drink booze and take drugs by night, write his book by day. Just like Jack Kerouac, he said.

The subject of his book had changed again. Now it was to be a straight-out memoir, the life and times of Max Perkal, tentatively titled *Cha-cha in Blue: Confessions of a Downbeat Daddy-o*.

I wished him luck. The cab arrived, bipped its horn. We shook hands at the door.

Chapter 18

By Monday afternoon, Kevin Simmonds and Les Newcombe were the most famous men in the country. Kevin's fingerprints had been found on a cricket stump next to the battered body of a warder at Emu Plains Prison. There was much speculation as to how come the two had busted out of Long Bay Jail on the Friday, then travelled thirty miles out of town in the other direction to kill the warder two days later. Must have been revenge, they said. Every cop in the country was alerted to look out for the bodgie escapees.

It became the biggest police action in Australia's history, bigger even than the hunt for Ned Kelly. The cops appealed to the public for help, and simultaneous sightings of Les and Kev came in from Mascot, Parramatta, Randwick, Albury, Melbourne, Chinchilla, Bathurst, St Ives, Fremantle and Broken Hill.

Carloads of cops were whizzing around suburbs and country towns all over Australia, following tip-offs, armed up for a big shoot-out. All police leave was cancelled, and any cop who'd ever arrested either of them was given special protection. There were calls in state parliament to bring in the army.

There was no shortage of rumour and speculation: Newcombe and Simmonds had left the country, they were being hidden by the underworld, they were planning a fight to the death in the bush somewhere, they were going to raid the jails and free all their cronies and then go on a criminal rampage. Single women were warned to keep their doors locked. The NSW premier Joe Cahill died that week and hardly got any press at all.

For my part, I just hoped they stayed the hell away from me. A cop was parked outside Perkal Towers the whole time.

Then, after seven days at large, Les Newcombe was pinched at Centennial Park. Kev remained on the tear.

The day after Les was arrested, a bloke in overalls knocked on my door, asked if I was Glasheen, said he had a car for me. A dark green Vanguard was parked out front.

I said, 'Hardly the equivalent of the Holden.'

'I'm just delivering it like I was told to. Do you want it or not?'

'I'm not sure. Can't Sidoti do better than this?'

'There's an old Chev. Do you want that?'

'How old?'

'1934.'

'No. I suppose this'll have to do.'

He signed over the car to me. After he'd gone I had a closer look at it. It had fifty thousand on the clock, and the upholstery was in good nick. I glanced up and down the street. The surveillance car was gone.

Sidoti came knocking on my door the next day. I said, 'What do you want?'

'Can we go somewhere for a drink?'

'I'd rather not be seen with you.'

'You got the car.'

The Vanguard, yeah, I got it.'

He smiled. 'I know, I know, it's not a Holden. But that's just to keep you mobile while I find something better. Hey, can I come inside?'

I shook my head. 'Say what you have to say from where you are.'

'It's been a while since you've seen your mate Slaney, hasn't it?'

'Not long enough.'

'Have you seen today's paper?'

'Not yet.'

He took a rolled up *Telegraph* out of his back pocket and gave it to me. 'Look at page three.'

I did. There was a small story at the bottom under the headline 'Allegations Against Sydney Detectives'. It said how a group of concerned 'important citizens, lawyers and policemen' had presented a dossier to the Minister of Police in which it was alleged that 'a certain clique of senior policemen in the NSW Police Force' had been involved in serious criminal activities over a long period of time. No names were mentioned.

I read it and said, 'So what?'

'So, that's Slaney they're talking about. It's as I predicted, he's a shot duck.'

'Maybe.'

'Oh he is, all right, you can be certain. And so here we are, me in need of money and you in need of friends.'

'I don't want a friend like you.'

He went on like I hadn't spoken at all. 'This isn't the sort of thing best discussed out here.'

I thought about it then stood aside. 'You've got two minutes.'

Sidoti walked in. 'I'll be quick. Slaney's finished. So here's what I propose: you give me five thousand pounds, to cement our friendship, and you keep whatever else you're holding. Please don't try to tell me you haven't got that much. You were to give Slaney ten thousand pounds, isn't that right?' He was grinning at me.

I went over to the couch, reached behind and took out the gun I'd stashed there. I pointed it at Sidoti's head. He stopped grinning.

'Come back and I'll kill you. Understand? I'm not giving you any money and I'm not doing any deal with you, now or ever.'

He slowly shook his head. 'I'm surprised you're not scared of what I can do to you. You really ought to be.'

I moved in closer and put the gun to his temple. 'Get out.'

He moved back a couple of feet, his eyes on the gun. 'There's something we've been sort of skirting around, isn't there? Your time in jail.' He paused. 'Hector Rackley.'

'Who's he?'

'The bloke who *allegedly* escaped from Oberon while you were there.' He was watching me closely. I didn't answer.

'There hasn't been a single trace of him since he absconded, not a whisper. And old Hector's a pretty distinctive individual. It makes me wonder if the Bathurst blokes weren't on the wrong track. What if Rackley didn't actually run away at all? Maybe they just haven't looked for him in the right place. Just a thought.'

He walked over to the door and stopped again. 'And here's something else for you to consider. Don't think the Ray Waters matter has blown over. Coppers have very long memories, and they *always* get quits with anyone who hurts one of their own. That said, I could *still* be a good friend. Or a very bad enemy. Cheerio.' He walked out the door.

My appeal came up at Central Court the following Monday. Before I left home I glanced in Ulmer. *The best insurance against adversity is to lead a blameless life.*

My brief had persuaded me to go quietly on the frame-up, stick with the guilty plea, and leave it to him to argue against the severity of the original sentence. Which I did. In court he claimed that, given my previously unblemished record, six months' hard labour was inappropriate, and that the time I'd already done was about right. The crown prosecutor made a half-hearted case against it, said it was a pretty low act stealing from a charity, but the appeal was upheld. I was put on a bond of good behaviour for three years. I told his honour I'd do my best, and in a way I meant it.

I eased up on the reefers and dexes a bit, swam laps and did some fishing around Botany Bay. I backed Macdougal in the Melbourne Cup and it came in first. I practised my guitar picking, got all the way to page six of *The Mickey Baker Jazz Guitar Book.*

'Talking the Blues' worked its way down the Top 40 charts and then dropped out of sight. Johnny Ray came out for a Lee Gordon tour, and on his return to the States got lumbered for putting an improper proposition to a vice-squad cop in a Detroit dunny. The so-called youth drug, Substance H-3, was exposed as nothing more than novocaine and a 'secret acid'. A couple of days later Cary Grant announced he had been taking the acid, known as LSD, for years. It was the secret of his youthful vigour, he said. I read that and thought maybe Dick and I should look into it after all. Like Dick said, there was no limit to the sales possibilities with patent medicines, provided you had a decent testimonial.

Johnny O'Keefe followed the lead set by Max and Lee Gordon and had his own nervous breakdown. But he one-upped the others: he had his breakdown on stage at a charity turn in Canberra. After two weeks at the bug farm he took off to America, telling everyone he was going to knock them on their arses over there, you watch.

I got a phone call from the record company accountant. He said they were calculating royalties and there'd definitely be something coming my way for 'Talking the Blues'.

'It did pretty well, all told,' he said. 'It's a pity about that other song coming out when it did. "Talking the Blues" was just starting to look like being a real hit.'

'What other song?'

'"Tie Me Kangaroo Down Sport". Now, *that's* a property I'd like to have. Probably be a hit in England too. It knocked your number right off the map.'

'But "Talking the Blues" was in the Top 40 for months!'

'Well, you must understand the charts are more an *estimate*.'

'They're bullshit?'

'I'd say they are a careful blending of real sales figures and wishful thinking.'

'So what do I get?' I said.

I heard him shuffling papers. 'The record has sold 18,417 copies so far.' He coughed. 'That's a very respectable figure.'

'How much?'

'We calculate your share of the royalties at . . .' He turned another page. 'At eighty two pounds, three shillings and ninepence.'

'You can't be serious!'

'Would you like a cheque? Or I could pay you out of petty cash if you prefer.'

In the second week in November Kevin Simmonds surfaced again. A couple of park rangers at Kuringai Chase happened upon him in the bush digging an underground hideout. He pulled a gun on the rangers and took their ute. Later he broke through a police roadblock on the central coast, took off into the scrub. Five hundred cops with dogs and machine guns chased him for days through snake- and leech-infested rainforest, but couldn't track him down. Rain bucketed down in the search area, and each morning the police announced that Simmonds couldn't possibly remain at large another twenty-four hours, but he did, day after day.

His notoriety turned into a kind of hero worship. Anonymous posters supporting Simmonds appeared around town, and letters poured in to the papers. An international fan club was formed. There was a body of opinion that said Kev was an underdog hero, and the cops should shut down the manhunt, more or less let him get away. In a lead story in the *Daily Mirror*, a government psychiatrist advised all Simmonds sympathisers to seek immediate psychiatric treatment. The next day he received death threats.

Channel Seven mounted a television camera on a helicopter and covered the manhunt live from the headquarters at Wyong. I watched it all on TV. They interviewed the Commissioner for Police, then they interviewed Ray Kelly at the rain-soaked field headquarters. In the background you could see a bunch of burly blokes standing around smoking and drinking from tin mugs. One of them was Fred Slaney.

Then the cops got a tip-off from a farmer at Kurri Kurri, miles away from where they'd been searching. An hour later they ran Simmonds to ground, brought him into Kurri Kurri lockup to be charged. It was all over the papers and television. Kevin, grubby, unshaven, bare-footed, being led in by two big coppers, Fred Slaney on one side, Ray Kelly on the other.

When Slaney appeared at Perkal Towers a week later, I was still eating my breakfast. He went to the sideboard and poured himself a drink.

'Surprised to see me?' he said.

'No. Yes. People said you were on the way out.'

'They spoke too soon. I hope for your sake you don't believe all you hear.'

'I don't.'

'You've got my money then?'

I didn't like the way he said my money and I didn't like him helping himself to my booze either.

'Well? Have you got it?'

'Yeah, I've got it.'

'Good. I want you to act as banker for me for a while longer. I'm not quite out of the woods yet, but I soon will be. In the meantime, I'd rather not be holding anything supplementary to my wages.'

I shook my head. 'That bloke you're supposed to have sorted out has been around making threats.'

'Sidoti?'

'He's been here twice. He knows about the money and he wants it.'

'He's gone.'

'Oh yeah, sure.'

'There's no need to take that tone with me, you cop-killing bastard. I don't owe you any explanations, but I'll tell you anyway. Sidoti's been reassigned. He's out at Walgett locking up drunken Abos, which is where he's likely to stay for the rest of his career.'

'What about his mate Rheinberger?'

Slaney gave an eerie laugh. 'That bloke's as silly as a hatful of arseholes. He's been committed for psychiatric assessment.'

I didn't wonder.

Slaney went on, 'And just for your information, Billy Glasheen, you were deeply implicated in the Newcombe and Simmonds escape. Your name got a lot of traffic around headquarters, and if it hadn't been for my good offices Ray Kelly would have taken you down to CIB and flogged the bejesus out of you. Jesus Christ, didn't you wonder how come you weren't pinched? So don't get all snooty with me. If I say I want you to be bagman, you'll fucking well do it. I'll be in touch when the time comes.' He started for the door.

I said, 'Hang on. Sidoti may be in Walgett but he can still do me harm. If I'm to mind this money, then you better mind me.'

He nodded.

'I have an idea,' I said. 'I need a photograph of Waters, one that no one else has seen. Have you got anything like that?'

Slaney looked vaguely suspicious but he said, 'I may have.'

'And a sample of Waters' handwriting.'

He opened the door. 'I'll see. Don't try to contact me.'

I moved out of the flat at Perkal Towers. Before I left I dug up the money in the back yard, but left the drops at Cooper Park and the golf course, figuring they were as safe there as anywhere else.

I took out a lease on a one-bedroom place down on Bronte Beach, above the fish and chip shop. The front room looked out over the beach, towards Tamarama and Bondi. It was all right, except that the sun shone in from the crack of dawn.

A week after I moved, Slaney showed up, even though I hadn't given him my new address. He poured himself a scotch, then gave me a photograph. It was a snapshot of him with Ray Waters. Waters' arm was around Slaney's shoulder. They were in the bush somewhere, holding .303s, a pile of dead kangaroos in front of them.

'This might do,' I said. 'How about the handwriting sample?'

He handed me a copy of an old police report written by Waters. 'Is that what you wanted?' he said.

'Yeah. This photograph, has anyone else got a copy of it?

'My missus took the picture. That's the only print.'

Next I visited Jim Swanson, my old cellmate from Long Bay. He was eager to make a few bob. I gave him the photo of Waters, the report, and some other photos I'd pinched from Max's flat. Do your stuff, I said.

I finally got a call from Uncle Dick. He was in Sydney and wanted to see me. He came over to my place the same day. I sat him down, opened a bottle of beer. He had the Fay Small papers with him.

He'd spent the previous couple of months getting his legal affairs sorted out and putting the business back into shape. He was sorry he hadn't contacted me sooner but he'd been too busy, he said.

After another minute of chat he said, 'Well, I've had a look at these papers.'

'And?'

'Tell me about the woman who gave you this stuff.'

I gave him the bare bones of the Irving affair. When I finished he said, 'And there was an . . . involvement between you and the popsy?'

'Why?'

He shook his head, smiled. 'You must be a better Romeo than anyone gave you credit for, young feller.'

'What do you mean?'

'Well, it would appear this lassie has done you a good turn. What did she tell you about this stuff?'

'Nothing much. She shot through in a hurry, left a note, said I may as well have it, said you might find it amusing.'

'*I* might?'

'Yeah, I told her about you. So what does it all mean?'

'It means, nephew, we're back in business.'

'How so?'

He flipped the lid on the port and handed me the ledger book.

'Open it anywhere. Pick any name at random.'

I opened it up a few pages in, chose the third name from the top. *Charles Gaucroger, electrician, Pagewood.* I handed it back to Dick, pointing to my selection.

'All right. Hand me the phone, Bill, would you?'

Dick dialled the number alongside the name. He asked to speak to Charles Gaucroger, and when told he was speaking to him, identified himself as Richard Glasheen, representing the New South Wales Association for the Welfare of Hospitalised Children. He asked the bloke did he have kids himself. Dick said they can keep you busy, can't they Charles? Not to mention worrying about their health and such. Dick wondered if Charles was aware of the work done by the Hospitalised Children's Association in providing educational facilities for kiddies in hospital. Apparently he was. Dick asked the bloke if he knew of the association's magazine, *Helping Hand.* They were getting the next issue ready now, Dick said. It had a colouring-in section at the back for the young ones, tremendous stuff. It so happened, he said, that they had one advertising space left, and if Charles would care to take out an advertisement he could help himself and help the association carry on its valuable work.

Dick made the sale. He hung up and looked at me, pleased as punch with himself.

'So?' I said. 'What's the big deal there? You made a bogus sale.'

'Pick another name. You ring this time. Try to sell them, say, space in the journal for the Association for the Preservation of Injured Native Parrots.'

'There's no such thing, is there?'

'It doesn't matter. Try it anyway.'

'I'm no good at that sort of caper. What's your point exactly?'

'If you were to ring, you'd make the sale. Wouldn't matter which name you rang. You know why? All those people listed there, every one of them is a blue-ribbon egg.'

'Egg?'

'An easy mark. Wouldn't say no to a shit fight. You could sell them swimsuits in the wintertime, overcoats the following summer. They'd buy last year's calendar from you. I'm talking about *repeat* business, Bill. Someone has compiled this list over years and years. And I'll give you London to a brick, these names have been taken *off* any register of clients held at, where did they work?'

'Victory Press.'

'Yeah. These eggs have been poached.'

'But we have nothing to sell.'

'You think so?' He reached into the case, picked out a bunch of roneoed newsletters, passed them across to me. 'These were in the suitcase too. It's our product.'

I fanned out the little collection of badly reproduced newsletters, looked through the top few. *Siren: The Returned Ambulance Drivers Association Newsletter*; *The Plumbers and Gasfitters Gazette*; *Newsletter of the Legion of Mary*; *Hoist: The BWIU Newsletter*; *Fleece: The Journal of the Association of Breeders of British Sheep*. I picked that one out. 'I know this mob,' I said. I thumbed through the six-page newsletter.

'There aren't any adverts in this!'

'That, nephew, is the whole point. There are over thirty of those pissy newsletters there. Run off on broken-down Gestetners and such. You know where this is heading?'

'The publishing game? What do we know about printing and all that shit?'

'We leave that to the pros. We act as middle men, place ourselves between the mugs on this list and those organisations. We do it all from the comfort and safety of our office, via the Al Capone. Even if only a quarter of them say yes, we'll be in business.'

'I'm not sure.'

'Telephone selling isn't such a bad way to turn a quid. No one can thump you over the phone.'

'Yeah, but, taking advantage of people's goodwill . . .'

'Can't you see what's happening here? These people, maybe they're mugs, but they can afford to be because they're making good money. Which means further up the food chain, somebody will be making real money. This new decade could be a good time for men with get up and go, like us. Forget about lucky monkeys' paws and betting systems that don't work.'

'I happen to have received a glowing testimonial to the worth of that system.'

'Even Perkal backs winners occasionally. But never mind that, it's all here, the makings of a bonzer business.'

'I'll have to think about it for a while. Maybe consult the oracle.'

'Consult who?'

'That book you gave me.'

'What book was that?'

'The Business of Life.'

'I gave it to you?'

'Yeah, last year. You said it had been your guide for years. You said it may help me make my fortune.'

'Did I? Is it any good?'

In the run-up to Christmas 1959 the *Sun Herald* ran a feature on the theme 'What will the 1960s bring?' They asked some prominent people to make predictions. An architect said inner Sydney would change completely; the squalid old terraces and stuffy Victorian architecture would make way for clean, modern buildings like the new Blues Point Tower. Someone else said skirts would get shorter, and a bloke from the Metalworkers Union said the same about the working week. Brian Henderson felt the Canadian three-step was ripe for a big comeback.

They even asked Max Perkal what he tipped. Rock'n'roll was over, he said. Tahitian surf-mambo rock would be the next big thing, you could bet on it. There was a picture of him in a sarong, with no shirt on, wearing a lei and sunglasses, playing a new Fender electric guitar.

I spent a morning doing my financial inventory for 1959, totted up as best I could every zack I'd received during the year, be it earned, won or stolen. The total wasn't in the Col Joye class, but it wasn't too bad either. Then I added up all I'd spent and all I was yet to spend, including the nine thousand pounds I was holding for Slaney. I subtracted one figure from the other. I was ahead overall, but not by much, less than what I'd have made as a foreman in a stove factory.

I consulted T. W. Ulmer. *Yesterday's history, tomorrow's a mystery.* What's the good of that? I thought. I stood up, went out the back, dropped the book into the rubbish bin, went back inside.

Two minutes later I went out and retrieved the book. I wrote a note saying 'This may help you make your fortune cookies', put it inside the book, took the package to the post office and sent it off to Number One Son.

One day in mid-December, I was outside the City Mission trying to hail a cab. A group of Salvos were preaching, selling the *War Cry* and singing songs. A few idlers were hanging around. Amongst the brethren was a nice-looking young woman strumming a guitar, singing 'Make Room in the Lifeboat for Me'.

Behind me a preacher was haranguing the crowd. "'Woe to those who rise early in the morning, that they may run after strong drink, and those who tarry late into the evening till wine inflames them! They have lyre and harp, timbrel and flute and wine at their feasts but they do not regard the deeds of the Lord, or seek the work of his hands." Friends, that's what the good book says about drink, about the terrible price to be paid for permitting alcohol to mar God's handiwork, to stupefy the brain and to confuse the judgement.'

I turned around, had a look. The preacher was in Salvo rig and holding a bible. I called out from where I stood, 'Murray, you old reprobate!' The crowd turned to stare at me. I said to those near me, 'He's an old mate of mine.'

Murray glanced quickly at me then away, consulted his bible again. 'The good book prophesied, "The drunkards of Ephraim will be trodden under foot."'

'Murray! It's me, Billy.'

He waved the book in my direction. '"They are confused with wine, they stagger with strong drink. They err in vision."'

The crowd laughed. I waited until Murray had finished the sermon and the group had sung 'Old Rugged Cross'. I circled around the back and put my hand on Murray's shoulder.

'Oh, hello, Bill. How's things?'

'Not bad. Thanks for making a mug of me in front of everyone, by the way.'

He looked pained. The guitar strummer came up, smiling. Murray said to her, 'Hon, this is an old friend of mine, Bill Glasheen. Bill, this is my fiancée Denise.'

'How are you, love?' I said.

'Very well, thank you.' She looked from me to Murray. 'How do you two know each other?'

'From the old days,' said Murray. 'I think the Captain wants you to help pass the box around, sweet.'

She nodded, looked at me again, said, 'Nice to meet you, Bill. Perhaps you'd like to join us after the meeting back at the citadel?'

'Love to, but I've got a prior commitment with the drunkards of Ephraim. Cheers.'

When she'd gone I said, 'Hey, Murray. She's a good sort, all right, but what's your lurk? You following someone? Beaut disguise, a Salvo!'

'He sighed. 'Things have changed. I've, well, to put it plainly, I've been, you know, saved. It's not a con, I'm through with that life.' He glanced quickly at me. 'I suppose you think I'm a mug.'

'No.' Thinking, yes.

'Before, when I disappeared, did anyone tell you what happened?'

'No.'

'I went on a bender. I got crook. I checked into the Salvos, the House of Bricks. I dried out. Stayed a couple of days more, and then a few more after that, just stringing along. But then things changed. I kind of woke up, started seeing things clearly for the first time in my life.'

'Was the fair Denise part of this?'

'We had long talks about spiritual matters, yes, and she opened my eyes to many things. Then God bestowed on us the gift of earthly love.'

'Women love a man in uniform.'

Murray looked me dead in the eye and said, 'Bill, I haven't had a drink or a bet since August, and now I've started preaching. They say I have a gift for it, that I seem to fill with the Holy Spirit when I preach.'

'Fair dinkum?' I said. 'Well, I'm glad I saw you, Murray, because I've got something for you, some money. That chick we were looking for? She turned up, sure enough. But guess what? Turns out she—'

'I know. She'd taken money from your client. That's the real reason he wanted to find her.'

'How did you know?'

'It was obvious. No one pays that much for love. Not those people anyway. So she paid you off, did she?'

'You really are a good sleuth, Murray. Yeah, she paid me off and I managed to collect from Irving as well. Then I had a bet with that money and won. And there was this other stuff she left with me, turns out it's potentially the most valuable of the lot. Any way you look at it, you're entitled to a whack.'

He shook his head. 'It wouldn't benefit me. You keep it.'

Jim Swanson returned the snapshot I'd given him, along with another one. This new version still had fat old Ray Waters in the foreground, but Slaney had been removed from the picture and replaced with Sammy Davis Jr. Waters and Davis were smiling at the camera, their arms around each other's shoulders. The rifles and dead kangaroos were gone, and instead of being in the bush they appeared to be standing in front of a big sign which read *The Sands, Las Vegas: A Place in the Sun*. On the back of the snapshot was written, 'Fred, wish you were here. All the best, Ray.'

Jim said, 'Is that what you wanted?'

'This is a work of genius.'

I handed the photograph to Slaney next day in the back bar at City Tatts. He looked at it and grinned, said, 'Who did this?'

I shook my head. 'Never mind. Will it pass muster?'

He held it up to the light. 'I wouldn't want any experts looking at it too closely, but it should make for some pretty interesting rumours as to the Chief Superintendent's current whereabouts.' Slaney put the photograph in his pocket.

Just before Christmas Kevin and Les appeared in court charged with the murder of Cecil Mills, the Emu Plains warder. The jury took nine hours to find them not guilty of murder, but guilty of manslaughter. The judge was spewing. He gave them both the maximum sentence, life imprisonment, saying, 'If you only serve thirty years of this sentence it will still be an injustice.'

I had a shitty Christmas. No one called by and my telephone didn't ring all day. I took a few drinks and sat around wondering how come a go-ahead, youngish feller like me had to spend Christmas alone. Then at six o'clock Fred Slaney rang me, said he was putting me on notice. He'd be around at ten next morning to collect his money.

I kept drinking with the television on as it slowly got dark outside, feeling that same depression I'd felt every single Christmas night in my life. Except this time was worse. The only human contact I'd had all day was with Fred Slaney.

When it was fully dark I got a shovel and locked up, thinking, I'll get this over and done with. I went out to the car and stopped. For all that I wanted to believe paying Slaney off would be the end of it, somewhere in my head there was a voice telling me different. Telling me it wouldn't be over tomorrow, regardless. He'd keep coming back. It wouldn't be over until I was lying dead in the foundations of a building somewhere, under fifty tons of concrete.

I put the shovel away again, went inside to the bathroom, took a long, hard look in the mirror. I saw the face of a tired man. Nothing new. There was something else there, something I couldn't quite put my finger on. That quiet voice came again. It said, 'Egg.'

That night I phoned Jim Swanson. I wished him Merry Christmas then said, 'Hey, remember that magazine picture you showed me in jail, that cockatoo you photographed?'

'It was a ground parrot.'

'Whatever. Do you still have the gear you used?'

'All it takes is a good camera, a long lens and a lot of patience, and I've still got them. Why?'

'Do you feel like earning some real money?'

He didn't answer straight away. 'I was sort of trying to resist temptation. What do you want me to do, exactly?'

'Help me beat the devil.'

On Boxing Day Slaney was still half pissed. 'Time for my Christmas present,' he said, pouring himself a scotch.

'Did you do that thing with the photograph?'

He nodded. 'A great success. Rumours are flying around like crazy. All contradictory, of course, but the smart money is saying that Waters is *not* resting with Jesus, as was previously rumoured, but is in fact living large in America. So. My money.'

'It's not here. I'll have to go and dig it up.'

He turned to face me, quickly. 'I told you to have it ready.'

He was tense, and it occurred to me then that a nine-thousand quid pay-off was big by anyone's standards, even his.

'It's not far. You can wait here if you like.'

Slaney stared hard at me. I tried to look casual, waiting for the answer I wanted.

'I'll come with you.'

Right answer.

We took the Vanguard to Cooper Park. I dug up the first jar, gave the money to Slaney.

He thumbed quickly through it and said, 'There's only two thou' here.'

'Next stop Royal Sydney Golf Club,' I said.

He looked at me, said nothing, nodded slowly.

I found the buried jar without trouble, gave the next bundle to Slaney. He counted it.

'That makes four thousand. A long way to go.'

'Back to my flat.'

'Why didn't you give it to me before?'

'Saving the best till last.'

Back at Bronte, Slaney poured himself another scotch the minute we got inside. 'Hurry up. I want to shoot through.'

The telephone started ringing. It rang twice, then stopped. Slaney looked at it, then at me. The telephone rang again, another two rings, then stopped.

He stood up quickly, said, 'What's going on?'

I didn't answer him. I went to the sideboard, got the bundle of money I'd left there, and gave it to him.

He looked at it dubiously, gave it a bit of a shake. 'This isn't five grand.'

'No. That's exactly one thousand, two hundred pounds. Counting what I gave you last March, that makes six thousand pounds all up. And that'll be all you get from me..'

He went very still. 'You don't have the rest?'

'Maybe, maybe not. Either way, you're not getting it.'

Slaney dropped his voice. 'And why would that be?'

'I view this business differently now.'

'*Do* you just?'

'Your leverage over me was Ray Waters' murder. But I didn't kill him. I may have been guilt-ridden, but I wasn't guilty. But I was involved in fencing the J. Farren Price stuff all right, and by some weird bent cop reckoning I suppose I was fair game on that score.'

He didn't say anything, just kept staring at me.

I went on. 'The six grand I'm giving you is my share of the J. Farren Price take. Maybe the money was bad. Maybe it's like they say, the law of karma. Anyway, I don't give a rat's. You take it, fuck off, don't come back. If you're not happy with that, we'll have it out right now.'

Slaney took a sip of his drink, then started clapping slowly.

'Terrific performance, Glasheen. Except for the shaking knees. Otherwise, very convincing.'

I looked down. They were knocking all right.

'You have every reason to be nervous. You're one bloke who won't be seeing in the new year.'

I shook my head. 'You think I'd try this on without insurance?'

'What's that supposed to mean?'

'You were photographed receiving that money from me. The phone a minute ago was the signal. We got a result. Copies are being run off. They'll be sent to a certain solicitor, with instructions, along with stat decs from me. In the event of my death, et cetera, et cetera. So that's where we stand. You might well kill me. But you'll land in the shit. Whichever way it goes, you're finished extorting money out of me.'

I looked at him and he stared back at me. We held the stare for I don't know how long.

Slaney looked away first. 'Listen to you getting all self-righteous. Do you think I go around demanding thousands of quid from law-abiding citizens? In this town, you can't keep working hot and not deal with someone, sooner or later. Goes with the job. As you bloody well know.'

'I'm quitting that job. I intend to lead a blameless life from now on.'

'Bully for you!' Slaney looked at the bundle of money in his hand. 'And I take it you've got a gun hidden somewhere handy, ready for a fight to the death, should it come to that.'

I shrugged.

He shook his head. 'You read too many comics. Well, as it

happens you got me in the festive spirit. And to tell you the truth, I never really expected you to raise even this much.' He put the money in his jacket pocket.

'You agree then?'

'Let's just say I'm letting you win this round, on points. Every lag who's just got his head out the noose swears blind he's learned his lesson. But they never do. So when you stuff up next time—and you will—that's when I'll be asking for the other four thousand. And God help you if you can't produce it then.'

He stood up, drained his glass, made for the bottle again. But I got to it before he did.

I pointed at him. 'Don't help yourself to my booze again,' I said, 'unless invited.'

Slaney guffawed. 'This business has been the making of you.'

Chapter 19

NEW YEAR'S DAY, 1960

Four of us were on a fly-fishing trip around the western slopes. So far, the fishing had been poor everywhere we went. We each put fifty quid in the pot, to go to the one who caught the biggest fish that day.

At midday we came to a small, fast stream running out of a narrow valley. Jim Swanson caught a fat trout with his first cast. This is more like it, he said, and headed off upstream. The other blokes went downstream, and I tried my luck in a string of pools near the car.

At two o'clock Jim came back with a three-pounder. The other two had a couple of smaller, though well-conditioned fish. One of the blokes said it was funny, this pissy creek had better fish than any body of water we'd seen all week. Jim opened his fish up with a knife. Firm pink flesh; and in the gut, bits of yabby tail, bugs, and some meaty-looking stuff.

I looked around, said, 'What's the name of this creek?'

No one knew.

'What's up there?' I pointed to the high granite bluffs a mile or so away.

Jim gave me a look. 'You should know, Bill. That's the edge of the Oberon Plateau.' He pointed to a line of plantation pines on the horizon. 'This creek runs down from up there.'

My knees went weak. I sat down on the bank. My breathing grew shallow and I could hear my heart racing. I looked again at the bluffs, back at the river, heard the casuarinas hissing in the breeze. Some rosellas flew down the corridor formed by the tall trees, then peeled off, disappeared behind the branches opposite me. Gradually my heartbeat slowed and I felt a kind of weariness come into my arms and legs, not unpleasant, like I'd just had a Chinese pipe.

I kept sitting there. Behind me Jim and the others built a fire and cooked up the fish. When they were done, they called to me to come have a feed. I said I wasn't that hungry, thanks. Go on, they said, there's plenty here, this is good tucker. I told them no, you never know what those effers have been eating.

But I had a pretty fair idea.

There was a small disturbance in the shadowy water on the other side, then a flash. I saw a fish dart out from the shadows, take a bug on the surface, go back and wait, do it again. I walked up the bank, got the rod, and made an almost perfect cast just to the left of where I thought the fish was lurking.

It took the fly and went berserk. The blokes came over to cheer me on. I wound the line in and picked up a fish scarcely more than eight inches long. The others hooted and clapped, said did I want the money now or did I expect to bag an even bigger one?

I told them to get rooted. I cradled the fish in my hand and removed the hook from its mouth. I turned it over. The right-side fin had been snipped off. A 1959 fingerling.

The State Fisheries releases hundreds of thousands of trout fingerlings into streams and dams each year. Most never make it to adulthood. They are devoured by hawks or cormorants, or by wild trout who are enthusiastic predators on the young. Those wily enough to escape face other perils—the streams can get too warm, too muddy or too slow for them, or dry up completely. A few get caught by fishermen.

I fanned out the trout's tail. There was a chunk taken out of it. Maybe you could read the letters BG. Or maybe it was just the result of an encounter with a creature with larger teeth than its own. The fish was pumping its gill plates, the equivalent of gasping for breath. I bent down and, still cradling it in my hand, moved it back and forth a few times to wash the water through its gills.

I opened my hand completely, said, 'Happy new year, slippery.'

The fish stayed there for a few seconds, gave one careful sweep of its tail. Then it lost itself in the dark water faster than my eye could follow it.

GET RICH QUICK

978-1-891241-24-6, paper, 256 pages, $13.95

Winner of the Ned Kelly Award for Best First Crime Novel

'A marvellous read and a truly distinctive piece of Australian crime writing.' – Sydney Morning Herald

Billy Glasheen is a likeable guy, with a gift for masterminding elaborate scenarios—whether it's a gambling scam, transporting a fortune in stolen jewels, or keeping the wheels greased during the notorious down-under tour by Little Richard and his rock 'n' roll entourage. But trouble follows close behind—perhaps because Billy's schemes always seem to interfere with the plans of Sydney's big players, an unholy trinity of crooks, bent cops, and politicians on the make. Suddenly he's in the frame for murder, and on the run from the police, who'll happily send him down for it. Billy's no sleuth, but there's nowhere to turn for help. To prove it wasn't him, he'll have to find the real killer.

THE DEVIL'S JUMP

978-1-891241-20-8, paper, $14.95

"Think of a hopped-up James M. Cain." – Kirkus Reviews

August 1945: the Japanese have surrendered and there's dancing in the streets of Sydney. But Billy Glasheen has little time to celebrate; his black marketeer boss has disappeared, leaving Billy high and dry. Soon he's on the run from the criminals and the cops, not to mention a shady private army. They all think he has the thing they're after, and they'll kill to get hold of it.

Unfortunately for Billy, he doesn't know what it is they're looking for . . . all he knows is, he'd better find it fast.

THE BIG WHATEVER

Introduction by Luc Sante

978-1-891241-44-4, paper, 310 pages, $14.95

"Peter Doyle does for Sydney what Carl Hiaasen does for Miami." – Shane Maloney

When Billy Glasheen picks up a trashy paperback he finds in his cab, its plot seems weirdly familiar. One of the main characters is based on him. Only one person knows enough about his past to have written it—Max, his double-crossing ex-partner in crime. But Max is dead. He famously went up in flames, along with a fortune in cash, after a bank heist. If Max is somehow still alive, Billy has a score to settle. And if he didn't get fried to a crisp, maybe the money didn't either. To find out, Billy has to follow the clues in the strange little book—and outwit the drug lords, cops, and robbers who are also on Max's trail.

With its ingenious novel-within-a-novel structure, *The Big Whatever* is both a grab-you-by-the throat crime story and an original take on early 70s pop culture. In his introduction, Luc Sante—renowned for his histories of the underworld (*Low Life, The Other Paris*) and for his penetrating analysis of crime fiction greats from Georges Simenon to Richard Stark—makes a powerful case for Peter Doyle's distinctive contribution to contemporary crime writing.

ALSO FROM VERSE CHORUS PRESS

COORPAROO BLUES & THE IRISH FANDANGO
G. S. Manson
978-1-891241-32-1, paper, 240 pages, $13.95
"Rough and gritty, but also vital." – Sydney Morning Herald

BRISBANE, 1943. Overnight a provincial Australian city has become the main Allied staging post for the war in the Pacific. The social, sexual, and racial tensions created by thousands of US troops are stirring up all kinds of mayhem, and Brisbane's once quiet streets are looking pretty mean.

Enter P.I. Jack Munro, an ex-cop with a nose for trouble and a stubborn dedication to exposing the truth. He's not a particularly good man, but he's the one you want on your side when things look bad.
When Jack is hired by a knockout blonde to find her missing man, he turns over a few rocks he's not supposed to. Soon the questions are piling up, and so are the bodies. But Jack forges on through the dockside bars, black-market warehouses, and segregated brothels of his roiling city, uncovering greed and corruption eating away at the foundations of the war effort.

Written in the spare, style of all great pulp fiction, G.S. Manson's fast-paced debut captures the high stakes and nervous energy of wartime, when everything becomes a matter of life and death.

ABOUT PETER DOYLE

Born in Maroubra, in Sydney's eastern suburbs, Peter
Doyle worked as a taxi driver, musician, and teacher
before publishing *Get Rich Quick* (1996), which won
the Ned Kelly Award for Best First Crime Fiction. Its
sequel, *Amaze Your Friends* (1999), grabbed the Ned
Kelly Award for Best Crime Novel. Two more books
in the series, *The Devil's Jump* (2001) and *The Big
Whatever* (2015) followed, as did a Ned Kelly Lifetime
Achievement Award.

No one knows Sydney (especially its murky past)
like Peter Doyle. He combed through the archives of
the Sydney police department to put together a highly
acclaimed exhibition of crime-scene photographs and
mug shots, as well as an accompanying book, *City of
Shadows: Sydney Police Photographs 1912-1948*, and
its sucessor, *Crooks Like Us*.

Doyle teaches writing at Macquarie University.